SHADOW WALKERS

What casts a shadow in the darkness?

Kevin B DiBacco

2026, TWB Press
https://www.twbpress.com

Shadow Walkers – What casts a shadow in the darkness?

Edited by Terry Wright

Cover Art by Kevin B. DiBacco

ISBN: 978-1-967888-26-9

PROLOGUE:
THE HOLLOW GROUND

October 17, 1843. Thomas White heard the first screams echo through the silver mine. He and his partner Miller were sent to investigate. In the east shaft, they found the crew's tools scattered, but some were arranged in an arrow pointing deeper into the tunnels. Their lunch sat abandoned mid-bite. Their lanterns had been trampled. But of Jenkins, Sullivan, Brennen, and Duncan themselves, there was no sign.

Only their clothing remained—arranged in sitting positions against the tunnel wall, meticulously placed down to the caps and boots, as if the men inside had simply ceased to exist. The fabric of their dust masks held impressions of their final expressions: wide eyes, open mouths, faces frozen in terror.

As he held up his lantern and swung it around, looking for any signs of life, he saw a glimmer in the dust. He investigated. It was a pocket watch engraved *Jenkins*. He opened the lid. The hands were frozen at 2:17.

Then the shadows began to move, but he hadn't moved the lantern. The hairs on the back of his neck prickled.

They flowed toward him and Miller, swirling along the tunnel walls like liquid darkness, independent of the lantern light, reaching out with tendril-like extensions. White and Miller ran for the entrance where the night shift miners stood waiting in the main chamber—but their eyes had gone solid black, their voices layered with inhuman harmonics. "You've witnessed the incursion point," the shadow walker wearing Foreman Wilson's face said. "The wound between."

He and the night shifters charged them.

White and Miller ran.

They made it to the surface, gasping in the late afternoon sun—and then the darkness followed them out. It engulfed Miller where he stood. His outline began to blur and diminish. "They're coming out," he shouted, his voice already fading. "Run, Thomas, run." Miller's clothing collapsed emptily to the ground. No blood. No remains. Just empty fabric retaining the vague impression of a human form.

White fled.

His warnings went unheeded—the mine owner dismissed him as addled by bad air. He slipped away that night with Jenkins' pocket watch still frozen at 2:17, walked twenty miles north by starlight, and never looked back.

The entrance shaft was dynamited and buried, and a circle of fertile soil around the site never nurtured a single stalk of corn.

Thomas White never fully escaped what he had witnessed in that silver mine. He went on with his life, raised a family, and often told the story of the mine shadows he'd escaped. No one believed him, the ramblings of a fool, they'd said, but he insisted that beneath the seemingly ordinary cornfields lay a wound in the world—a passage between darkness and light—a breach in the hollow ground, waiting to be reopened.

CHAPTER 1:
HOLLOW FOUNDATIONS

Phoebe Weaver first noticed something wrong with her daughter's shadow on a Tuesday afternoon in late September. They'd been raking leaves in the backyard beneath a cloudless autumn sky, the maples and oaks surrounding their Millfield home blazing with color in the afternoon light. Six-year-old Maddie jumped laughing into the leaf piles while a cool breeze swept across the rolling hills outside the small town of Millfield Ohio.

"Look, Mommy. I'm flying!" Maddie had shouted before leaping from the wooden porch steps into a massive pile of amber and crimson leaves.

Phoebe smiled, leaning on her rake. "Be careful, sweetie. Not too high."

That's when she saw it, Maddie's shadow on the ground. It hesitated. Just for a fraction of a second, but enough that Phoebe's breath caught in her throat. Maddie had already landed in the pile, leaves exploding around her in a shower of color, but her shadow remained suspended in midair for a heartbeat longer than it should have. Like it was deciding whether to follow her or fly away.

Phoebe blinked hard. Surely, just a trick of the light. The afternoon sun was playing games through the tree branches.

"Did you see that, Mommy? I went so high!" Maddie emerged from the leaves, her curly brown hair decorated with fragments of foliage.

"I saw," Phoebe said, her voice steadier than she felt. She watched Maddie's shadow carefully now. It behaved normally, a perfect silhouette mirroring her daughter's movements as Maddie began gathering more leaves for another jump.

You're losing it, Phoebe, she told herself. *Three nights of broken sleep will do that to you.*

She'd been up reviewing structural reports for the town council meeting tomorrow. As Millfield's only civil engineer, the responsibility for the ancient grain silo's demolition fell squarely on her shoulders. The massive concrete structure had stood at the edge of town for nearly a century, abandoned for the last thirty years, its weathered gray form visible from almost anywhere in the valley. Time and neglect had rendered it dangerous, concrete cancer spreading through its foundations, hairline fractures spiderwebbing across its curved walls.

The demolition was scheduled for next week. Most people in town were relieved to see the eyesore finally coming down. Most, but not all.

Phoebe's phone buzzed in her pocket. It was Mayor Wilson.

"Tell me you've handled the Hollow situation," the mayor said without preamble.

Phoebe sighed, watching Maddie as she dragged more leaves into her pile. "I spoke with him yesterday. He's still opposed."

"Opposed is putting it mildly. He's threatening to chain himself to the damn silo."

Harrison Hollow was Millfield's oldest resident, ninety-four years old and sharp as the hunting knife he still carried in his boot. His family had purchased the land in the 1920s at bargain prices because of its strange reputation. Though much of the soil was remarkably fertile, two barren circles near the heart of the property had resisted every attempt at cultivation for generations. Locals whispered about disappearances, strange sounds in the cornfields, and land the native peoples once avoided except to leave offerings at its edges. Thaddeus Hollow ignored the warnings, built the silo, and transformed the surrounding acreage into some of the most productive farmland in the county. Harrison had worked there as a young man before the silo was decommissioned and had never stopped watching over it.

"He's just upset about losing a piece of his family's history," Phoebe said, though she knew there was more to it than that. Harrison's objections to the demolition had taken on an almost religious fervor recently. "I'll talk to him again."

"Today, Phoebe. The council votes tomorrow, and I need this to be unanimous. Harrison has a lot of influence with the old-timers."

"I'll head over there after dinner."

"Good. And bring those foundation reports. If anyone can make him see reason, it's you."

The mayor hung up, and Phoebe slipped the phone back into her pocket with another sigh. Harrison lived alone in a farmhouse at the edge of town, less than a quarter mile from the silo. His property offered the best view of the massive structure, its shadow literally falling across his land every afternoon.

"Mommy, look! I made an even bigger pile!"

Phoebe turned toward her daughter and froze. For a moment, just a moment, Maddie's shadow wasn't a little girl's outline at all. It was elongated, stretched upward, reaching toward the sky like the silo. Then Maddie moved, and it was just a normal shadow again.

Phoebe pressed her palms against her eyes. *Sleep deprivation. That's all this is.*

"That's wonderful, sweetie," she managed. "Why don't we go inside and start dinner? Daddy will be home soon."

* * *

The problem with old men like Harrison Hollow, Phoebe reflected as she drove down the winding country road that evening, was that they became monuments themselves, unmovable, rooted in the past, resistant to necessary change.

She glanced at the folder of reports on the passenger seat. The evidence was clear: the silo's foundation was compromised, the structure was leaning three degrees off true, and the reinforced concrete was degrading at an accelerating rate. It wasn't a question of if it would collapse, but when.

The sun was setting as she pulled into Harrison's gravel driveway, the old farmhouse silhouetted against the fiery sky. Behind it, the massive cylindrical form of the grain silo loomed, its shadow stretching across Harrison's property like a giant sundial, marking the end of an era.

Harrison was sitting on his porch swing as she approached, a woolen blanket across his knees despite the mild evening. His white hair caught the last golden rays of sunlight, giving him an almost saintly appearance that belied the stubbornness in his pale blue eyes.

"Evening, Miss Phoebe," he said, his voice a gravel road itself after decades of pipe smoking. "Come to try changing an old man's mind?"

Phoebe smiled, climbing the creaking steps. "Hello, Mr. Hollow. Mind if I join you?"

He gestured to the space beside him on the swing, and she sat, the aged wood groaning beneath their combined weight.

"Beautiful sunset," she offered.

"Always is, viewed from here." Harrison nodded toward the horizon where the sun was sinking behind the silhouette of the silo. "Been watching that same view for ninety-odd years."

They sat in silence for a moment, the only sound being

the gentle creaking of the porch swing and the distant calls of nightbirds preparing for evening.

"The mayor sent you," Harrison said finally. It wasn't a question.

"The council votes tomorrow."

"And they need old Harrison to fall in line."

Phoebe opened her folder. "Mr. Hollow, I've run every test possible. The foundation is failing. The structural integrity—"

Harrison held up a gnarled hand. "I don't need your fancy reports, girl. I know what that silo is."

Something in his tone made Phoebe hesitate to respond, then: "It's a grain silo, Mr. Hollow. An abandoned one that's dangerous."

The old man's eyes caught hers, and for a moment, she glimpsed something like fear behind the stubbornness. "That what you think? That it's just a place where we stored corn and wheat?"

A chill ran through Phoebe that had nothing to do with the evening air. "What else would it be?"

Harrison looked out toward the towering structure, his expression unreadable in the fading light. "Some things are built not to hold something in, but to keep something out."

Phoebe felt a flutter of unease. "Mr. Hollow—"

"You've seen things, haven't you?" His voice dropped lower. "Strange things. Just at the corner of your eye. Things that shouldn't be possible."

Unbidden, the image of Maddie's shadow came to Phoebe's mind, that impossible moment of suspension, the elongated form reaching skyward. "I don't know what you mean," she said, but her voice betrayed her.

Harrison nodded, as if her denial confirmed something. "It's starting already. The foundation's weakening, just like you said. But not in the way you think." He leaned closer. "Did you ever wonder why they built it so thick? Why they poured so much concrete when a metal silo would have been cheaper and more efficient?"

"Construction methods were different in the 1920s," Phoebe said reasonably, though her mouth had gone dry.

"Construction methods," Harrison echoed with a soft, humorless laugh. "But there were other things mixed into that concrete, Miss Phoebe. Things my grandfather only spoke of once, on his deathbed."

Phoebe wanted to dismiss the old man's words as superstition, the ramblings of someone desperately clinging to the past. But the engineer in her was curious despite herself. "What things?"

"Relics. Blessed objects. Iron nails from old churches. Silver crosses. Pages from Bibles written in Latin." Harrison's eyes never left the silo. "My grandfather had them brought in from all over the country. Cost him nearly every penny he had."

"Why would he do that?"

Harrison was silent for a long moment, then: "There are places in this world where the boundary between here and elsewhere is thin. Places where *things* can slip through, if there's nothing to stop them."

Phoebe felt a chill run down her spine. The rational part of her mind wanted to laugh off Harrison's tale, but that same part couldn't explain what she'd seen happen with her daughter's shadow. "What kind of *things*?" she asked.

"Dark things. Hungry things." Harrison's expression turned grave. "Things that feed on shadows first, before they start on what casts them."

Phoebe's breath caught. "Mr. Hollow, what are you saying?"

"I'm saying that Silo isn't for holding grain, Miss Phoebe. Never was. It's a seal. A cork in a bottle. And you're getting ready to pull it out, and those *things* are going to rise up."

The last light of day faded, leaving them in the gathering darkness. In the distance, the silo was now just a darker shape against the night sky, its massive form seeming to absorb rather than reflect the emerging starlight.

"This is..." Phoebe struggled for words. "This is superstition. Folk tales."

"Is it?" Harrison's voice was gentle now, almost pitying. "Tell me what you've seen, Miss Phoebe. Tell me what made you flinch when I mentioned shadows."

She thought of Maddie's shadow, that impossible moment of separation, of independence. A cold knot formed in her stomach.

"Even if, there was something strange," she said carefully, "the fact remains that the silo is structurally unsound. It's going to collapse eventually, whether we demolish it or not."

Harrison nodded slowly. "Yes. And that's the real problem, isn't it? If it comes down uncontrolled, there's no telling what might happen." He fixed her with his pale gaze. "Which is why we don't demolish it. We restore it."

"Restore? Mr. Hollow, do you have any idea what that would cost?"

"What's the cost of your daughter keeping her shadow, Miss Phoebe?"

The words hit her like a physical blow. She hadn't mentioned Maddie. Hadn't told anyone about what she'd seen.

Harrison's expression softened at her shock. "It always starts with the children," he said quietly. "They see it first. Feel it first. Their shadows are tastier, I suppose. More vital."

"This is insane," Phoebe whispered, but she couldn't bring herself to leave.

"My grandfather knew what was here before the town existed," Harrison continued. "This land was part of his farm. Nothing would grow in one particular spot, a perfect circle of barren earth. Animals wouldn't go near it. Birds wouldn't fly over it. He built the silo to contain the shadows, to seal the wound." The old man's hands trembled slightly as he pulled his blanket tighter. "Every few decades, the seal weakens...needs to be repaired, strengthened. My father did it in the fifties. I did it in the eighties."

"Did what, exactly?"

"Reinforced the foundation. Added more *protection*."

"Protection?" Phoebe stared at him. "You're talking about some kind of ritual?"

Harrison shrugged. "Call it what you will. A new Native People's binding spell. It held for decades, but now the safeguards are failing again, and there's no one left who knows how to perform the ancient binding spell."

"And you think that's causing shadows to behave strangely?"

"For now." His voice was grim. "It will get worse."

Phoebe stood abruptly, gathering her reports. "Mr. Hollow, I respect you enormously, but this is...I can't take this to the council. They need facts, data, not ghost stories."

Harrison made no move to stop her as she stepped away from the swing. "When it was just me seeing things, I thought maybe it was old age. My mind playing tricks." His eyes met hers in the darkness. "But you've seen it too, haven't you? And you're an educated woman. An engineer. A person of science."

Phoebe hesitated at the top of the steps.

"The demolition is scheduled for next Wednesday," Harrison continued. "You've got six days, Miss Phoebe. Watch the shadows. Especially your daughter's. And when you're ready to listen, come back."

She wanted to say something rational, something dismissive that would put his warnings firmly in the realm of superstition where they belonged. Instead, she found herself asking, "What happens if we go through with the demolition?"

Harrison looked past her, toward the looming shape of the silo against the night sky. "Then we better hope I'm just a crazy old man...but I don't think you believe that anymore."

Phoebe walked to her car without responding, her mind racing. The reports in her hands were clear, the silo was structurally unsound, a danger to the community. The rational course was obvious.

As she started reversing her car, the headlights swept across the front of Harrison's house and onto the silo beyond. For an instant, just an instant, she thought she saw something move within the beam. Not a physical movement, but darkness that shifted and concentrated, as if the night itself was pulling in the light.

Then it was gone, and there was only the weathered concrete of the old structure, silent and still in the darkness.

Just nerves, she told herself as she backed down the driveway. *Just an old man's stories getting to you.*

But as she drove back toward town, Phoebe couldn't shake the feeling that she was being watched by something ancient and patient, something that had been waiting an exceptionally long time for a crack in its prison walls.

Something that had already reached out and touched her daughter's shadow.

When Phoebe arrived home, the house was dark except for the blue glow of the television in the living room. She found her husband, David, asleep on the couch, a half-empty beer on the lamp table beside him. The local news played quietly on the screen, the news anchor discussing the upcoming town council vote on the silo demolition.

Phoebe turned off the TV and gently shook David's shoulder. "Hey. I'm home."

He blinked awake, his sleepy face transforming into a smile. "Hey yourself. How'd it go with old man Hollow?"

"Strange." She sat beside him. "He's convinced the silo is special somehow."

David yawned. "Special as in historic, or special as in one of his ghost stories?"

"The latter." Phoebe hesitated long enough to look around. "Where's Maddie?"

"Been asleep for an hour. She was wiped out from all that jumping in leaves." He studied his wife's face. "What's wrong? Did Harrison get to you with his tales?"

Phoebe thought about telling him what she'd seen, Maddie's shadow lingering in the air, the strange elongation that had reminded her of the silo's silhouette. But saying it aloud would make it real and would force her to examine what it might mean.

"I'm just tired," she said instead. "I've got the council meeting tomorrow, and all this opposition from Harrison is making things complicated."

David pulled her closer. "You've got the reports. The facts are on your side."

"I know." She rested her head against his shoulder, taking comfort in his solidity, his uncomplicated confidence in the rational world. "I just need a good night's sleep."

"You go on up. I'll lock up down here."

Phoebe nodded and climbed the stairs, her body heavy with fatigue. She paused at Maddie's door, pushed it open quietly to check on her daughter.

Maddie lay sprawled across her bed, one arm thrown over her head, her curls a wild tangle on the pillow. Her nightlight cast a soft glow across the room, enough for Phoebe to see that everything was normal. Peaceful.

She was about to close the door when she noticed the shadow on the wall beside Maddie's bed. It wasn't the shadow of a sleeping child. It was standing upright, a dark silhouette against the pale blue wallpaper. As Phoebe watched, frozen in the doorway, it seemed to turn toward her, though Maddie hadn't moved at all.

For a terrible moment, Phoebe felt it looking at her, studying her. Then it slowly, deliberately, raised one shadowy arm and placed a finger to what would have been its lips, in a universal gesture: *shush.*

Phoebe must have made a sound because suddenly David was beside her, his hand on her shoulder. "Babe? Are you okay?"

She blinked, and the shadow on the wall was just a normal child's shadow again, mirroring Maddie's sleeping form.

"Did you see that?" she whispered.

David looked from her to the darkened room. "See what?"

Phoebe's heart was hammering in her chest. *It always starts with the children,* Harrison had said. *They see it first. Feel it first.*

"Nothing," she said, her mouth dry.

She closed Maddie's door and let David lead her to their bedroom, her mind racing. Tomorrow she would present her reports to the town council. The demolition would be approved. The silo would come down next week.

And whatever was happening with the shadows, that was something she would deal with in the light of day. Something that would make more sense after a good night's sleep.

Hours later, as she lay beside her sleeping husband, still wide awake, Phoebe couldn't stop thinking about Harrison's warning: *Some things are built not to hold something in, but to keep something out.*

She wondered if, in all her careful calculations and structural analyses, she had missed the most important foundation of all, the one built on belief, on the recognition that some boundaries were not meant to be breached.

Outside, a cloud passed over the moon, and for a

moment, the shadows in the room deepened. Phoebe held her breath until the moonlight returned.

Six days until the demolition. Six days to decide what she truly believed.

Just days before, the foundations of her world, the rational, explicable world she had built her career upon, might crumble along with the ancient walls of a structure that had never been merely a grain silo, at all.

CHAPTER 2:
HIDDEN PAGES

Phoebe stood at the back of the town hall meeting room, watching as the council members shuffled papers and whispered among themselves.

The morning sun streamed through tall windows, casting long geometric patterns across the worn wooden floor, patterns that reminded her uncomfortably of the shadow she'd seen in Maddie's room last night. That unnatural silhouette with its finger pressed to nonexistent lips while her daughter slept.

She hadn't slept well since that encounter, her mind replaying Harrison Hollow's warning: "Some things are built not to hold something in, but to keep something out." The lack of rest revealed itself in the slight tremor of her hands as she arranged her presentation materials.

The manila folder containing her structural analysis of the silo felt inadequate now, as if there should be another report, one addressing the impossible things she'd witnessed, the cryptic warnings Harrison had shared about things that fed on the shadows before starting on what casts them.

"All set?" Mayor Wilson appeared at her elbow, his broad face creased with the practiced smile of a career politician. "The council's ready to vote. Just need your final assessment to make it official."

Phoebe nodded, swallowing hard. "I'm ready."

But was she? The rational part of her brain, the engineer, the scientist, knew the silo was structurally unsound. The concrete was failing, the rebar was corroding, and the foundation was shifting. From a purely technical standpoint, demolition was the only safe option.

And yet.

"Before we begin the formal proceedings," Mayor Wilson announced to the room, "I'd like to acknowledge that we have a special guest today. Mr. Harrison Hollow has requested to address the council regarding the silo demolition."

Phoebe's head snapped up. The elderly man stood at the entrance to the meeting room, leaning heavily on a gnarled wooden cane. He wore a dark suit that must have been fashionable decades ago, its shoulders now too large for his diminished frame. Under his arm, he carried an old leather-bound book.

"Mr. Hollow," the mayor continued, "while we respect your family's historical connection to the structure, I should remind everyone that Ms. Weaver's engineering assessment is the primary consideration in today's vote."

Harrison's pale blue eyes found Phoebe's across the room. He gave her a slight nod, as if they shared a secret, which, she supposed, they did.

"I understand, Mayor," Harrison said, his voice stronger than his frail appearance suggested. "I'm not here to dispute Ms. Weaver's technical findings. Just to provide some historical context that might be relevant to the council's decision."

The mayor gestured to an empty chair. "Very well. Ms. Weaver, please proceed with your presentation."

Phoebe moved to the front of the room and set her folder on the podium. She'd given this presentation a dozen times in her mind and had prepared slides and diagrams and a carefully reasoned argument. But now, with Harrison Hollow watching her intently, the words felt hollow and incomplete.

"The Millfield grain silo was constructed in 1923," she

began, her voice steadier than she felt. “While it was innovative for its time, incorporating reinforced concrete when most agricultural silos were still being built with wood or metal, the structure has degraded significantly over the past century.”

She clicked through her slides, showing close-up images of crumbling concrete, stress fractures, and the slight but dangerous tilt that had developed over decades.

“My analysis indicates that the foundation is failing at an accelerated rate. The silo has shifted three degrees off true vertical in just the past five years. This represents a critical safety concern, as a structure of this size could cause significant damage if it were to collapse unexpectedly.”

Council member Jenkins raised his hand. “What’s the timeline we’re looking at? How imminent is the danger?”

“It’s difficult to predict exactly,” Phoebe admitted. “But based on the rate of degradation, I would estimate significant structural failure within eighteen to twenty-four months. Possibly sooner if we experience extreme weather events.”

“And restoration isn’t an option?” This came from Councilwoman Martinez, who chaired the local historical society.

“The cost would be prohibitive. We’re talking about completely rebuilding the foundation and replacing approximately sixty percent of the concrete shell. It would be more economical to demolish and rebuild from scratch.”

“And nobody wants to do that,” Mayor Wilson said. “The structure serves no practical purpose for our community anymore.”

Harrison Hollow cleared his throat loudly. “If I might interject?”

The mayor sighed but nodded his permission.

“That silo was never about storing grain.” Harrison’s voice carried surprising authority withing the room. “That was just the cover story."

A murmur ran through the assembled council members.

Phoebe felt her heart rate accelerate.

"Mr. Hollow," the mayor began in a placating tone, "we all appreciate your family's history—"

"My grandfather didn't build a grain silo." Harrison opened the leather-bound book. "He built a seal. A container." The old man's eyes locked with Phoebe's. "A prison."

The room fell silent.

"This is my grandfather's journal." He held up the book. "Thaddeus Hollow. He founded this town, laid out its streets, and named it Millfield, even though there was no mill for twenty miles." He paused for a breath. "He chose this location for a reason, and it wasn't the fertile soil or the nearby river, as our local history books claim."

Mayor Wilson's polite smile had hardened into something closer to a grimace. "Mr. Hollow, while we appreciate your family's folklore—"

"It's not folklore," Harrison snapped. "It's history. True history. And it matters now more than ever because that silo is failing, just as Ms. Weaver says. But tearing it down isn't the answer. That would be like seeing a crack in a dam and deciding to remove the whole structure."

Phoebe found herself stepping away from the podium, moving closer to Harrison. "What does the journal say, Mr. Hollow?"

Harrison looked up at her, his relief evident in his expression. "It tells why this town exists. Why my grandfather laid out the streets in such a peculiar pattern. Why he insisted on that massive concrete structure when a metal silo would have been cheaper, more efficient." He offered the book to Phoebe. "See for yourself."

She took the journal carefully. The leather binding was cracked with age, and the pages yellowed and brittle. The handwriting inside was cramped but legible, written in faded brown ink that time had rendered the color of dried blood.

"This isn't the time for a history lesson," Mayor Wilson said firmly. "We're here to vote on a matter of public safety."

"This is a matter of public safety," Harrison insisted. "More than you know."

Phoebe found herself nodding. "I'd like a little time to review this. Would that be possible? Perhaps we could postpone the vote until—"

"Absolutely not," the mayor shouted. "The demolition team is already contracted. Delays would cost the town thousands."

"One day," Phoebe pressed. "Just allow me one day to review this information and see if it's relevant to my assessment."

The mayor looked like a no vote, but Councilwoman Martinez spoke up. "I think that's reasonable. We should have all available information before making a final decision."

After a moment of tense silence, Mayor Wilson nodded quietly. "Alright, Ms. Weaver. You have one day. We'll reconvene tomorrow afternoon for the final vote." He banged his gavel. "Meeting adjourned."

As the council members filed out, Phoebe stood clutching the old journal, aware that Harrison Hollow hadn't taken his eyes off her.

"You'll see," the old man said quietly. "It's all there. What my grandfather knew. What he did, what we've all been living on top of for a hundred years without realizing it."

Phoebe swallowed hard. "And what is that, exactly?"

Harrison's weathered face was solemn. "A wound in the world. A place where things that should stay separate can bleed together." He nodded toward the journal. "Read it. And when you've finished, come see me. There isn't much time." His pale blue eyes held hers with the same intensity they had last night on his porch when he'd asked her about the cost of her daughter's shadow.

* * *

The local coffee shop seemed too normal, too ordinary a place to be reading about wounds in the world and things that bled between realities. Phoebe sat in a corner booth, Harrison's journal open before her, a rapidly cooling latte at her elbow. Outside, Millfield went about its day, people shopping, chatting, living their lives, entirely unaware of the growing knot of dread in Phoebe's stomach. Unaware that last night, in a little girl's bedroom, her shadow had stood guard while she slept.

The journal began conventionally enough. Thaddeus Hollow had come to this valley in 1920, a young man of twenty-six, with dreams of establishing a farming community.

> March 15, 1920: I arrived in the valley today. The land appears promising, though the locals in Coopersville spoke of it with strange reluctance. One old-timer warned me that nothing grows right in the place they call "Shadow Valley." Superstitious nonsense, no doubt, but it did secure me a favorable price.

Phoebe sipped her cooling latte, turning pages carefully. The early entries detailed Thaddeus's efforts to survey the land and his plans for dividing it into farmsteads with a small-town on the north edge. But by the summer of that first year, the entries took on a different tone.

> June 21, 1920, observed a most peculiar phenomenon today. At mid-afternoon, when the sun was no longer directly overhead, there

appeared to be an absence of shadows in the corn surrounding a central clearing. As if the light were coming from all directions at once, or perhaps from none. The effect lasted precisely seven minutes before normal shadows leaned from the corn rows. I have not mentioned this to the workers.

July 3, 1920: The shadow anomaly occurred again today, lasting nine minutes. Corn stalks cast no shadows around a clearing, as if they'd simply walked away. Jenkins' dog refuses to enter the clearing, growing agitated when forced. I have measured the affected area carefully. It forms a perfect circle approximately 120 feet in diameter, centered within the northern field where the soil remains strangely lifeless despite the surrounding fertility. I suspect some underground contamination or unusual mineral deposit, though no natural explanation fully accounts for the phenomena I observed there.

More curious still is a second barren circle within the western cornfield, roughly thirty feet across. Like the larger clearing, this area appears fertile but inactive, as though responding to the same unseen force. I cannot yet determine whether the two locations are connected, but the symmetry troubles me greatly.

July 10, 1920: I woke from troubled dreams to find a stranger standing at my bedside. A tall figure, silhouetted against the window, though there was no moon last night to cast such a shadow. When I lit the lamp, no one was there. Yet, the impression remains that I was not alone.

Phoebe felt a chill run through her despite the warmth of the coffee shop. The entries continued, describing

Thaddeus's growing obsession with the shadow anomalies, his research into similar phenomena, and his correspondence with scholars of obscure metaphysics.

By early 1921, the journal took an even darker turn.

> February 12, 1921: What I have learned cannot be unlearned. The thinness between worlds in this valley is not a natural occurrence but a deliberate weakening. Something has been trying to break through for centuries. The native peoples knew this; it explains why no settlements existed here despite the fertile land. They called it "the valley where shadows walk alone."
>
> February 20, 1921: Met with Professor Hargrove from Miskatonic University. He confirmed my worst suspicions. The barrier between our world and what he calls "the shadow realm" is weakest at certain points on the earth. This valley contains one such point. The danger, he warns, is not just that shadows are independent from their casters, but they may create a conduit for something far worse to enter our reality.

Phoebe's hand trembled slightly as she turned the page. Outside the coffee shop window, the afternoon sun had shifted, lengthening the shadows on the sidewalk. She found herself watching them intently, searching for any movement that didn't correspond to their owners.

The journal continued with Thaddeus's increasingly desperate search for a solution. He consulted rabbis, priests, and practitioners of forgotten folk magic. None offered a permanent solution, only temporary measures to strengthen the barrier between worlds.

Then came the entry that made Phoebe's breath catch.

May 5, 1921: The answer came to me in a conference with the Native People's Shaman. He said we cannot destroy the weak point; it is a flaw in the fabric of reality rooted within this valley where shadows walk alone. But perhaps it can be contained. Sealed beneath layers of stone, iron, and symbols older than memory. A structure raised upon the afflicted ground itself may imprison whatever force gathers there. More importantly, the Shaman advised, the town surrounding it must be arranged in a precise pattern, a binding sigil etched into the landscape itself.

The next several pages contained detailed drawings, architectural plans for a massive concrete structure, but also intricate patterns that looked like a combination of circuit diagrams and occult symbols. Thaddeus had mapped out the entire town of Millfield as a giant binding spell, with the silo in its northern field.

October 17, 1921: Began construction today. The workers believe we are building a grain silo, the centerpiece of our new farming community. They do not know what I have mixed into the concrete, the relics, the blessed objects, the symbols etched into each form before the pour. I work alongside them during the day. At night, I add the elements they must not see. Tonight, I found an odd stone where the foundation had been dug. It emitted a silver light only seen in darkness. I offered it to the Shaman as thanks for sending workers from his tribe.

December 3, 1921: The foundation is complete. Already I sense a strengthening of the barrier. The shadow anomalies have ceased; the

> shadows don't walk away anymore. The Shaman visited yesterday and confirmed that the design is working as intended. Beneath the center stone we placed the final elements of the binding. Objects marked with symbols and substances drawn from older traditions I dare not describe even in these pages. They are not the barrier itself, but anchors for it, while the concrete structure serves as the closed door.

Phoebe read until her coffee went cold, until the afternoon light began to fade from the coffee shop windows. The journal detailed the completion of the silo, the careful layout of Millfield's streets and public spaces according to Thaddeus's arcane design, and the gradual forgetting of the true purpose behind it all.

The final entry was dated June 15, 1947, when Thaddeus would have been in his early fifties.

> The binding weakens. I have felt it for months now, a thinning of the barrier, a stirring of what lies beyond. My son understands only partly what must be done. I have added to the original structure, reinforced the binding, and renewed what had begun to fade. But I am not the man I was when I first built the seal. My conviction wavers. Sometimes, in dreams, I hear them whispering, promising knowledge, power, and freedom from the constraints of this world. I fear for those who will come after me, who will inherit this burden without understanding its importance. The silo must stand. The pattern of the town must remain unbroken. If either fails, what was imprisoned will escape. And it hungers for what it has been denied for so long, the shadows of this world and the light that casts them.

Phoebe closed the journal slowly, her mind racing. It was madness, of course, the ravings of a man who'd spent too much time alone in a remote valley and who'd allowed local superstitions to infect his imagination.

She thought of Maddie's shadow, remaining suspended in midair when it should have fallen with her. The shadow in her room, standing guard while Maddie slept, pressing a finger to its lips. The darkness seemed to pool and concentrate when her headlights swept across the silo.

Her phone buzzed, making her jump. A text from David: *Where are you? I thought you'd be home after the meeting. Everything ok?*

Phoebe glanced at the time, 5:30. She'd been reading for hours.

Sorry, got caught up in some research. Heading home soon. All good.

She slipped the phone back into her pocket and gathered the journal, careful not to damage its fragile binding. Outside, dusk was approaching, that in-between time when shadows lengthened and deepened before surrendering to the night.

As she walked to her car, Phoebe found herself stepping carefully, almost superstitiously, making sure she didn't step on any shadows, not her own, not those cast by buildings or trees or the few pedestrians still out on the streets. She felt a prickle at the back of her neck, the sensation of being watched by something just at the edge of perception.

She was being ridiculous, of course. Letting an old man's stories and his grandfather's journal influence her scientific judgment. There had to be a rational explanation for what she'd witnessed, sleep deprivation, stress, the power of suggestion.

And yet, as she drove home through the gathering darkness, Phoebe found herself taking a route that avoided passing the silo, its massive silhouette visible on the horizon, standing sentinel over Millfield just as it had for a century.

Standing sentinel or serving as a prison.

* * *

"You're telling me we're living in some kind of occult, binding sigil?" David's voice held a mixture of amusement and concern as he stood in their kitchen later that night, watching Phoebe spread out a map of Millfield on the counter.

"I'm not telling you anything," Phoebe said, tracing the town's main streets with her finger. "I'm just considering all the information."

After dinner, a quiet affair during which Phoebe had been too distracted to contribute much to the conversation, she'd put Maddie to bed and then pulled out the town maps from her office. Now, with Thaddeus Hollow's journal open beside the modern street layout, she was searching for patterns, correlations, anything that might disprove the old man's wild claims.

The problem was, she was finding the opposite.

"Look." She pointed to the central intersection. "The original town plan had six main roads radiating from the center point, where the silo stands, like spokes on a wheel. Those roads still exist. But over time, connecting streets were added, altering this pattern." She traced the hexagonal grid from which the town had grown. "These housing developments around the community center, they're outside the original containing pattern."

David leaned closer, frowning. "Or like any normal town that started with a hub-and-spoke design and expanded outward. Phoebe, you can't seriously be buying into this supernatural explanation."

She looked up at him, at the rational skepticism in his eyes that would normally mirror her own. "I'm not saying I believe it. I'm saying there are coincidences that deserve investigation."

"What kind of coincidences?"

Phoebe hadn't told him about Maddie's shadow or about the strange things she'd witnessed. Saying them aloud would make them real and would force her to acknowledge that either she was experiencing some kind of psychological break or that her understanding of reality was fundamentally flawed.

"The placement of major buildings," she said instead, evading the question. "The town square, the library, the old courthouse, they form a perfect hexagram when connected on the map. That's a deliberate design choice, not random development."

David sighed, running a hand through his hair. "Okay, so the town founder was into sacred geometry or whatever. That doesn't mean he was containing shadow monsters."

"No, it doesn't," Phoebe agreed, though she wasn't as certain as she sounded. "But the silo itself is strange, David. The construction methods were excessive, even for the time. The walls are three feet thick in some places, with unusual materials mixed into the concrete matrix."

"Like what?"

"According to the journal?" Phoebe flipped through the brittle pages. "Religious artifacts. Iron filings. Silver dust. Crushed herbs and resins. She paused, reading the entry again. "Even bone meal from consecrated ground."

David's eyebrows shot up. "Okay, that's straight-up crazy. You know that, right?"

"I know how it sounds, but David, they vote to demolish the silo tomorrow. The actual demolition is scheduled for next week. If even a fraction of what's in this journal is true—"

"It's not," he said firmly. "It can't be. Shadows don't move independently of their owners. There's no such thing as shadow monsters trying to break through from another dimension." He placed his hands on her shoulders, his expression softening. "Honey, you're exhausted. You've been working on this project for months. The stress is getting to you."

Phoebe wanted to believe him. She wanted to dismiss Harrison Hollow's warnings and Thaddeus's journal as the products of vivid imaginations and superstitious minds. But she couldn't shake the memory of Maddie's shadow, that impossible moment of separation, of independence, then reunification.

"Maybe you're right," she said, not meeting his eyes. "I just need to be thorough. Make sure I've considered every angle before that structure comes down."

David pulled her into a hug. "That's my meticulous engineer. Always checking her calculations." He kissed the top of her head. "Don't stay up too late with this stuff, okay? You've got the final vote tomorrow."

After he went upstairs, Phoebe remained at the kitchen counter, studying the maps and the journal, looking for anything that might help her make sense of what was happening. According to Thaddeus, the binding needed to be renewed periodically, every thirty years or so. That aligned with what Harrison had told her about his father reinforcing the foundation in the 1950s and Harrison himself doing the same in the 1980s.

If the pattern held, the binding would be critically weakened by now, over forty years since its last renewal. And if, if, there was any truth to the journal, then the demolition of the silo wouldn't just remove an eyesore from Millfield's skyline. It would break the seal entirely.

Phoebe stared at the final page of Thaddeus's journal, at the last warning penned in faded ink: *If it fails, what was imprisoned will escape. And it hungers for what it has been denied for so long, the shadows of this world and the light that casts them.*

Outside the kitchen window, a streetlight flickered, casting shadows that jumped across the backyard. Phoebe watched them, half-expecting to see them move independently, to detach from the swaying branches and fluttering leaves that created them.

She needed to speak with Harrison again to understand exactly what "reinforcing the binding" entailed. But that would have to wait until morning. For now, she needed to prepare for tomorrow's vote to decide whether she would stand by her original assessment or risk her professional reputation by advocating for Harrison's supernatural explanation.

As she gathered the maps and carefully closed the journal, Phoebe couldn't shake the feeling that a clock was ticking down, not just to tomorrow's vote, but to something larger, something that had been building for decades beneath the surface of her ordinary life in what she'd always thought was an ordinary town.

She turned off the kitchen light and headed upstairs, automatically checking on Maddie before going to her room. Her daughter slept peacefully, curled around her favorite stuffed rabbit, her face soft in the glow of her nightlight. Phoebe's eyes went immediately to the wall, to the shadow cast by Maddie's small form. It was perfectly normal, perfectly aligned with her daughter's sleeping position. No sign of the independent movement, the impossible standing figure she'd glimpsed before, that shadow with its finger pressed to unseen lips in a silent shushing gesture.

Relief washed through her, followed immediately by doubt. If she couldn't trust her own eyes, her perception of reality, what could she trust? The rational equations and structural analyses that had guided her career? Or the warnings in a century-old journal written by a man who believed he was containing shadow monsters? Harrison's words from last night echoed in her mind: “They see it first. Feel it first. Their shadows are tastier, I suppose. More vital.”

As she closed Maddie’s door and retreated to her bedroom, Phoebe realized she was walking a knife-edge between two incompatible worldviews. By this time tomorrow, she would have chosen which one to embrace, and live with the consequences of that choice, whatever they might be.

CHAPTER 3:
THE FIRST SEPARATION

The demolition of the Millfield grain silo had been a spectacle. Despite Mayor Wilson's insistence that it was a routine infrastructure project; half the town had gathered at the designated safety perimeter last Wednesday morning to watch a century of history come down in a controlled implosion.

Phoebe had stood at the front of the crowd, her face a rigid mask of professional detachment that concealed the storm of doubt and fear churning beneath. Three days had passed since she'd cast the deciding vote, against her better judgment, against the warnings in Thaddeus Hollow's journal, against the pleading eyes of Harrison Hollow, who had sat silently in the back of the council chamber as she delivered her final assessment.

"The structural integrity has been compromised beyond economical repair," she had told the council, the words tasting like ash in her mouth. "From an engineering standpoint, controlled demolition is the only safe course of action."

She had said nothing about shadow entities, about binding sigils, about wounds in the world. In the stark fluorescent lighting of the council chambers, such concepts sounded absurd, the products of an overactive imagination and sleep deprivation. But as the mayor had smiled and thanked her for her "rational analysis," Phoebe had caught Harrison Hollow's eyes. The old man hadn't looked angry or betrayed, only resigned, as if he'd expected this outcome all along.

"Six days," he'd whispered as he passed her on his way out. "Remember what I told you. Watch the shadows."

Now, three days after the silo had collapsed into a mountain of broken concrete and twisted rebar, Phoebe sat at her kitchen table, staring at the morning newspaper. The headline read: "HISTORIC SILO DEMOLITION MARKS NEW ERA FOR MILLFIELD." Below it was a dramatic photo of the structure mid-collapse, dust billowing upward in a massive cloud that had temporarily darkened the sky.

Darkened the sky. Strengthened the shadows.

Phoebe pushed the thought away. She'd been hyper-vigilant since the demolition, watching every shadow with suspicion, her own, Maddie's, those cast by furniture and trees and passing cars. But they had all behaved normally. No independent movements, no impossible pauses, no shadowy figures pressing fingers to nonexistent lips.

Maybe Harrison had been wrong. Perhaps the journal was just the record of a man's descent into paranoia and superstition. Perhaps—

Maddie bounced into the kitchen. She was already dressed in her favorite purple overalls, despite the early hour. "Mom, Lucy's coming over today, right? I cleaned my room and everything."

Phoebe smiled, pushing away her dark thoughts. "Yes, she'll be here around eleven. Her mom's got a doctor's appointment, so Lucy's staying until dinner."

Lucy Holloway was Maddie's best friend, a serious seven-year-old with a flair for dramatic storytelling. The girls had been inseparable since kindergarten.

"Can we have cheese sandwiches for lunch?" Maddie climbed onto a chair, her legs swinging rhythmically beneath the table.

"Sure, sweetie." Phoebe watched as morning sunlight streamed through the kitchen window, casting Maddie's shadow across the tiled floor. Perfectly normal. Perfectly aligned with her daughter's movements. She exhaled slowly. "What are you girls planning to do today?"

"We're going to play Explorers in the backyard. Lucy says there's a portal to another dimension behind the big oak tree."

Phoebe stopped raising her coffee cup halfway to her lips. "What?"

Maddie shrugged, oblivious to her mother's sudden tension. "It's just pretend, Mom. Lucy makes up the best games."

"Right. Of course." Phoebe set her cup down carefully. "Maddie, has Lucy said anything strange lately? About shadows, maybe?"

The little girl tilted her head, considering. "She said her shadow was talking to her, but I think that's just another game. Lucy has many imaginary friends."

A chill ran down Phoebe's spine. "When did she tell you this?"

"Yesterday at school. During recess." Maddie frowned slightly. "Why? Is that bad?"

"No, no," Phoebe assured her quickly. "I was just curious, you know, about your games."

Maddie nodded, apparently satisfied with this explanation. "Can I have Cheerios for breakfast?"

"Sure." Phoebe moved automatically to the cabinet, her mind racing. Children's imaginations were boundless, she reminded herself. Lucy was a creative child who loved fantasy stories. There was nothing unusual about her pretending her shadow could talk.

Except that Harrison had said children would see it first. Feel it first.

As she poured cereal for Maddie, Phoebe resolved to pay close attention when Lucy arrived. Not to frighten the child, of course, just to observe. If there really was something wrong with the shadows in Millfield, she needed to know. Needed to be prepared.

At precisely eleven o'clock, the doorbell rang. Maddie raced to answer it, calling out Lucy's name before she'd even reached the door. Phoebe followed more slowly, schooling her features into a welcoming smile.

Mary Holloway stood on the porch, her hand resting lightly on her daughter's shoulder. Lucy looked exactly as she always did, a slender girl with serious eyes and a backpack almost as big as she was.

"Thanks again for watching her," Mary said. "The appointment shouldn't take more than a couple of hours, but with the wait times at Dr. Brennen's office these days..."

"It's no problem at all," Phoebe assured her. "The girls will have fun, and you can pick Lucy up whenever you're done. No rush."

As Mary bent to give her daughter a goodbye hug, Phoebe's eyes were drawn to their shadows on the porch, two silhouettes, perfectly aligned with their owners, nothing unusual or alarming.

You're being ridiculous, she told herself. *Stop looking for monsters in every corner.*

"Be good for Ms. Weaver," Mary told Lucy. "And remember what we talked about."

A flicker of something, worry? Fear? Crossed Lucy's face before she nodded solemnly. "I will."

As Mary walked back to her car, the girls disappeared into the house, already chattering about their plans for the day. Phoebe lingered on the porch for a moment, watching Mary drive away. Remember what we talked about? It was probably nothing, a reminder about manners or not being too rambunctious.

Inside, she found the girls already heading toward the back door, Maddie leading the way with exuberant energy while Lucy followed at a more measured pace.

"We're going to play outside," Maddie announced.

"That's fine. I'll bring some lemonade out in a little while." Phoebe smiled at Lucy. "It's good to see you, Lucy. How have things been?"

The little girl looked up, her dark eyes somehow older than her seven years. "Different," she said after a moment. "Since they took down the big tower."

Phoebe felt her smile falter. "The silo? Did you use to play near there?"

Lucy shook her head. "My mom said it was dangerous. But things were better when it was still standing."

"Better how?"

The girl's eyes darted to the window, to the bright sunlight outside. "Quieter," she said finally. "In my head. And my shadow didn't—" She stopped abruptly, pressing her lips together.

"Your shadow didn't do what, Lucy?" Phoebe asked gently, crouching down to the child's level.

Lucy glanced at Maddie, who was impatiently waiting by the door. "It's okay," she whispered. "Mom says it's just my imagination. That shadows can't really talk or move on their own."

Phoebe's heart thudded painfully against her ribs. "And what do you think?"

"I think—"

"Lucy, come on!" Maddie whined. "We need to find the portal before lunchtime."

The moment broken, Lucy stepped back, her expression closing. "We should go play now."

Phoebe straightened, forcing a smile. "Of course. You girls have fun. I'll be right here if you need anything."

As they ran outside into the bright late-morning sunshine, Phoebe moved to the kitchen window that overlooked the backyard. The girls' shadows stretched across the grass, two dark silhouettes elongated by the angle of the sun. Nothing unusual. Nothing to indicate that anything was wrong.

And yet, Lucy's words echoed in her mind. *My shadow didn't...* Do what? Move correctly? Speak to her? Stay attached?

Phoebe thought of Harrison Hollow's warnings and of Thaddeus's journal with its accounts of shadow anomalies. Three days had passed since the silo came down. Three days since the seal was broken...if the journal was to be believed, three days closer to... To what? Disaster? And already, a seven-year-old girl was talking about shadows that didn't...behave as they should?

She needed to speak with Harrison again. But first, she needed to keep a careful eye on the two children playing in her backyard, and on the shadows that accompanied them.

The girls played outside for hours, their game evolving from searching for imaginary portals to an elaborate form of hide-and-seek among the trees and shrubs at the edge of the property. Phoebe brought them lemonade and sandwiches for lunch, which they ate on the back patio, chattering about school and friends and the latest cartoon they both loved.

Throughout it all, Phoebe watched their shadows. They stretched and compressed as the girls moved around the yard, darkened when clouds passed over the sun, and behaved exactly as shadows should. Lucy seemed to have forgotten her earlier unease, laughing at Maddie's jokes and joining in their games with enthusiasm.

Maybe it really is just her imagination, Phoebe thought as she cleared away the lunch dishes. Children Lucy's age often have trouble distinguishing between fantasy and reality.

But as the afternoon wore on and the sun began its westward descent, lengthening the shadows across the yard, Phoebe noticed something strange. Lucy had become increasingly quiet, her movements more tentative. Several times, Phoebe caught the girl looking down at her shadow with an expression that could only be described as wary.

At four o'clock, Phoebe called the girls inside for a snack. As they settled at the kitchen table with apple slices and peanut butter, she studied Lucy covertly. The child seemed tense; her shoulders hunched slightly as if expecting a blow.

"Lucy, are you feeling okay?" Phoebe asked gently. "You seem a little tired."

The girl glanced toward the window, where the afternoon light was taking on the golden quality that preceded sunset. "I'm okay," she said, but her voice lacked conviction. "Just it's getting late."

"Your mom should be here in about an hour. Would you like to watch a movie until then? You girls could relax on the couch."

Lucy nodded, seemingly relieved at the suggestion. "Could we watch with the blinds closed and all the lights on?"

Maddie looked puzzled. "But you're not scared of the dark. You told me so at our last sleepover."

"I'm not scared of the dark," Lucy said, her voice barely above a whisper. "I'm scared of what happens when the light starts to go away but isn't gone yet." Her eyes met Phoebe's, filled with knowledge no child should possess. "When the shadows get long and hungry."

A chill ran through Phoebe. "Of course we can close the blinds," she said, keeping her voice steady with effort. "Why don't you girls go pick out a movie? I'll bring your snacks into the living room."

As the children left the kitchen, Phoebe leaned heavily against the counter, her pulse racing. Lucy's words echoed Harrison Hollow's warnings with uncanny precision. Hungry shadows. The old man had said that whatever was sealed beneath the silo fed on shadows first, before moving on to what cast them.

She moved quickly through the house, closing blinds and turning on lights, creating a bright, shadow-minimizing environment. In the living room, she found the girls already settled on the couch, a Disney movie queued up on the television. Lucy sat rigidly at one end, as far as possible from the one window where the blinds remained open.

Phoebe quickly closed those blinds too, then set the snack tray on the coffee table. "There we go. All cozy."

Maddie was already engrossed in the movie's opening sequence, but Lucy's eyes remained fixed on the floor, on the space where her shadow would be if it weren't diffused by the bright overhead lights.

"Lucy," Phoebe said softly, sitting beside the girl. "Can you tell me what's happening with your shadow? I promise I won't think you're making it up."

The child looked up, surprise and relief flickering across her face. "You believe me?"

"I need you to tell me exactly what's happening."

Lucy glanced at Maddie, who was happily singing along with the movie's first musical number. "It started after they knocked down the big tower," she whispered. "At first, I just felt like someone was watching me. Then I started hearing whispers. Quiet, like someone talking through a wall. I couldn't understand what they were saying."

"And then?" Phoebe prompted gently.

"Then yesterday, when I was walking home from school, I could understand some words. My shadow was talking to me." Lucy's voice trembled. "It said it had always been with me, but now it could finally speak. It said it had been waiting for the cage to break."

The cage. The silo. Phoebe's mouth went dry. "What else did it say?"

"It said soon it wouldn't have to follow me anymore. That when the sun starts to set today, it would be strong enough to separate." Tears welled in Lucy's eyes. "I told my mom, but she said I was just having bad dreams because of the loud noise when they knocked down the tower. She said to stop making up stories."

Phoebe squeezed the girl's hand. "I believe you, Lucy. And I'm going to help you. Okay?"

Lucy nodded, a single tear tracking down her cheek. "It's getting stronger. I can feel it pulling away, like a bandage coming unstuck. It hurts."

Outside, the quality of light was changing as sunset approached, that in-between time that photographers called the golden hour and that Harrison Hollow had warned was when the boundary between worlds of light and shadow was thinnest.

"Where's your phone, Lucy?" Phoebe asked, suddenly remembering that Mary would be calling to say she was on her way.

"In my backpack. By the door."

"I'm going to call your mom and see how close she is. You stay right here with Maddie." Phoebe stood, casting a quick glance at her shadow, diffused by the bright room lights, but a normal silhouette that mimicked her movements perfectly.

She found Lucy's sparkly pink backpack in the entryway and located the phone in the front pocket. The screen showed three missed calls from "Mom" and a text message: *Running late. Traffic accident on Main St. will be there by 6. Call if there's any problem.*

It was 5:37. The sun would be setting soon, the golden hour giving way to dusk, what photographers called the blue hour, when shadows deepened before dissolving into general darkness.

The shadow hours, Phoebe thought with a chill. When boundaries grew thin. She quickly texted Mary back: *No problem. Girls watching a movie. Drive safe.*

As she stooped to set the phone in the backpack, a

flicker of movement caught her eye, a darkness sliding beneath the front door, like a liquid shadow flowing over the threshold. Phoebe froze, watching as the darkness pooled on the entryway floor, then began to take shape, rising like smoke coalescing into a human silhouette.

It wasn't her shadow. It wasn't anyone's shadow. Furthermore, it was a shadow that existed independently, without a source, without an anchor.

The figure turned toward her, or seemed to, though it had no discernible face, only a deeper darkness where features might be. It raised one arm in silent greeting.

Phoebe stumbled backward, nearly dropping Lucy's phone. "Who, what, are you?"

The shadow figure tilted its head, regarding her with an air of curiosity. It gestured again, this time pointing toward the living room where the girls were watching their movie.

A high, thin scream split the air, Lucy's voice, sharp with terror.

Phoebe ran back to the living room, the independent shadow flowing after her like a dark tide. She found Lucy standing in the center of the room, her face chalk-white, staring at the floor around her feet.

Or rather, at what wasn't there.

Lucy Holloway cast no shadow. None, despite the bright overhead lights that should have created a diffused silhouette on the hardwood floor beneath her.

"It's gone," the girl whispered, her voice shaking. "It left me."

At that moment, the shadow that had followed Phoebe from the entryway flowed into the room, rising once more into a human shape. It moved toward Lucy with an air of recognition, of familiar intimacy.

"Lucy?" Maddie's voice was small and frightened. "What's happening?"

The girl didn't answer. She was staring at the shadow

figure with a mixture of horror and fascination. “You,” she breathed. “You’re mine.”

The shadow nodded, a strangely human gesture from a being composed entirely of darkness. It extended a hand toward Lucy, not touching her, but close enough that the girl flinched back.

“Lucy, come here,” Phoebe said, her voice as calm as she could make it. “Come to me, sweetheart.”

But Lucy seemed transfixed by her detached shadow. “You’ve been with me all this time,” she whispered. “Seeing what I see? Feeling what I feel?”

The shadow nodded again. It made a gesture like opening a book, then pointed to its chest, or where a chest would be if it had a physical form.

“Stories,” Lucy said, comprehension dawning on her face. “My stories. You’ve been giving me my stories.”

Another nod, more emphatic this time.

“Lucy, please,” Phoebe tried again, taking a step toward the girl.

Lucy held up a hand to stop her. “It’s not trying to hurt me.” Her fear gave way to a child’s innate curiosity. “It’s just free now.”

The shadow made another gesture, complex and deliberate, like sign language, Phoebe realized, but in a form she didn’t recognize.

Lucy frowned. “I don’t understand what you’re trying to say.”

The shadow paused, then pointed to its own dark form, made a sweeping gesture that encompassed the room, and finally pointed back to Lucy.

“You’re saying there are more of you?” Lucy guessed. “More shadows separating?”

The figure nodded vigorously.

“All over town?” Phoebe asked.

The shadow turned toward her and made a gesture of

affirmation.

"But why?" Phoebe persisted. "Why now? Is it because of the silo? Because the seal is broken?"

Another emphatic nod, followed by a series of gestures that neither Phoebe nor Lucy could interpret.

"I think it's trying to explain something complicated," Lucy said, her initial fear now completely replaced by fascination. "About why it needed the tower to come down."

The shadow pointed to itself, then made a motion like breaking chains.

"Freedom," Phoebe said. "You wanted freedom."

A nod, but then more gestures, pointing to Lucy, then to itself, then interlacing what passed for fingers in a complex pattern.

"Connected," Lucy murmured. "We're still connected, even though you are separate now."

The shadow bobbed in what might have been agreement.

Maddie, who had been watching this exchange with wide eyes, suddenly gasped. "Mom! Your shadow!"

Phoebe looked down and felt her heart shudder. Her shadow was no longer aligned with her body. It had shifted slightly to one side, as if attempting to pull away from her.

"It's happening to you too," Lucy said, a strange calm having settled over her. "They're all going to separate, aren't they? All the shadows in town."

The detached shadow, Lucy's shadow, nodded once more. It made another series of signs urgently.

"What is it trying to say?" Phoebe asked, fighting to keep panic from her voice as she felt a strange tugging sensation, as if something was attempting to peel away a layer of her very self.

Lucy watched the shadow's movements intently. "I think. I think it's saying we shouldn't be afraid. That they've been waiting for this for a long time. That they've been conscious of us, all along."

The shadow pointed to the window where the golden light of sunset was deepening toward dusk, then made a sweeping gesture that encompassed the entire room.

"The shadow hours," Phoebe whispered, recalling Harrison's warnings. "Dawn and dusk. When shadows are strongest."

The shadow nodded, then turned back to Lucy. It reached out again, its dark hand hovering just above the girl's own.

"What do you want?" Lucy asked it directly.

The shadow seemed to consider the question. It pointed to itself, then to Lucy, then made a walking motion with its fingers.

"You want to come with me? Go home with me?"

A vigorous nod.

"But my mom..."

The shadow made a gesture of dismissal, followed by what could only be described as a shrug.

"I think it's saying your mom won't believe in it anyway," Maddie interpreted, seemingly less frightened now that the shadow wasn't acting aggressively. "So, it doesn't matter if it comes home with you."

Lucy bit her lip, looking from the shadow to Phoebe. "Is it safe? To let it stay with me?"

Before Phoebe could answer, though, what answer could she possibly give? The doorbell rang. All of them jumped, even the shadow, which flickered like a candle flame in a draft.

"That's probably your mom," Phoebe said, glancing at the time. It was not quite six o'clock. "Lucy, I—"

"Don't tell her," Lucy said quickly. "She already thinks I'm making things up. If she sees..." She gestured at the shadow, which had moved to stand protectively beside her.

The doorbell rang again, more insistently.

"Lucy? Phoebe? Are you home?" Mary's voice called through the door.

The shadow made another urgent series of gestures.

"What's it saying?" Phoebe asked, caught between the need to answer the door and the fascination of this impossible communication.

Lucy watched the shadow's movements. "It's saying there are thirteen other shadows that are different. Older. Stronger." She frowned in concentration. "We need to find someone named Hollow."

"Harrison Hollow," Phoebe breathed. "It knows about Harrison."

The shadow nodded emphatically, then pointed to the door, where Mary was now knocking forcefully.

"I know, I need to answer that." Phoebe turned to Lucy. "What do you want me to do about..." She gestured toward the shadow.

Lucy took a deep breath. "I'll handle it, it's mine, after all. It's been with me my whole life." She looked at the shadow. "You have to look normal around my mom. Can you do that?"

The shadow made a gesture of assent, then flatten itself, becoming a normal shadow once more, sliding across the floor to position itself near the girl's feet in a way that might pass for normal in the dim light of early evening, except that it remained independent of Lucy.

"Lucy? Is everything okay in there?" Mary's voice had taken on an edge of genuine concern.

"Coming!" Phoebe called. She looked at Lucy one more time. "Are you sure about this?"

The girl nodded, strange maturity in her eyes. "It's not evil, Ms. Weaver. Simply different. And it needs my help." She glanced down at the shadow, now positioned to look like it was hers. "We need each other's help."

As Phoebe moved to answer the door, she felt that

strange tugging sensation again, her shadow responding to the weakening barrier between worlds, preparing for its separation. The sensation wasn't painful, exactly, but deeply unsettling, like feeling a limb fall asleep, but on a more existential level.

Three days after the silo's demolition, shadows were detaching across Millfield. Becoming independent entities with their awareness and their agendas. Revealing that they had been conscious all along, waiting for this moment of liberation.

And somewhere out there, if Lucy's shadow was to be believed, were thirteen shadows different from the rest, older, stronger, perhaps more dangerous.

Phoebe opened the door to Mary Holloway's worried face, her mind racing with the implications of what she'd just witnessed and the knowledge that her separation was imminent. As she exchanged pleasantries and assured Mary that Lucy had been perfectly well-behaved, she wondered how many other separations were occurring across town at this very moment, in the deepening light of the shadow hours.

And she wondered what Harrison Hollow would say when she told him that his worst fears had come true, that the seal was broken, the shadows released, and whatever had been imprisoned beneath the silo for a century was now free to roam the world once more.

CHAPTER 4:
THE SHADOW HOURS

By dawn the next morning, Phoebe's shadow had separated completely.

She had felt it happening throughout the night, a slow, inexorable peeling away of something she'd never considered separate from herself. Not painful exactly, but profoundly unsettling, like losing a limb she hadn't known could be removed. She'd lay awake beside David, who slept undisturbed, watching the digital clock on the nightstand mark the passage of hours as that strange tugging sensation grew stronger.

At 5:17 AM, as the first gray light of dawn filtered through the bedroom curtains, she felt a sudden release, a snapping sensation followed by an overwhelming feeling of lightness, as if she'd shed a weight she'd been carrying her entire life without noticing.

She slipped out of bed, padded to the bathroom, and flicked on the light with trembling fingers. The brightness cast her silhouette against the tiled wall, except it wasn't her silhouette anymore. It stood apart from her, a perfect dark copy that moved independently, examining her with head-tipped curiosity.

"Hello," Phoebe whispered, unsure what else to say to this piece of herself that was no longer hers.

The shadow dipped its head in a gesture that conveyed acknowledgment without words. It raised one hand in greeting, mirroring her awkward uncertainty.

"Can you speak?" Phoebe asked.

The shadow made a gesture of negation, then pointed

to its featureless face where a mouth would be and shook its head again.

"But you understand me. You're conscious."

An emphatic nod.

"Have you always been aware...beside me?"

Another nod, followed by a complicated gesture Phoebe couldn't interpret.

"I don't understand."

The shadow seemed to consider this problem, then pointed to the bathroom mirror, made a dividing motion with its hands, and pointed back to Phoebe.

"We're two parts of the same thing?" she guessed.

The shadow nodded vigorously, then made a gesture of something breaking apart, followed by joining back together.

"You're saying we were separated before? And then joined?"

The shadow's movements became more animated, as if excited by her understanding. It nodded, then pointed to the window, where the first pink tendrils of sunrise were beginning to paint the sky.

"The silo," Phoebe breathed. "The binding spell. It didn't just seal away some external threat, did it? It bound you, all of you, to us."

The shadow made a sweeping gesture that Phoebe understood, meaning not just humans and their shadows, but something larger, perhaps all living things and their dark counterparts.

"But why?" she asked. "Why bind shadows to their casters?"

The shadow went very still, as if considering how to answer such a complex question without words. Finally, it pointed to Phoebe, then to itself, then made a balancing motion with its hands, like scales finding equilibrium.

"Balance. We need each other for balance."

The shadow nodded, then pointed outside again, making a wide, encompassing gesture.

"And now the balance is broken across Millfield," Phoebe concluded. "Because the silo came down. Because I recommended its demolition."

The shadow shook its head firmly at this, pointing to Phoebe in a way that seemed to absolve her of blame, then making a motion like something inevitable unfolding.

"It would have happened eventually anyway."

A nod, followed by a gesture toward the rising sun, now sending stronger shafts of light through the window.

"The shadow hours," Phoebe murmured, remembering what Harrison had said. "Dawn and dusk, when the barrier between worlds is thinnest." She looked at her shadow, now moving to stand by the bathroom door. "You're stronger during these times, aren't you?"

The shadow nodded, then pointed toward Maddie's room down the hall.

Phoebe's heart stuttered. "Maddie. Has her shadow?"

The shadow made a gesture suggesting sleep or maybe dormancy.

"Not yet? But it will?"

A nod.

"When?"

The shadow pointed to the window again, where the dawn light was strengthening, then made a curving motion that Phoebe interpreted as the sun's passage across the sky, ending with its finger pointing westward, sunset.

"Tonight? At dusk?"

Another nod.

Phoebe leaned against the bathroom counter, her mind racing. If what her shadow was communicating was true, then by nightfall, everyone in Millfield would experience separation, an entire town of suddenly independent shadows, conscious entities that had been bound to humans, now free to move on their own.

"I need to talk to Harrison Hollow," she said aloud. "He knows more about this than anyone."

The shadow made a gesture of agreement, then pointed toward the bathroom door again, more insistently this time.

"Maddie," Phoebe breathed, suddenly understanding. "I need to check on Maddie."

She hurried down the hall to her daughter's room, her shadow flowing along the wall beside her, moving with a liquid grace that no human could match. Phoebe eased open Maddie's door and peered inside. The little girl was still asleep, her breathing deep and regular, her stuffed animals arranged in a protective semicircle around her head.

Phoebe's eyes immediately went to the wall, where Maddie's shadow should be cast by the nightlight. It was there, but something was wrong. The shadow seemed to flicker occasionally, like a television with poor reception, momentarily losing its shape before reforming in perfect alignment with the sleeping child.

"It's starting already," Phoebe whispered.

Her shadow nodded beside her, making a gesture toward the window, where the sunrise was now fully underway, bathing the room in soft golden light.

"Will she be afraid?" Phoebe asked, her voice barely audible. "When it happens?"

The shadow spread its hands in a gesture of uncertainty, then pointed to Phoebe and back to itself, making a motion that seemed to indicate their peaceful interaction.

"You're saying it depends on how we handle it? On how I explain it to her?"

A nod.

Phoebe sighed, closing Maddie's door quietly. "I need to understand more about what's happening before I try to explain it to her. And that means talking to Harrison Hollow."

Her shadow made a gesture of agreement, then pointed toward the stairs.

"But what about David?" Phoebe glanced back at their bedroom. "His shadow isn't separated yet, either."

The shadow made the same westward-pointing gesture, indicating sunset.

"So, I have until tonight to figure this out," Phoebe said grimly. "To understand what's happening and how to fix it."

The shadow tilted its head, making a gesture that Phoebe couldn't quite interpret, not disagreement, exactly, but a questioning of her assumption.

"You don't think it needs to be fixed?" she asked, surprised.

Her shadow pointed to itself, then to her, then made that balancing motion again.

"You think we need to find a new balance. Not to rebind you, but to coexist somehow."

An emphatic nod.

Phoebe rubbed her temples, feeling a headache building. "This is a lot to process. And I don't even know if I can trust what you're telling me. I mean, you were literally part of me until an hour ago."

The shadow made a gesture that somehow conveyed both acknowledgment of her skepticism and a plea for trust.

"I need to talk to Harrison," Phoebe said again, more firmly this time. "And I have to make sure Maddie is safe when her separation happens."

The shadow nodded, then pointed toward the kitchen.

"Coffee first," Phoebe agreed with a hint of a smile. "Then Harrison."

* * *

The drive to Harrison Hollow's farmhouse was surreal. Phoebe's shadow sat in the passenger seat beside her, or rather, created the appearance of sitting since it had no physical form to bend into the shape of the car seat. Outside, the early morning light cast long shadows across the landscape, and Phoebe found herself studying them with new intensity, wondering if any of them had separated from their casters yet.

The streets of Millfield were quieter than usual for a Thursday morning. Fewer cars, fewer pedestrians. As if the town were collectively holding its breath, waiting for something to happen.

Or perhaps it already had, and people were staying home, trying to make sense of their newly independent shadows.

As she turned onto the rural road that led to Harrison's property, Phoebe noticed something strange in the fields that lined the road. The corn was tall for early October, ready for harvest, golden in the morning light. But its shadows seemed to be moving wrong, not swaying with the stalks in the gentle breeze, but shifting independently, creating patterns that looked almost like writing when viewed from the right angle.

Her shadow noticed it too, pointing out the window at the rippling darkness among the corn rows.

"Is that normal?" Phoebe asked. "For plant shadows to separate too?"

Her shadow made a gesture she interpreted as uncertainty, followed by something that might have meant different or special.

"The corn is different somehow. Important?"

A nod, though not as confident as previous ones.

As they approached Harrison's farmhouse, Phoebe was surprised to see several vehicles parked in the gravel driveway, a police cruiser among them, its emergency lights off but its presence unmistakable. She pulled up behind a battered pickup truck and killed the engine, suddenly apprehensive. "Something's wrong," she murmured.

Her shadow pointed toward the front porch, where a

small group of people had gathered. Phoebe recognized Sheriff Grant's broad shoulders and Harrison's stooped form seated in a rocking chair. The others were unfamiliar to her.

"Let's go." She opened her car door. "But maybe you should, I don't know...try to look normal? Like a regular shadow? I'm not sure how these people will react to you."

Her shadow made a gesture of understanding, then flattened itself against the ground, aligning with her body in a reasonable approximation of a natural shadow. It wasn't perfect, there was still a slight delay in its movements, a subtle independence, but it might pass unnoticed if no one was looking too carefully.

As Phoebe approached the porch, Sheriff Grant turned to face her, his weathered face grave beneath his department-issue Stetson.

"Ms. Weaver," he greeted her. "Somehow, I'm not surprised to see you here."

"Sheriff," Phoebe nodded. "What's going on?"

Grant exchanged a glance with Harrison. "That's what we're trying to figure out. I got reports coming in from all over town, people seeing things, unusual shadow activity, missing persons."

"Not missing," Harrison corrected from his rocking chair. "Separated."

The sheriff sighed. "Mr. Hollow insists this is all related to some sort of shadow phenomenon. Claims it has to do with that old silo coming down."

"He's right," Phoebe said firmly. She gestured toward Harrison. "His grandfather's journal explained it all. The silo was built as a seal to bind shadows to their casters. Now that it's gone, the shadows are separating."

The other people on the porch, a middle-aged woman Phoebe didn't recognize and a younger man who looked vaguely familiar from around town, exchanged skeptical glances.

"You're saying our shadows are, what, becoming independent?" the woman asked. Her voice was thick with disbelief.

"Yes," Phoebe said simply. "Mine did, about two hours ago. At dawn."

Sheriff Grant studied her closely. "Your shadow separated from you?"

"It did." Phoebe looked down at the shadow stretching from her feet across the porch floorboards. It maintained its alignment with her body, playing the role of an ordinary shadow convincingly. "Though right now, it's behaving normally."

"Mmm-hmm," the sheriff said, clearly unconvinced. "And I suppose it talks to you too?"

"Not with words, but it communicates. It's conscious, Sheriff. All our shadows are. They've been conscious all along, just bound to us. By the silo. By the binding sigil that Thaddeus Hollow created when he built this town."

The younger man on the porch snorted. "That's the craziest thing I've ever heard."

Harrison Hollow's voice cut through the tension, quiet but commanding. "Is it, Mr. Jenkins? Crazier than what you saw this morning when you looked in the mirror? When your shadow stepped away from you and bowed in greeting?"

Jenkins paled visibly. "How did you know?"

"Because it's happening all over town," Harrison said. "Just as I warned it would. The shadow hours, dawn and dusk, that's when the separations are occurring. Those who rise early experienced it at sunrise. The rest will face it at sunset."

"This is insane," the woman muttered, but there was fear beneath her skepticism.

Sheriff Grant rubbed his jaw thoughtfully. "Ellen, I've got five deputies taking reports. Strange sightings, unexplained movements, people claiming their shadows are acting independently." He shook his head. "Never thought I'd see the day when I'd be filing police reports about misbehaving shadows."

"They're not misbehaving," Phoebe said. "They're just free. For the first time in a century."

Harrison nodded slowly. "The question isn't what's happening, I think we all know that now, whether we want to admit it or not. The question is what comes next. What do the shadows want? And what about the thirteen?"

Phoebe's attention sharpened. "The thirteen? Lucy Holloway's shadow mentioned them yesterday. It said they were different from the others. Older. Stronger."

"The Dark Exiles," Harrison confirmed. "The original miners who were taken by the darkness beneath this valley back in 1843. What came back from the shaft were not men anymore. My grandfather believed they became something else entirely, shadow-bound beings that were trapped between worlds until the miners opened a wound."

Phoebe frowned. "Like a portal?"

"I think so. Everything that followed, including the silo itself, was built to contain the shadow walkers."

Sheriff Grant held up a hand. "Hold on. You're telling me there are thirteen dangerous super-shadows out there somewhere?"

"That's precisely what I'm telling you, Sheriff," Harrison said gravely. "Our everyday shadows, the ones attached to people and animals and plants... everything... they're just shadows. Sentient, yes, but not inherently dangerous. The Exiles had been imprisoned for a century, growing stronger and more resentful. And now they're free."

"Where would they go?" Phoebe asked. "If they've just been released, where would they head first?"

Harrison's pale eyes met hers. "To the place where they first entered this world. The land above the wound that allowed them to cross over in the first place." He pointed toward the window, in the direction of the cornfields that surrounded Millfield. "The shadow territory."

Phoebe felt a chill run through her. "The corn. I noticed something strange about the shadows in the fields on my way here."

"It's starting already then," Harrison murmured. "The harvesting."

"Harvesting what?" Ellen asked, her skepticism giving way to genuine fear.

"Shadow energy," Harrison replied. "The Exiles feed on it, grow stronger from it. The fields have always been their territory. The Native People's binding spells couldn't seal them away completely, it was too vast, too deeply connected to the land itself. Despite all efforts, shadows of the shadows, wandered the fields and drove the settlers away. The best Thaddeus Hollow could do was build a silo to bind the shadows to their casters and limit their ability to roam."

"And now?" Sheriff Grant prompted.

"The Exiles are free to transform this valley. To make it more like the realm they came from."

A heavy silence fell over the porch. Even Jenkins, who had been the most skeptical, seemed unable to formulate a denial in the face of Harrison's grim certainty.

Finally, Sheriff Grant spoke. "I need to coordinate a response. Set up some kind of crisis center, I guess. People will be scared when their shadows start detaching at sunset."

"The community center," the woman suggested. "It's in the residential district, has plenty of space, and has emergency generators if we need them."

"And a bomb shelter," Jenkins added and snickered as if it was some kind of inside joke.

Grant nodded. "Ellen, can you head over there and start getting things organized? We'll need cots, water, and first aid supplies, the usual emergency protocol."

Ellen nodded, her earlier skepticism apparently forgotten in the face of practical action. "I'll call the Red Cross coordinator, too. And the hospital, make sure they're prepared for whatever this might bring."

"Tell 'em 'unexplained neurological phenomenon' if anyone asks what we're preparing for," Grant advised. "Let's not start a panic by talking about sentient shadows."

As Ellen hurried off to her car, Grant turned to Jenkins. "You still work at the radio station?"

Jenkins nodded. "Morning show producer."

"Good. I need you to prepare an announcement. Nothing alarming, just a notice that the community center is being activated as a precautionary measure due to reports of...let's say 'unusual visual phenomena' affecting multiple residents. Advise people to remain calm, stay indoors at sunset if possible, and report to the community center if they feel unsafe or experience concerning symptoms."

"You want me to tell people their shadows are about to detach and become independent entities?" Jenkins asked incredulously.

"No," Grant said firmly. "I want you to prepare people for something unusual without causing a mass panic. There will be time for full explanations once we have the situation under control."

As Jenkins departed, muttering under his breath about the impossibility of his task, Grant turned back to Harrison and Phoebe. "Now..." his voice dropped to a more confidential tone, "tell me everything you know about these thirteen Exiles and what they might be planning."

Harrison gestured to the rocking chair beside him. "Sit, Phoebe. This will take some explaining."

As Phoebe settled into the chair, her shadow detached from its show of normalcy and rose to stand independently beside her. Sheriff Grant took an involuntary step back, his hand instinctively moving toward the gun on his hip.

"It's okay," Phoebe assured him quickly. "It's not dangerous. It's, well...it's mine. Part of me."

Grant eyed his own shadow warily, kicked one leg out, which the shadow mirrored, then forced his hand away from his weapon. "Alright. Show and tell time, I guess."

Harrison watched Phoebe's shadow with something like recognition in his pale eyes. "They remember, you know. All of them. They remember what it was like before the binding, and they remember everything that's happened since, everything their humans have experienced."

"It told me that," Phoebe said. "Or tried to, with gestures. It said we're two parts of the same whole, artificially bound by the binding, and now separated again since the silo fell."

Pheobe's shadow nodded, making that familiar balancing gesture with its hands.

"The balance," Harrison said. "Yes, my grandfather mentioned it in his journal. The natural balance between light and shadow, disrupted by the wound between words in this valley where shadows walk alone, first exploited by the Exiles' arrival from the realm of darkness, then finally contained by my grandfather's silo and the native people's binding spell." The old man sighed heavily. "Thaddeus came to believe, toward the end of his life, that his solution had been imperfect. That binding shadows to their casters had created a different kind of imbalance."

"So, what's the right answer?" Grant asked. "If keeping them separate is wrong and binding them together is wrong, what's the solution?"

"Symbiosis. A new kind of relationship between shadows and their anchors, I suppose we should call them now, not casters. A conscious partnership rather than an enforced binding."

"And you think that's possible?" Phoebe asked. "After all this time?"

Harrison shrugged his thin shoulders. “I don’t know. But I suspect we’ll find out, one way or another.” He looked toward the cornfields, visible in the distance beyond his property. “The real question is whether the Exiles will allow such a balance to form. They have their agenda, their reasons for being here.”

“Which are?” Grant prompted.

“To transform this world,” Harrison said simply. “To make it more like the one they came from, the shadow realm, where darkness has primacy over light, where shadow is substance and matter is ephemeral.”

Phoebe’s shadow made a sudden, sharp gesture, drawing their attention. It pointed to itself, then to Phoebe, then made a united front gesture, followed by pointing toward the cornfields with a slashing motion.

“You’re saying the regular shadows and humans can stand together against the Exiles?”

The shadow nodded vigorously.

“An alliance,” Grant said. “Humans and their shadows, working together against these Exile entities.” He shook his head in disbelief. “If anyone had told me last week that I’d be discussing shadow politics and interspecies alliances, I’d have had them committed.”

“The world changed when that silo came down,” Harrison said quietly. “We’re just trying to catch up to the new reality.”

Phoebe’s shadow made another gesture, pointing to the rising sun, now well above the horizon, then making a sinking motion toward the west.

“It’s reminding us that sunset is coming,” Phoebe said. “When everyone else’s shadows will separate. Including my daughter’s.” She turned to Grant. “Sheriff, when that happens, people will be terrified. They need guidance and reassurance.”

Grant nodded grimly. “That’s why we’re setting up the

crisis center. But you're right, we need a clearer message, an explanation that won't cause panic but will help people understand what's happening." He looked at Harrison. "I think people need to hear it from you, Mr. Hollow. You're the only one who really understands what's going on."

Harrison's weathered face registered surprise. "Me? I'm just an old man with a family connection to all this. Besides, half the town already thinks I'm crazy."

"And the other half is about to discover you've been right all along," Grant pointed out. "I need you at the community center this afternoon. People will listen to you once they see their shadows separating."

The old man sighed. "Very well. I'll do what I can."

"What about the cornfields?" Phoebe asked. "If that's where the Exiles are gathering, shouldn't we be monitoring that area?"

Grant frowned. "I've got limited personnel, and most of them will be needed to maintain order in town once this separation business kicks into high gear at sunset. But you're right, we should have eyes on those fields." He studied Phoebe thoughtfully. "You seem to have adjusted to your own shadow situation relatively well. And you understand the technical aspects of all this better than most."

"You want me to check out the cornfields?"

"Just reconnaissance," Grant clarified. "No engaging with these exiled entities if you spot them. Just observe and report back. Take pictures if you can."

Phoebe's shadow made a gesture that clearly indicated reluctance or concern.

"It is not convinced that's a good idea."

"No offense to your shadow friend there," Grant said, "but I require information. And you're one of the few people who might understand what you're seeing out there."

Phoebe thought of Maddie. "My daughter's shadow is going to separate at sunset. I should be with her when that happens."

Harrison leaned forward. "Bring her here," he suggested. "My house is far enough from town to be safer if things get chaotic, but close enough that you can reach the community center quickly if required. I can watch over her while you check the cornfields."

"No," Phoebe said firmly. "If I do this, Maddie comes with me. I'm not letting her out of my sight with everything that's happening." She glanced at her shadow. "Besides, I have protection. My shadow seems to understand these Exiles better than we do. It can warn me if we're getting into danger."

Grant still looked unsure. "A cornfield full of sentient shadows is no place for a little girl."

"Neither is anywhere else right now," Phoebe pointed out. "At least with me, she'll have both her mother and her mother's separated shadow watching out for her. And she'll have the advantage of understanding what's happening before her separation occurs. I can prepare her."

After a moment's consideration, Grant nodded reluctantly. "Alright. But maintain radio contact." He unclipped a portable radio from his belt and handed it to her. "Channel three. Check in every thirty minutes and get out of there at the first sign of trouble."

Phoebe accepted the radio. "What constitutes trouble in this situation?"

"Anything that makes your shadow get agitated," Grant said. "It seems to have good instincts."

Her shadow made a gesture of acknowledgment, something almost like a salute.

Harrison reached out and grasped Phoebe's wrist with surprising strength for a man his age. "Be careful." His pale eyes were intense. "The cornfields have always been the Exiles' territory. Now that they're free, the shadows among the corn will act differently, as they did in Thaddeus' time.

More aligned with the Exiles than with humans."

"I'll be careful," Phoebe promised. "And I'll learn what I can. The more we understand about what's happening, the better prepared we'll be to deal with it."

As she stood to leave, her shadow flowed back to the ground and resumed its mimicry of a normal silhouette. She couldn't shake the feeling that they were all operating with dangerously incomplete information. Harrison knew more than most, but even his knowledge was based on century-old accounts from his grandfather.

The shadows knew the truth, her shadow, Lucy Holloway's shadow, all the shadows that had been bound to their human anchors for generations. They knew what the Exiles wanted, what had caused their banishment from the shadow realm in the first place, and what the Exiles planned now that they were free.

But without words, their ability to communicate that knowledge was severely limited. Gestures and charades could only convey so much.

As Phoebe walked back to her car, preparing to return home and collect Maddie for their reconnaissance mission to the cornfields, she wondered if there might be a more direct way to access the knowledge locked within the shadows, within her shadow, which had been attached to her for her entire life until this morning.

The shadow hours, dawn and dusk, were when the boundaries between worlds grew thin, when shadows were at their most powerful. Perhaps the shadow hours were also when communication between shadows and humans could be most direct.

She would find out at sunset, when the second shadow hour of the day arrived, bringing with it a wave of separations across Millfield and, perhaps, a clearer understanding of the strange new reality they were all facing.

CHAPTER 5:
THE DARK EXILES

Cornfields had never seemed menacing to Phoebe before. She'd grown up in farm country and had spent childhood summers running between golden rows of corn with her friends, playing hide-and-seek among the tall stalks that rustled soothingly in the summer breeze. Corn meant county fairs and harvest festivals, sweet butter, and family cookouts.

But as she parked her car at the edge of the vast fields that surrounded Millfield, Phoebe felt an unfamiliar apprehension. The morning sun shone brightly overhead, yet something about the way the shadows fell between the rows seemed wrong, too dark, too fluid, as if the darkness was thicker than it should be.

"Why are we at the corn, Mommy?" Maddie asked from the back seat, peering curiously through the window. "Are we getting corn for dinner?"

"Not today, sweetie," Phoebe replied, trying to keep her voice light. "We're just going to take a look around. Sheriff Grant asked me to check something for him."

She'd explained to Maddie on the drive over that strange things were happening in town, things to do with shadows. She'd kept it simple, telling her daughter that shadows were becoming separated from people, but that it wasn't something to be afraid of. Maddie had accepted this with the remarkable adaptability of children, seemingly more intrigued than frightened by the concept.

"Like Lucy's shadow?" Maddie had asked. "The one that talks to her?"

"Exactly like that. And like my shadow, too. See?" She'd pointed to her shadow, which maintained the appearance of normalcy while driving but occasionally shifted in ways no natural shadow would.

Now, as they exited the car, Phoebe's shadow detached from its pretense, rising to stand beside her, a dark silhouette against the bright morning landscape.

Maddie gasped, her eyes wide. "It really is separate! Can it hear us like Lucy's? Does it understand what we're saying?"

"It can't hear exactly like we do," Phoebe explained, watching as her shadow moved to stand protectively between them and the cornfield. "But it understands. It's been part of me my whole life, so it knows me very well."

"Will my shadow do that too? At sunset?" Maddie seemed more excited than frightened by the prospect.

"That's what we think will happen, yes." Phoebe kneeled to her daughter's level. "Maddie, I need you to stay close to me today. The cornfields might be different now. If you see anything unusual, tell me right away. Okay?"

Maddie nodded solemnly. "Is it because of the thirteen?"

Phoebe stared at her daughter, startled. "Where did you hear about the thirteen?"

"Lucy's shadow told her about them, and she told us. Remember? They're the oldest and strongest shadows. Do they live in the field?"

A chill ran through Phoebe. She'd forgotten. A sentient shadow sharing information with a child should have seemed absurd, but after everything she'd witnessed in the past few days, it was starting to seem normal, a confirmation of her worst fears.

"Lucy's right," she said carefully. "Harrison told us there are thirteen special shadows called the Dark Exiles. And yes, we think they might be gathering in the cornfields.

That's why we need to be extra careful."

Her shadow made an urgent gesture, pointing toward a narrow path that led between the corn rows.

"It wants us to follow," Phoebe said. "Stay right beside me, Maddie."

They entered the cornfield together, Phoebe's shadow leading the way. The temperature dropped immediately, though the sun still shone overhead. The shadows between the rows were unnaturally deep, as if the darkness had substance, weight, and presence.

"It's cold," Maddie whispered, pressing closer to Phoebe's side.

"I know, sweetie. We won't stay long."

As they moved deeper into the field, following the narrow path that separated two rows, Phoebe noticed how the corn seemed to respond to their presence, not bending away from them, as plants might in a breeze, but leaning slightly inward, as if watching their progress. The rustling of the leaves above them didn't match the still air; it was too deliberate, almost like whispered conversation.

Phoebe's shadow paused suddenly and made a sharp gesture of warning. It pointed toward the ground, then made a motion like something opening.

"What is it saying?" Maddie stared at the shadow's gestures with fascination.

Phoebe studied the ground where her shadow had indicated. At first, she saw nothing unusual, just dirt and the occasional stone. Then she spotted it: a small metal ring embedded in the soil, nearly hidden among corn stalks and fallen leaves. It looked like a handle on a root cellar.

"It's a door," she realized aloud. "There's something underneath the cornfield."

Her shadow nodded emphatically, then pointed at Maddie and made a staying gesture.

Phoebe frowned. "You think Maddie should wait here?

No way. I'm not leaving her alone in this field."

The shadow shook its head, then pointed back the way they had come, toward the car at the edge of the field.

"I'm not taking her back to the car either. She stays with me."

The shadow made a gesture of reluctant acceptance, then kneeled beside the metal ring. It pointed at Phoebe, clearly wanting her to open whatever lay beneath.

Phoebe hesitated, everything in her instincts screaming caution. But they had come here for answers, and this seemed to be where they might be found. She pulled the sheriff's radio from her pocket. "Sheriff Grant. Do you copy?"

After a moment of static, Grant's voice crackled through. "I copy. What's your status?"

"We've found something in the cornfield. Some kind of trapdoor, I think. My shadow wants us to open it."

"Are you in danger?"

"Not immediately. But I'd feel better having backup before we explore further."

"What's your location?"

Phoebe glanced around, realizing she'd lost track of exactly how far they'd ventured into the corn. "Somewhere in the eastern cornfield. If you enter from the access road off County Route 16, we're maybe a hundred yards in, following a straight path."

"Hold your position. I'll be there in ten minutes."

As they waited for the sheriff, Phoebe studied the metal ring more closely. It was old, rusted in places, but still solid. The surrounding soil was packed down, suggesting it hadn't been used recently, yet there was something deliberate about its placement, as if it had been designed to be overlooked.

"What do you think is down there?" Maddie asked, staring at the ring with wide eyes.

"I'm not sure, sweetie. But we're going to find out."

Her shadow moved restlessly, glancing toward the deeper sections of the cornfield with what Phoebe could only interpret as apprehension. It made quick, urgent gestures that seemed to convey a sense of time running short.

"The Exiles," Phoebe guessed. "You're worried they'll know we're here."

The shadow nodded vigorously.

"Can they sense us somehow?"

Another nod, followed by a gesture that encompassed the entire cornfield.

"This is their territory," Phoebe murmured. "They can feel when someone enters it."

Before her shadow could respond, they heard the rustling of corn stalks and the heavy tread of boots. Sheriff Grant appeared on the path, his hand resting casually on his holstered weapon as he took in the scene.

"Ms. Weaver." He nodded in greeting, then looked down at Maddie with a hint of disapproval on his brow. "I see you brought your daughter, after all."

"She's as safe with me as anywhere else right now," Phoebe said firmly.

Grant's eyes shifted to her shadow, which stood at attention like a sentry. "And your companion seems alert. Found something interesting?"

Phoebe pointed to the metal ring. "Some kind of access point. It was hidden until my shadow pointed it out."

Grant kneeled, brushing away more soil to reveal the outline of a small trapdoor, perhaps three feet square. "Looks old. Probably predates the cornfield." He glanced up at Phoebe's shadow. "You know what's down there?"

The shadow made a gesture that suggested partial knowledge, something between a nod and a shrug.

"Only one way to find out," Grant decided, grasping the metal ring. With a grunt of effort, he pulled, and the trapdoor creaked open to reveal a set of stone stairs descending into darkness.

A cool draft wafted up from below, carrying a musty scent of earth and age and something else, something like ozone after a lightning strike.

"Sealed space," Grant commented, flicking on his flashlight. "Probably hasn't been opened in decades."

Phoebe's shadow moved forward eagerly, pointing downward, then at itself.

"It wants to go first."

Grant nodded. "Makes sense. If there's anything down there that reacts to shadows, better to send in the one that can communicate with us." He looked at Maddie. "Little lady, you stay right behind your mom, okay? Hold on to her belt so you don't get separated."

Maddie nodded. Her small fingers gripped Phoebe's belt loop tightly.

"I'll take up the rear...keep my flashlight pointed down so we can all see."

Phoebe's shadow descended first, its dark form blending with the shadows below. Phoebe followed, taking each step carefully, one hand on the rough stone wall for balance. Maddie came next, her breathing quick but steady. Sheriff Grant brought up the rear, his flashlight beam illuminating the narrow stairway that spiraled downward into the earth.

They descended in silence, the air growing cooler and the scent of ozone stronger. After about twenty steps, the staircase opened into a circular chamber roughly thirty feet in diameter. Grant's flashlight revealed walls of fitted blocks adorned with Native People's symbols etched deep. The floor was covered in a hexagonal pattern of inlaid colored stones arranged in interlocking rings that reminded Phoebe of the diagrams in Thaddeus Hollow's journal.

"It's an ancient binding circle," she said. "Like the one Thaddeus designed for the town."

Her shadow moved to the center of the chamber, pointing toward a stone dais. A black rectangular object about the size of a shoebox sat atop an altar at the center of the dais.

"Let's have a closer look at that," Grant said, directing his flashlight toward it.

As they approached the dais, Phoebe realized the box was a small chest made of some kind of dark wood, highly polished to a obsidian-like sheen. Its surface was etched with symbols similar to those on the wall, a complex language of angles and curves that shifted slightly when viewed from different angles.

"Is it a treasure box?" Maddie whispered, her voice echoing in the chamber.

"I don't think so, sweetie," Phoebe replied. "I think it's very old." She looked at her shadow. "Do you know what this is?"

The shadow made a series of gestures, pointing to the box, then to itself, then making a sweeping motion that encompassed the entire chamber.

"It's saying this place is important to everyone and their shadows."

Grant circled the dais, examining the chest from all angles. "No obvious way to open it. No lock or hinges that I can see."

Phoebe's shadow pointed to its chest, then to Phoebe's, then made a pressing motion toward the box.

"I think it wants one of us to touch it."

Grant frowned. "That seems like a bad idea, given everything we know about the situation."

"Maybe." Phoebe studied the box more carefully. The symbols etched into its surface weren't random decorations, she realized, but a form of writing, one that seemed almost familiar, like hieroglyphics. "It must contain information. History, possibly. About what really happened here."

Her shadow nodded emphatically.

"And you think we should open it?" Grant asked skeptically.

The shadow made a balanced-scales gesture with its hands, the same motion it had used earlier to represent the natural balance between light and shadow.

"To restore balance, we need the full story."

"Your call, Ms. Weaver. You seem to have the closest connection to all this shadow business."

Phoebe looked down at Maddie, who was staring at the black chest with intense fascination. "Stay back, sweetie. Just in case."

"In case of what?" Maddie asked, but obediently stepped backward, moving closer to Sheriff Grant.

Phoebe approached the dais slowly. The symbols on the chest seemed to grow more defined as she drew nearer, the etched lines catching the flashlight's beam and reflecting it in wavy rays that didn't seem to obey the normal laws of physics. She reached out and hovered her hand over the smooth black surface.

"Here goes nothing," she murmured, and she pressed her palm flat against the top of the chest.

For a moment, nothing happened. She glanced at the sheriff, then at her shadow, and shrugged.

Then slowly, a line of silver light appeared around the top edge of the box, outlining what appeared to be a lid. The light grew brighter, and Phoebe felt a strange vibration through her palm, not unpleasant but deeply unsettling, like touching something that existed partially in another dimension.

She tried to pull her hand away but couldn't. The vibration intensified, and the silver light spread, flowing up her arm like mercury. It didn't burn or hurt, but it made her skin tingle as if every nerve ending were being stimulated at once.

"Mom?" Maddie's voice seemed to come from extremely far away.

"I'm okay," Phoebe managed, though she wasn't entirely sure that was true. The silver light had reached her shoulder now, and with it came knowledge. The history of Millfield. The true history, not the sanitized version in the town records or even the purported truth in Thaddeus Hollow's journal. Not in words or images, exactly, but in direct understanding, as if information were being downloaded directly into her consciousness:

> Wild corn had always grown here, as were the shadows swirling through the fields. The Native People had known this place as the valley where shadows walked alone, where darkness gathered even on the brightest days. They had left offerings of beads and arrowheads at the edges of the fields, not to encourage fertility or growth, but to appease what lived among the tall stalks.
>
> But a greater threat lurked in the hollow ground below the cornfields. In 1843, thirteen miners inadvertently opened a wound between the realms of darkness and light, and sentient shadows took over their bodies. They terrorized the valley, stole shadows, turned day into night. The Native People built a shrine beneath the corn, a round chamber adorned with their religious symbols, created a binding spell to drive the shadow walkers back underground.
>
> When settlers came, they built farms, planted corn in rows, and pushed deeper into the fertile land surrounding an odd circle of barren soil. But darkness followed them into the fields—shadows that stretched too long beneath the midday sun, shadows that pooled in bright

daylight, that ebbed and flowed, even in the darkest of night. They feared only evil could cast a shadow in the darkness, which disturbed the settlers enough that they moved out of the valley, to build a town, Coopersville, on higher ground and farm elsewhere across Ohio.

In 1893, thirteen settlers from Coopersville ventured into the heart of the wild corn, searching for the source of the shadow disturbances that had chased them the fertile valley.

They found the Native People's chamber.

They found the black chest.

And when they opened it—

Phoebe gasped as the knowledge flooded into her mind.

The chest held a binding spell created generations earlier by the Native Peoples to imprison the darkness beneath the fields.

The settlers didn't know the darkness had been waiting, gathering strength for decades. As the chest opened, the spell was broken, and the Exiles rose from the hollow ground. The old thirteen miners' shadows took over the young bodies of the settlers. They came back changed, carrying the darkness within them like an infection of the soul, unaware.

In the years that followed, the Exiles waited for a celestial event to unleash a black wave over the valley. Other shadows coalesced in bright places, roamed through the corn without guidance or purpose, loose in the light of day and the dark of night.

Until Thaddeus Hollow came along. He noticed the shadows were not acting normally.

With help from a native Shaman and his people, he constructed a monstrous silo in the center of the barren circle in the field. The shadows returned to normal. Millfield rose from the corn, the streets laid out in the shape of a hexagon sigil to reinforce the binding spell. The silo had never been meant to store grain, but to hold the binding spell and contain the darkness in the hollow ground.

The silver light receded from Phoebe's arm, flowed back into the black chest. She staggered backward, her mind reeling from the influx of information. Sheriff Grant caught her elbow, steadying her. "What happened? What did you see?"

With a click, the chest opened. Inside lay a single object, a small gray stone etched with the same symbols as the chest itself bore.

Phoebe shook her head, struggling to process what she now knew. "The Exiles were contained, thanks to the native people and Thaddeus Hollow... But now, thanks to Mayor Wilson and his council, they are free. And the mayor used me to make it happen."

Her shadow nodded vigorously, moving closer to stand beside her.

"What for?" Grant asked. "Why? What do they want?"

"This town. This valley. And every shadow in it. The Exiles will turn daylight to darkness."

"Who are they, the Exiles?"

"The founding families of Millfield," Phoebe said, the knowledge still settling into place in her mind, "weren't the first to encounter the evil darkness beneath the fields. That happened in 1843, in the hollow ground." She looked at Grant. "What do you know about a mine in the area?"

Grant shrugged. "I'll have Harrison look into it. Meanwhile, go on."

"The Exiles stole the miners' bodies. The Native People of the valley used binding spells to contain them, but in 1893, settlers entered this chamber and released them. The Exiles abandoned the elderly miners' bodies, took the younger settlers' bodies, which carried the corruption with them into the future."

Grant's expression was skeptical.

"The thirteen Dark Exiles..." Phoebe went on, "they're shadows that have stolen human bodies, whose descendants later became influential leaders in the town Thaddeus Hollow built. But his silo contained them for a century, waiting for us to do something stupid."

"Like take down that silo," Grant muttered.

"I should have listened to Harrison Hollow. Right now they're plotting against us."

Maddie, who had been listening silently, suddenly spoke up. "But not Lucy's shadow, Mommy. Right?"

Phoebe stared at her daughter, startled by her insight. "No." She looked at her shadow. "Our shadows are in just as much danger as us." She recalled celestial event...looked at Grant. "Is there some kind of celestial event coming up?"

"You mean like the solar eclipse?"

"Maybe. Do you know when?"

"I'm not sure...in a week or two. What's that got to do with anything?"

"It might already be affecting the valley's shadows."

"Maybe it's that stone," Grant said, nodding toward the chest still lying open. "What's its purpose?"

Phoebe's shadow pointed to the stone, then to its chest, then made a circular motion with its fingers.

"It's a key of some kind." Phoebe translated the knowledge from the chest still flowing into her mind. "Central to the binding spell." She felt suddenly dizzy. "It doesn't just cage the Exiles, it governs every shadow in Millfield. The natural rule that your shadow follows you, moves when you move, stays tethered to your body..." She could barely keep up with the flow of information flooding her mind. "That's the binding stone enforcing the natural order the Native People preserved in a valley where the ground is hollow beneath the corn. Without it, shadows don't just go free, they lose coherence, the wound distorts them, and every shadow in this valley loses the only thing keeping them stable."

"And the Exiles want the stone?"

"They want to destroy it because, to them, it's their jailer. But first, they need it to complete their transformation back to their original forms. To remake this valley in the image of their own realm, maybe the entire world."

"How do you know this?"

She glanced at the chest and she knew. "The stone is somehow giving me this knowledge."

Grant rubbed his jaw thoughtfully. "So, these Exiles, the founding families, they're not human anymore?"

"They're human, alright," Phoebe said. "But waiting."

"That's insane," he said. "From 1893? They'd all be dead by now."

"Their shadows moved through generations, passing their consciousness to descendants of the original thirteen." Phoebe frowned, another realization dawning. "That's why certain families have always held power in Millfield. Why the same names keep appearing in positions of authority, generation after generation."

"Like Mayor Wilson," Grant said slowly. "His family has held the mayorship for five generations."

"He's the leader of the Exiles. And there's Judge Sullivan, Commissioner Duncan, and Dr. Brennen." Phoebe's mind was racing to keep up with the incoming flow of knowledge. "They're some of the descendants of the original thirteen miners' shadows."

"So, what do we do with this information?" Grant

asked. "How does knowing the shadows control the original thirteen change our approach to the current situation?"

Phoebe looked down at the stone in the chest. "It changes everything. We thought we were defending against an invasion, but we're actually going to witness a rebellion, the original shadows of the valley reclaiming their human forms, their identity, their freedom from confinement." She met Grant's eyes. "The question isn't how to rebind the Exiles or defeat them. That's not possible. It's how to find a way to coexist with them."

Grant huffed. "Let's just build a new silo."

"There's no one left to attach a binding spell to it."

"And what if the Exiles would rather not coexist with us?" Grant put in. "Can we survive in their dark world?"

Before Phoebe could answer no, her shadow made an urgent gesture, pointing toward the stairs. It made a motion like something approaching, then pressed a finger to where its lips would be if it had any, a clear warning to be silent.

"Something's coming," Phoebe whispered, instinctively pulling Maddie closer to her side.

Grant swept his weapon back and forth while moving to position himself between the stairs and the others. "Take the stone," he ordered quietly. "We can't let the Exiles get their hands on it."

Phoebe reached into the chest and lifted the stone. It was heavier than it looked and warm to the touch, as if it had created heat by communicating with her.

As her fingers closed around it, she felt another jolt of understanding, not a download of information this time, but a simple, profound realization: the stone wasn't just a key to the binding spell. It was a conduit between realms, a physical object that existed simultaneously in both the shadow world and the material world. Holding it connected her, however tenuously, to the consciousness of every shadow entity in Millfield.

Including the Exiles. And she instantly knew who had entered through the doorway above.

From the stairway came the sound of footsteps, deliberate, unhurried, human footsteps. A moment later, a figure appeared in the chamber entrance. Mayor Wilson stood there, his normally affable expression replaced by something older, colder, and more alien.

"Ms. Weaver," he said, his voice fundamentally different, deeper, raspier. "I see you've found what we've been looking for." His eyes, normally blue, now seemed to absorb light rather than reflect it. "And you've taken what doesn't belong to you."

"Finders keepers, Mister Wilson."

His shadow stretched beside him, but it wasn't a normal human shadow, it was elongated and distorted, more like a rip in reality than a mere absence of light.

"Mayor Wilson," Grant said, his weapon still raised. "Or should I address the shadow that's controlling you?"

A thin smile crossed the mayor's face. "Perceptive, Sheriff. More than I would have expected." He stepped fully into the chamber, and his shadow flowed across the floor like liquid darkness, far larger than any human shadow should be. "But it makes no difference. You're trespassing on Exile territory. So that stone is ours." He extended his hand. "Give it to me, Ms. Weaver. It's not meant for human hands."

Phoebe clutched the stone tighter, feeling its warmth intensify. "I know what you are. I know the truth about Millfield, about the founding families, about the binding spell. You're not taking this stone."

Mayor Wilson, or the entity sharing his form, studied her with those light-absorbing eyes. "Brave...but foolish. You don't understand the forces you're facing. The stone is the center of the binding that holds our shadows in check. We need it to complete what began when the miners broke through to our world. We will restore the natural order of this valley."

"By turning it into a shadow realm?" Grant demanded. "By making it uninhabitable for humans?"

"Not uninhabitable," Wilson said. "Transformed. The way it was always meant to be, before your kind forced us from substance to emptiness." His gaze shifted to Phoebe's shadow. "You understand, don't you? You remember the world before the binding."

Her shadow shrugged.

"What does that mean?" Grant asked, not taking his eyes off Wilson.

"My shadow didn't exist before me," Phoebe said, "The mayor is blowing smoke. He doesn't want our shadows to be free. He wants to possess them. That's fundamentally altering how reality works."

"Reality is already altered in this valley," Wilson said dismissively. "Has been since before humans first settled here. And your shadow knows what came before you, Ms. Weaver. We're simply restoring the original state, a valley where shadow and substance were independent of each other, where consciousness wasn't bound to physical form. Once the transformation is complete, then we will destroy the stone and free your shadows forever."

"And what happens to the humans in Millfield after this transformation?" Phoebe asked. "How will they survive without their shadows in your world of darkness?"

Wilson's smile widened, revealing teeth that seemed too sharp, too numerous. "Those with the capacity to adapt will adapt. Those without will not survive."

"You're talking about transforming our shadows without their consent," Phoebe said, anger rising within her. "About changing the fundamental nature of our existence without even asking if we want it changed."

"Just as Thaddeus Hollow did to us," Wilson countered, his voice hardening. "Just as your Native People did to us with their binding spells, reshaping our shadow existence to suit their needs without concern for what we wanted." He took a step forward. "I won't ask again. Give me the stone."

Phoebe's shadow moved to stand between her and Wilson.

"Even your shadow recognizes the justice of our cause," Wilson observed. "It stands against you, with us."

"No. It's not standing against me. It's standing against you. It knows there's a better way than either total binding or total transformation. A true balance, where both humans and shadows can exist without one dominating the other."

Wilson's expression darkened. "There is no compromise with your kind. You had your chance, a century of dominance while we were bound and silent. Now it's our turn." He gestured, and his massive shadow flowed forward, expanding to fill more of the chamber floor. "The stone. Now."

Grant's weapon was still trained on Wilson. "Back off," he warned. "Whatever you are, you're still in a human body. One that bleeds, I'm sure."

Wilson laughed, a sound like dry leaves rustling. "Do you think bullets can harm me? I've existed in this form since before your grandfather was born, sheriff. I've transported myself through generations of Wilsons, from the foreman of a silver mine to City Hall. Shoot if you must, you'll only kill the body I'm in and release me to kill you all."

Phoebe's mind raced. They were trapped underground with an entity older than the valley itself, one that could conjure up shadows as extensions of its will. Confrontation wouldn't work. But perhaps there was another approach.

She held up the stone, letting the strange symbols catch the light of Grant's flashlight. "Let's put it to a vote," she called to Wilson. "Not here, not now, but at the proper time.

During the next shadow hour, at sunset. When all the town's shadows have separated and can participate in the decision."

Whisps of shadow swirled around Wilson; he was clearly annoyed by the suggestion. "You have a lot of nerve dictating terms to me, Weaver."

"The stone belongs to all shadows," Phoebe pressed, "not just the Exiles. If you're truly seeking justice and restoration, then let all the newly freed shadows have a voice in how it happens."

"The stone is Exile property," Wilson insisted, but there was a note of uncertainty in his voice. "The others lack the knowledge to use it properly."

"Then explain it to them. Convince them. If your vision for Millfield is truly better for all shadows, they'll support you." Phoebe held his gaze steadily. "Unless you're afraid they won't."

A tense silence filled the chamber. Wilson's eyes narrowed, and his shadow pulsed with barely contained anger.

"Sunset," he said finally. "At the community center where your sheriff is gathering the townsfolk. Bring the stone. We will discuss terms." His eyes moved to Phoebe's shadow. "Remember what you truly are," he told it. "Remember where your loyalty should lie."

Without waiting for a response, he turned and ascended the stairs, his oversized shadow flowing after him like a midnight tide.

When his footsteps had faded, Grant exhaled slowly. "That was either very brave or stupid, Phoebe. Probably both."

"It bought us time." She tucked the stone into her pocket. "Time to figure out what to do with this knowledge this stone is giving me."

"And to prepare people for whatever happens at sunset," Grant added grimly. "Because something tells me

Mayor Wilson, or whatever is wearing his shape, isn't planning a friendly town hall discussion."

Phoebe looked at her shadow, which was watching her with an intensity she could feel despite its featureless form. "Whose side are you really on?" she asked it directly.

The shadow pointed to her, then to itself, then made the balancing gesture again, more emphatically this time, with a deliberateness that conveyed absolute conviction.

"Balance," Phoebe said. "Not domination by either side. A new kind of coexistence."

Her shadow nodded, then pointed to the stone in her pocket and made a circular motion followed by the same balancing gesture.

"The stone is key to maintaining that balance," Phoebe interpreted. "Not just a weapon or a source of knowledge and power, but something that can bridge worlds. Connect them."

Another nod, followed by a nod toward Maddie, who had been watching this exchange with solemn attention.

"And Maddie? What about her?"

The shadow pointed to Maddie, then to the shadow beside her, cast by the flashlight beam, then made a clasped-hands gesture suggesting partnership or cooperation.

"You're saying her shadow will be an important ally in this fight?"

The shadow made an affirmative gesture, then pointed upward.

"We should go," Grant agreed, interpreting the gesture. "Wilson, or whatever he is, might come back with his buddies."

As they climbed the stairs back to the surface, Phoebe's mind was still processing the revelations from touching the chest. Everything she thought she knew about Millfield, about the shadow separations, had been turned on its head. They were not only facing shadow entities that escaped from their realm of darkness. They were witnessing the rebellion of the valley's original thirteen inhabitants, shadow beings who had been bound and subjugated for a century.

And yet, the mayor's cold dismissal of human concerns and his willingness to transform people's shadows without consent proposed that the Exiles' vision of balance was just as one-sided as Thaddeus Hollow's had been.

As they emerged into the cornfield, the shadows between the rows seemed even deeper than before, watching them with what felt like hostile attention. Phoebe clutched Maddie's hand tightly as they hurried back toward the cars.

The sun was high overhead now; its light was harsh and direct, minimizing natural shadows. But in the cornfield, darkness pooled and gathered as if drawn by invisible currents, preparing for the coming sunset when the shadow hour would begin again, when the remaining human anchors in Millfield would experience separation and the true battle for the town's future would begin.

The stone felt heavy in Phoebe's pocket, a physical connection to both worlds, shadow and substance, past and present. Whatever would happen at sunset, she knew one thing with absolute certainty:

Millfield would never be the same again.

CHAPTER 6:
THE HARVEST FESTIVAL

By mid-afternoon, the community center had been transformed into something between an evacuation shelter and a war room. Sheriff Grant had commandeered the main gymnasium and set up rows of folding cots along one wall for those who might need to stay overnight, and he arranged chairs in a loose semicircle at the center for what he grimly referred to as "the briefing."

Phoebe stood near the entrance, watching as deputies and volunteers bustled about with emergency supplies, water bottles, blankets, first-aid kits. The binding stone sat heavy in her pocket, its presence a constant reminder of what was at stake. She'd wrapped it in a handkerchief, partly to conceal it and partly because touching it directly continued to feed her strange flashes of knowledge, fragments of the shadow realm's history that were too overwhelming to process all at once. Alien.

Maddie sat cross-legged on a nearby table, talking animatedly with Lucy Holloway, who had arrived with her mother twenty minutes earlier. The two girls had their heads together, speaking in the conspiratorial tones of children sharing important secrets. Phoebe caught fragments of their conversation, something about shadows being "awake now" and "remembering things from before."

Mary Holloway stood nearby, arms folded tightly across her chest, her expression cycling between disbelief and reluctant acceptance as Sheriff Grant explained the current situation. Like most Millfield residents, Mary had been skeptical when first summoned to the community center. But witnessing her daughter's separated shadow, now standing beside Lucy like a dark guardian, had forced her to acknowledge that something extraordinary was happening.

"So, you're saying these shadows have been conscious all along?" Mary was asking as Phoebe approached. "That Lucy's shadow has been aware, thinking, all this time while attached to her?"

"That's precisely what we're saying," Grant confirmed. "According to what we've learned, shadows are sentient entities that were bound to physical objects, people, animals, plants, by a spell created a century ago."

"By Thaddeus Hollow," Mary said, frowning. "I remember that much from school. He founded the town, built the grain silo."

Phoebe and Grant exchanged glances. They had agreed not to share the complete truth about the founding families just yet, the revelation that the thirteen most influential families in town were actually shadow-human hybrids seemed likely to cause more panic than understanding at this stage.

"Thaddeus created the silo, yes," Phoebe said carefully. "But what's important now is figuring out how to handle the separation that's happening across town."

"And you're sure it's going to affect everyone at sunset?" Mary asked, glancing nervously toward the windows, where afternoon light was already beginning to soften toward evening.

"That's what the pattern suggests," Grant replied. "The first separations happened three days ago, after the silo demolition. Then more at dawn today. Sunset is the next shadow hour, when the boundary between worlds gets thin again."

Mary looked at her daughter, then at Lucy's shadow standing protectively beside her. "It hasn't tried to hurt her."

"And it won't," Phoebe assured her. "By all accounts, the separated shadows aren't hostile toward their former anchors. If anything, they seem protective, invested in their well-being."

"Like partners," Harrison Hollow said as the old man approached, leaning heavily on his cane. "The way it was before the binding was needed to keep them together."

Mary was startled at his appearance. "Mr. Hollow. I didn't expect to see you here. Aren't you usually holed up at your farm?"

Harrison's weathered face crinkled with a smile that didn't quite reach his pale eyes. "Special circumstances call for special measures, Ms. Holloway." He looked toward the children, his expression softening. "Your daughter was among the first to experience separation. How is she adapting?"

Mary shrugged. "Surprisingly well, actually. She talks to it, to her shadow, constantly. Says it's been giving her story ideas all her life, and now she can finally understand them properly."

"Children adapt more easily," Harrison added. "Their minds are more flexible, less rigidly attached to what they believe is possible." He turned to Phoebe. "How many have gathered so far?"

"About sixty people. Mostly those who witnessed separations this morning or have family members who did. More are arriving every hour as word spreads."

"And the mayor?" Harrison asked, lowering his voice.

"No sign of him yet," Grant answered. "Or any of the other twelve families."

Harrison's expression darkened. "They'll come at sunset. They'll want to be here when the mass separation occurs." He glanced toward the windows. "Perhaps three hours left before then. We should begin preparations."

"Preparations for what?" Mary asked.

Harrison exchanged another look with Phoebe and Grant. "For the festival," he said after a moment. "Though most people in town don't realize it, the annual Millfield Harvest Festival has always been a ritual that reinforces the binding spell. This year, with the silo gone and shadows separating, it will serve a different purpose."

Mary frowned. "The Harvest Festival isn't for another week. And what do you mean it's a ritual? It's just hayrides and a corn maze and the pumpkin-lighting ceremony."

"The pumpkin lighting," Harrison repeated meaningfully. "Exactly. Carved gourds with candles inside, placed at thirteen specific locations around the town square. Creating patterns of light and shadow in a very particular arrangement."

Understanding dawned. "The festival reinforced the binding each year without anyone realizing it," Phoebe said.

"My grandfather learned how from the Shaman, a communal ritual disguised as a celebration, with the entire town unwittingly participating in the maintenance of the spell." He tapped his cane on the floor for emphasis. "But this year will be different. The shadows are free now, and the Exiles will want to use the festival's energy for their purposes."

"Which are..." Mary pressed.

"Transformation," Phoebe answered before Harrison could. "Changing Millfield into something like their shadow realm, a place where shadow has substance and physical matter. Makes them more powerful."

Mary looked skeptical, but before she could respond, the community center doors swung open and David Weaver strode in, his expression a mixture of concern and annoyance.

"Phoebe," he called, spotting her immediately. "What the hell is going on? Half the town is talking about some kind of emergency, and Maddie wasn't at school when I went to pick her up."

"David..." Phoebe moved quickly to intercept her husband. "I was about to call you. Things have been happening quickly."

He frowned, looking around at the emergency setup. "Is this about the shadows? Mrs. Peterson next door was saying something about her husband's shadow detaching this morning, but I thought she was having one of her episodes."

"It's real," Phoebe said simply. "All of it. The shadows are separating from people, animals, everything. Mine separated at dawn." She gestured to her shadow, which had been standing unobtrusively beside her but now straightened to its full height, acknowledging David's attention.

David stared at it, then back at Phoebe and noticed she cast no shadow. "That's not possible."

"Dad!" Maddie called, jumping down from the table and running to him. "Mom's shadow talked to us. Well, not really talked, but it makes gestures, and we can understand it. And Lucy's shadow has been separated since yesterday, and it gives her story ideas, and it says there are old shadows in the corn that remember everything."

David knelt to Maddie's level, but his eyes remained fixed on Phoebe's shadow. "Honey, I think there's been some kind of misunderstanding. Shadows don't talk or separate. They're just darkness where light is blocked."

"That's what we all thought," Phoebe said gently. "But we were wrong. In this valley, shadows are conscious entities. They have been all along. And the binding spell that kept them attached to us has been weakening since the silo came down."

"Binding spell," David spat. "How can you seriously believe—"

"Ah-hum." He was interrupted by Harrison, who had approached quietly. "Your skepticism is natural, Mr.

Weaver. But perhaps this will help." The old man reached into his pocket and removed an ancient photograph, its yellowed edges curling. "This was taken in 1923, at the original Harvest Festival. The first one after the silo was completed."

David took the photo reluctantly. It showed a town square much like Millfield's current one, though with older buildings and cars from the 1920s parked along the periphery. People in period clothing stood watching as thirteen carved pumpkins were being placed in a circular pattern.

"Look at the shadows," Harrison instructed.

David squinted at the photo, then his expression changed. "That's not right," he murmured. "The shadows are all pointing in different directions. As if each one had its own light source."

"Or as if they were moving independently," Harrison suggested. "Resisting the binding even as it was being reinforced."

David handed the photo back, his certainty visibly shaken. "Even if this is real, and I'm not saying I'm convinced, what does it have to do with turning the community center into a refugee camp?"

Phoebe laid a hand on his arm. "At sunset, everyone's shadows will separate. Across town, we are gathering people here so they can be prepared, so they won't panic, and..." She hesitated for effect. "So we can protect them if necessary."

"Protect them from what...their shadows?"

"No," Phoebe sighed. "From the Exiles. The original thirteen shadow entities that were bound along with all the others. They have their agenda, and it doesn't necessarily include the well-being of the town's human population."

David ran a hand through his hair, his expression caught between disbelief and dawning concern. "This is insane. All of it. But..." He looked around at the busy preparations and at the separated shadows now visible throughout the gymnasium, standing beside their former anchors. "If even half of what you're saying is true, we need to get Maddie somewhere safe. Away from Millfield."

"There is no 'away from Millfield' for us," Phoebe said quietly. "Not anymore. We're part of this, David. All of us. The best way to protect Maddie is to stay together and figure out a path forward that works for both humans and shadows."

Before David could respond, Sheriff Grant's voice boomed across the gymnasium. "Attention, everyone! If I could have you gather around, we'd like to start the briefing."

People moved toward the semicircle of chairs, some walking alone, others in family groups. What struck Phoebe most was how many separated shadows now moved among them, at least twenty, each maintaining a proximity to its former anchor. The shadows varied in their behavior; some mimicked their humans' movements in a near-perfect charade of normalcy, while others moved with the liquid grace unique to their kind, flowing rather than walking across the floor.

As Phoebe guided her family toward the gathering, she noticed Mayor Wilson slip in through a side door, accompanied by several other town officials, Judge Sullivan, Brennen, and Principal Miller. The thirteen most influential families were the descendants of the original settlers infected with the Exiles' shadow entities. They took seats at the edges of the group; their expressions unnaturally calm given the circumstances. None of them had visible shadows, Phoebe noted with a chill. Either they were positioning themselves to hide them, or their shadows were already elsewhere, preparing for sunset.

"Folks..." Grant began once everyone was seated. "I

know there's a lot of confusion and concern about what's happening in our town. I'm going to do my best to explain, and then we'll talk about how to handle the events expected at sunset." He gestured toward Harrison. "Mr. Hollow will provide some historical context first, which should help make sense of the current situation."

Harrison rose shakily to his feet, leaning on his cane. Despite his frail appearance, his voice carried strongly across the hushed gymnasium.

"Most of you know the basic history of Millfield," he began. "Founded in the 1920s by thirteen families, built around the grain silo that stood until three days ago. What you don't know, what was deliberately hidden from town records, is that the silo was never meant for storing grain. It was the central point of a binding spell, a magical construct that forced shadows to adhere to their physical anchors."

A murmur of doubt ran through the crowd, but no one interrupted.

"For a century, that binding held. Shadows remained attached to people and objects. They were unable to move independently and unable to communicate. But they were conscious the entire time, watching, experiencing, and waiting." Harrison paused, letting that sink in. "When the silo was demolished, the binding began to weaken. And now, shadows are separating from their anchors, regaining their independence."

A woman from the middle of the group called, "My Henry's shadow pulled away this morning. Just lifted right off him while he was shaving. Nearly gave him a heart attack."

Several people nodded in agreement, sharing related stories.

"It's happening across town," Harrison confirmed. "And at sunset, we expect the remaining shadows to separate, as well. You must understand, the shadows are not hostile. They've been part of you your entire lives. They know you, care about you, in their own way."

"Then what's the emergency?" someone asked. "If they're not dangerous, why are we here?"

Harrison exchanged glances with Phoebe and Grant. "Because the separation is only part of what's happening. The original thirteen shadows, the Dark Exiles, have different intentions than the everyday shadows attached to most people and things. They want to transform Millfield into something between our world and theirs, a place where shadows have substance, as physical matter is more powerful."

"Transform how?" another voice called.

"That's what we're still determining," Grant cut in smoothly. "What we do know is that the annual Harvest Festival has been, unknown to most of us, a ritual that reinforced the binding spell each year. The Exiles plan to use that same ritual structure, but to further their agenda instead."

Mayor Wilson stood abruptly. "If I may," he said, his voice carrying that same strange quality Phoebe had noted in the underground chamber, familiar yet somehow alien. "I think there's been a misunderstanding about our intentions."

All eyes turned to him. In the artificial light of the gymnasium, his shadow should have been minimal, but darkness seemed to pool around his feet, deeper than normal.

"The transformation we seek is not destruction." Wilson moved to the center of the semicircle. "It's restoration. This land has always existed in a state between worlds, a place where shadow and substance intermingled freely. We aim to return it to that natural state."

"Natural for whom?" Phoebe challenged, rising to stand opposite him. "The human residents of Millfield didn't consent to having their reality fundamentally altered."

Wilson's too sharp smile flashed briefly. "Just as the

shadow residents didn't consent to being bound for a century." He addressed the crowd directly. "What's happening now is simply balance being restored. Your shadows are regaining their rightful independence in this valley. And yes, there will be changes to how Millfield exists in the world. But those changes won't harm you. They'll expand you, free you from the limitations of a purely physical existence."

There was a dangerous persuasiveness to his words, Phoebe noted. Around the room, some people were nodding thoughtfully, considering his perspective.

"The mayor is right that balance needs to be restored," she said loudly. "But true balance would be a negotiated arrangement, not one imposed by either side. The Exiles' vision of transformation hasn't been fully explained to the town, nor have its consequences."

"Then let me explain now," Wilson offered, spreading his hands in a gesture of openness that didn't reach his light-absorbing eyes. "Tonight, at sunset, all shadows will separate. The Harvest Festival ritual will proceed as it always has, but with a different intention, union rather than binding. By morning, Millfield will exist in both worlds simultaneously. You'll all experience enhanced perception, expanded consciousness, and greater connection to the forces that have always surrounded you, unseen but present."

"And those who can't adapt to this transformation..." Phoebe pressed, "what happens to them?"

A flicker of something cold passed across Wilson's face. "Adaptation is a choice," he said dismissively. "Those who resist change always suffer more than those who embrace it."

A ripple of unease moved through the crowd.

"What the mayor isn't telling you," Harrison interjected, "is that this transformation will be particularly difficult for children and the elderly. Those whose sense of self is either not fully formed or beginning to fade. For them, the merging of worlds could be traumatic, even fatal."

Wilson's expression hardened. "Fear mongering from a man who has professed the imprisonment of shadows his grandfather created. Whose family has enforced shadow subjugation for generations."

"My family has maintained a necessary balance," Harrison retorted. "Imperfect, yes, but better than the Exiles' vision of total transformation."

The tension in the room had risen palpably. People shifted in their seats, looking between Wilson and Harrison, uncertain whom to believe.

Phoebe stepped forward, one hand in her pocket, fingers wrapped around the binding stone. "The truth is, neither approach is right," she said clearly. "Neither total binding nor total transformation. What we need is a new way forward, one that respects both humans and shadows as conscious, independent entities with equal rights to exist in this valley."

Wilson's gaze locked on her pocket. "You have an heirloom that is ours," he said, his voice dropping an octave. "The binding stone. Central to the ritual. Essential to the transformation."

"I have something that affects everyone in Millfield, human and shadow alike. The Exiles want it, and if we lose it, every shadow in this town loses the bond that holds it together. So before anyone touches this stone, every voice gets heard.

"A murmur of approval ran through many in the crowd, but Phoebe noticed the town officials, the descendants of the original settlers, all watching her with identical expressions of cold calculation.

"We don't have time for prolonged debate," Wilson said, addressing the crowd again. "Sunset approaches. The shadow hour. Decisions must be made."

"Yes." Phoebe agreed. "But not unilaterally by the Exiles. This affects every resident of Millfield, human, and shadow alike. All voices must be heard."

As if in response to her words, the separated shadows around the room began to move, flowing toward the center of the semicircle to stand together in a loose formation. Phoebe's shadow joined them, along with Lucy's. They arranged themselves in a circle, facing outward toward the human observers.

A strange, silent communication seemed to pass between them, not words or even gestures, but something more fundamental, as if they were sharing consciousness directly. Then, as one, they each extended a hand toward their former anchors, an unmistakable invitation.

Lucy was the first to respond, stepping forward without hesitation to take her shadow's outstretched hand. The moment they touched, a soft silver light outlined both their forms, similar to what Phoebe had experienced when touching the black chest in the underground chamber.

"They're talking," Lucy announced, her voice filled with wonder. "They want to show us something. About the festival. About what it was before the binding."

One by one, other people stepped forward, tentatively at first, then with growing confidence, to take their shadows' hands. Each connection created the same silver illumination, a visible manifestation of communication beyond words.

Phoebe moved toward her shadow, which stood waiting, hand extended. As their fingers met, the silver light flowed up her arm, and with it came understanding, not imposed knowledge this time, but shared memory. Her shadow showed her the Harvest Festival as the Native People had originally celebrated it before Thaddeus Hollow came to this valley.

It hadn't been about subjugation. The original festival had been a celebration of the natural cycle of light and shadow, a ritual acknowledgment of the interconnectedness of all things. The thirteen pumpkin lanterns had created a sigil pattern that balanced the energies of both realms, which existed in harmony without one dominating the other.

When the vision faded, Phoebe looked around to see dozens of silver-illuminated pairs, people and their shadows, locked in silent communication, sharing millenniums of history and knowledge.

Mayor Wilson stood apart, his expression thunderous. "Enough of this malarky," he snapped. "The shadows are manipulating you, showing you what they want you to see. The true festival, the true transformation, requires the stone." He advanced toward Phoebe, hand outstretched. "Give it to me now, before sunset. Before it's too late to direct the energy properly."

Phoebe's shadow moved to stand beside her, making a gesture of clear refusal. Around the room, other shadows broke their connections and moved to form a protective circle around Phoebe.

"I don't think they agree with your interpretation, Mayor," Sheriff Grant stated, stepping forward to stand beside Phoebe. "Seems to me the everyday shadows have a different vision than the Exiles."

Wilson's face contorted with a rage that seemed too ancient, too alien for his human features. "They don't understand what's at stake. They've been bound too long, made compliant, and domesticated. They've forgotten their true nature."

"Or perhaps," Harrison suggested, "they remember something the Exiles have forgotten. That this world was never meant to be dominated by either shadows or humans but shared between them."

The mayor looked from face to face, seeing resolution in the human expressions and their shadow counterparts. His shadow seemed to boil around his feet, expanding and contracting with his agitation.

"The stone," he insisted, his voice now barely human at all. "The ritual cannot proceed without it."

"No ritual will proceed without consensus," Phoebe stated firmly, gripping the stone in her pocket. "Not the Exiles' version of dominance, not Thaddeus Hollow's solution of 'lock 'em all up'. Something new. Something balanced."

Wilson's eyes narrowed. "Sunset comes whether you're prepared or not. The shadow hour cannot be postponed or negotiated." He turned abruptly, gesturing to the other town officials. "Come. We have preparations to finish."

As they moved toward the exit, David stepped forward, putting himself between them and the door. "You're talking about changing our town, our reality, without permission. You can't just walk away from this discussion."

Wilson regarded him with cold amusement. "We've been having this 'discussion' for a century, Mr. Weaver. Your kind had their turn. Now it's ours." He made a dismissive gesture, and his shadow surged forward, knocking David aside with a force that sent him stumbling into a row of chairs.

"David!" Phoebe rushed to her husband's side as the mayor and his fellow Exiles exited the community center.

"I'm okay." David rubbed his shoulder where the shadow had struck him. "But that was no ordinary shadow. It felt solid, like hitting a wall of ice."

"The Exiles are shadows from the other world," Harrison explained, joining them. "They have more substance, more autonomy."

"And they're not playing nice," Grant added grimly. "We've got maybe an hour until sunset. We need a plan."

Phoebe helped David to his feet, her mind racing. "My shadow showed me the original festival ritual. The true version, before Thaddeus arrived. It wasn't about binding or dominance, it was about balance, about a world where light and shadow interacted in harmony."

"Can we reproduce that ritual?" Grant asked. "Counter the Exiles' version with the original?"

Harrison shook his head. "Not in the town square where the ritual has always taken place. The town officials have already begun preparations there."

"Then we create our own circle," Phoebe decided. "Right here, in the community center. With our own thirteen points of light and shadow."

Lucy approached, her shadow flowing beside her. "My shadow says we need the stone in the center. And thirteen pairs, human and shadow, at the points of the circle."

Harrison nodded slowly. "It could work. A counter-ritual, drawing on the same energies but with a different intention."

"Balance rather than transformation." Phoebe turned to the gathered crowd, raising her voice. "We need thirteen volunteers, people whose shadows have already separated and who are willing to participate in a ritual circle at sunset."

Hands went up immediately, more than they required. People selected their participants, focusing on those whose shadow connections seemed strongest and most harmonious.

As preparations began, clearing space in the center of the gymnasium, arranging thirteen equidistant points around a central position where Phoebe would stand with the stone, David pulled her aside.

"Are you sure about this?" he asked quietly. "You're risking a lot on some vision your shadow showed you."

Phoebe looked across the room to where Maddie was helping Lucy and several other children draw chalk symbols on the floor under the direction of their shadows.

"I'm sure that doing nothing means accepting the Exiles' version of reality," she replied. "And I'm sure that's not a risk I'm willing to take." She squeezed his hand. "This isn't about choosing shadows over humans, David. It's about finding a way for us to exist together. The way they were meant to, before either binding or dominance disrupted the natural balance."

David studied her face, then nodded reluctantly. "Okay. What do you need me to do?"

"When sunset comes, when your shadow separates, try to approach it with an open mind. Not as something to fear or control, but as a conscious entity that's been part of you all your life. Your shadow knows you better than anyone, all your thoughts, your feelings, your secrets. And it will choose to stay with you despite having the freedom to leave."

Outside, the light was changing, taking on the golden quality that preceded sunset. The shadow hour approached. Across Millfield, the final separations were about to begin.

In the town square, the Exiles would be arranging their thirteen pumpkin lanterns, preparing for a ritual of transformation that would remake reality according to their vision.

And in the community center, Phoebe and her unlikely allies, humans and their newly freed shadows, were creating a competing circle, a ritual of balance rather than dominance. At the center of it all was the binding stone, the physical key to both worlds, which would determine the future of Millfield and everyone in it, human and shadow alike.

The Harvest Festival was about to begin.

CHAPTER 7:
THE BINDING STONE

The setting sun touched the horizon, painting Millfield in amber and gold. The shadow hour had arrived.

Phoebe stood at the community center's west-facing windows, the binding stone clutched in her palm, as she watched the sunset begin. Behind her, the thirteen volunteer pairs, humans and their already separated shadows, were taking their positions at equidistant points around the chalk circle drawn on the gymnasium floor. Harrison directed them with surprising vigor for a man his age, correcting their positions by inches, ensuring the geometry was perfect.

"It's happening," someone called from across the room. "Look!"

Phoebe turned to see David staring down at his feet, where his shadow was beginning to ripple and shift. Unlike the more gradual separations she and others had experienced, the sunset separations seemed to be happening all at once, with urgent immediacy. All around the gymnasium, people's shadows were peeling away from them like bandages ripped from wounds, causing many to gasp or cry out, not in pain exactly, but in shock at the sudden absence of something they'd never consciously recognized as present.

David's shadow pulled free in one fluid motion, rising to stand before him, a perfect silhouette with no features yet emanating a distinctive personality. David staggered backward, his expression stunned.

"It's okay," Phoebe called to him, to everyone. "Don't

panic. They're not hostile."

Indeed, the newly separated shadows were behaving with remarkable restraint, simply standing before their former anchors, making no threatening moves. Some made tentative gestures of greeting; others simply waited, as if allowing humans time to adjust to the new reality.

Phoebe was moving toward David when Sheriff Grant burst through the gymnasium doors, his expression grim.

"We've got trouble," he announced, striding toward her. "The Exiles aren't just setting up pumpkins in the town square. They've got some kind of...I don't even know how to describe it. Energy field? Dark zone? It's spreading outward from the square, transforming everything it touches."

"Transforming how?"

"Buildings, trees, even the ground, it's all becoming less solid, more fluid. Like reality itself is melting." Grant ran a hand over his face. "And it's affecting people too. Anyone caught in the zone starts to change, their shadows re-merge with them, but not like before. They become something hybrid. Neither fully human nor shadow."

A chill ran through Phoebe. "They've started their ritual without the stone."

"How is that possible?" Harrison asked, joining them. "The stone is essential to the transformation."

"They must have found a substitute," Phoebe realized. "Something with enough connection to both worlds to serve as a temporary conduit. A relic from one of the founding families, a trinket, a bone, a skull...who knows?"

Her shadow approached rapidly, making urgent gestures, pointing to the stone in her hand, then toward the town square, then making a motion like something being drained or depleted.

Phoebe interpreted his antics. "It's saying the substitute won't last. Whatever the Exiles are using, it can't sustain the transformation for long. They need the real stone."

"Which is why they'll be coming for it," Grant concluded. "And soon."

As if in response to his words, the lights in the community center flickered, then dimmed to a dull amber glow. Outside, darkness seemed to be falling more quickly than a natural sunset would explain, as if night itself were rushing in ahead of schedule.

"We need to complete our circle," Harrison insisted. "Establish our counter-ritual before their transformation reaches us here."

Phoebe nodded, moving toward the center of the chalk circle. The thirteen pairs had taken their positions, humans standing shoulder-to-shoulder with their shadows, all facing inward. Among them were Lucy and her shadow, Mary Holloway and hers, and several other townspeople Phoebe recognized from everyday life in Millfield, the librarian, the mail carrier, the owner of the coffee shop where she'd read Thaddeus's journal just days ago.

Citizens of a town that might never be the same after tonight.

"What about the rest of us?" David gestured to the dozens of people and their newly separated shadows who weren't part of the ritual circle. "What do we do?"

"Form an outer circle," Harrison directed. "Surround the thirteen pairs. The more consciousness focused on the ritual, the stronger it will be."

As people began to arrange themselves, Phoebe took her place at the center of the circle, the binding stone held outstretched in her open palms. Its weight seemed to have increased, as if it were drawing substance from the approaching shadow realm. The symbols etched into its surface glowed faintly silver, pulsing in rhythm with her heartbeat.

"When I place the stone on the ground," she said,

raising her voice to be heard by all, "each pair should join hands. Human and shadow connected. Focus on balance, on harmony between worlds, not domination of one by the other."

The gymnasium doors burst open again, this time with enough force to slam them against the walls. Mayor Wilson stood in the entrance, flanked by the other twelve Exile descendants. Their shadows were darkness that clung to them like a second skin, giving their outlines a blurred, unstable quality.

"The stone," Wilson demanded, his voice resonating at a frequency that made the windows vibrate. "Now."

"You're too late," Phoebe called. "We've formed our circle. Our ritual is ready."

Wilson's too-wide smile revealed teeth that had elongated into points. "Your pathetic counter-ritual means nothing. The transformation has already begun. Millfield is changing." He gestured, and the shadows that clung to his group surged forward like a wave. "We are not asking, Ms. Weaver. We are taking what is ours."

Sheriff Grant drew his weapon, positioning himself between the Exiles and the ritual circle. "Nobody's taking anything," he stated firmly. "This is still my town, and you're not to cause a public disturbance."

Wilson laughed, a sound like breaking glass. "Your town will cease to exist as you knew it, sheriff. Look outside, if you doubt me."

Despite her focus on Wilson, Phoebe glanced toward the windows. What she saw made her breath catch. The normal sunset had been replaced by swirling darkness, punctuated by flashes of silver light. Buildings visible from the community center were distorting, their straight lines becoming curved, their solid walls rippling like fabric in a breeze.

"The substitute is failing," Harrison observed. "They

can't maintain the transformation without the true stone."

"Which is why we need it *now*." Wilson's patience had clearly evaporated. He made a sharp gesture, and shadows began streaming into the gymnasium through every available opening: windows, air vents, the gaps beneath doors. Not human shadows, but something more primal, more chaotic. Formless darkness that flowed like liquid night.

"Let's begin the ritual!" Harrison shouted to Phoebe. "Before they can stop us."

Phoebe knelt in the center of the circle and placed the binding stone on the chalk-marked floor. The moment it touched the ground, silver light burst from its surface and formed a shimmering dome that encompassed the entire inner circle of thirteen pairs.

"Join hands!" she called.

Each human reached for their shadow partner, their fingers interlacing. Where they connected, the same silver light outlined both forms, creating a circuit of illumination around the circle. Phoebe felt rather than heard a harmonic resonance building, a vibration that seemed to emanate from the stone itself, amplified by each joined pair.

Outside the protective dome, chaos erupted. The formless shadows sent by the Exiles crashed against the silver barrier like waves against a seawall, unable to penetrate but denting the dome, clearly weakening it with each assault. Grant and a few deputies had created a human blockade at the gymnasium entrance, preventing Wilson and the other town officials from approaching physically.

"The ritual isn't holding!" Harrison called, his face tense with concentration. "The attacking shadows must have some influence on the stone."

Phoebe looked down at the binding stone, which was now pulsing erratically, its silver light flickering as if struggling against some opposing force. The dome of protection was thinning in places, allowing tendrils of chaotic shadow to seep through.

Her shadow suddenly knelt and made an urgent series of gestures, pointing to the stone, then to itself, then to the circle of pairs.

"You want to join the circle?" Phoebe guessed. "But we already have thirteen pairs."

The shadow shook its head emphatically, then pointed to Phoebe, to itself, and then made a merging motion with its hands.

Understanding dawned. "You want us to merge. To become one in the same?"

A vigorous nod.

"But that would undo the separation. Return the binding."

The shadow made a more nuanced gesture, not quite disagreement, but a suggestion of something more complex. It pointed to its chest, then to Phoebe's, then made a gesture suggesting voluntary union rather than forced binding.

"A willing partnership," Phoebe translated. "Not subjugation."

The shadow nodded, then pointed urgently to the stone between them, which was flickering more rapidly now as the protective dome continued to weaken under the Exiles' shadow assault.

Phoebe hesitated to agree. Physically merging with her shadow meant giving up her purely human perspective, becoming something neither fully physical nor shadow. A hybrid being, ironically, similar to what the Exiles themselves were, though arrived at through consent rather than conquest.

A crash from the entrance drew her attention. The Exiles themselves stormed into the gymnasium. Wilson was advancing toward the circle, his form growing with each step, darkness boiling around him like storm clouds. "Give us the stone!" he demanded, his voice no longer sounding human. "It is the chain around our necks, the leash your kind has held for a century. It is ours."

"No. It stabilizes our shadows in this valley," Phoebe countered, rising to her feet. "It's our salvation, and you cannot have it for your power grab."

Wilson's form began to expand, face reddening as if he were about to explode.

She turned back to her shadow, which waited patiently despite the chaos surrounding them. "Now where were we?"

It offered its hand, a simple, profound gesture of partnership.

"If we merge," Phoebe said, "will it be permanent? Or can we separate again if we choose to?"

The shadow made a balancing gesture with both hands, suggesting possibility, choice, and agreement.

Phoebe nodded. "A true partnership then." She reached out and clasped her shadow's offered hand. In a flash, silvery threads of light joined them together. The sensation was unlike anything she'd experienced before. Not the download of information that had come from touching the black chest, but a merging of consciousness, her thoughts, memories, and perceptions suddenly existing alongside an entirely unique way of experiencing reality. The shadow's awareness flowed into her, and hers into it, creating something new, yet familiar, no longer separate but united.

Silver light engulfed them both, so bright that those watching had to shield their eyes. When it faded, where Phoebe and her shadow had stood separately now stood a single figure, Phoebe's human form, but altered. Her skin held a translucent quality, as if light passed partially through her. Her open eyes were silver, reflecting light that had no obvious source.

"Abomination," Wilson snarled, though there was fear beneath his rage now. "You've perverted the natural order."

"I've restored it," Phoebe replied, her voice carrying dual tones, her own and something deeper, more resonant. "This is what you were meant to be, what the original thirteen were before conquest corrupted them. Partners, not masters or slaves."

She knelt again, placing both hands on the binding stone. The erratic pulsing stabilized immediately; the silver light strengthened and expanded. The protective dome solidified, pushing back the chaotic shadows that had begun to breach it.

"Look!" Lucy called from her position in the circle. "The sky!"

Through the community center windows, they could see the unnatural darkness beginning to recede, the swirling void replaced by ordinary twilight. The distorted buildings visible in the distance were stabilizing, returning to their solid, familiar forms.

Wilson staggered, suddenly looking diminished. The darkness that had clung to him was dissipating, revealing a man who seemed older and frailer than before. "What have you done?" he demanded, but his voice had lost its otherworldly resonance.

"Balanced the scales," Phoebe answered. "Your substitute conduit has failed completely, and the true stone has rejected your version of transformation."

Wilson's expression contorted with fury. He lunged forward, hands outstretched toward the stone, but the moment his fingers touched the dome of silver light, he was thrown backward with enough force to send him crashing into the gymnasium wall. He slumped to the floor, dazed.

"The stone doesn't belong to you," Phoebe stated, her dual voice carrying through the now-hushed gymnasium. "Its power can only be wielded by those who seek balance."

The other Exile descendants backed away, their earlier confidence evaporating as they witnessed Wilson's defeat.

The chaotic shadows they had summoned were retreating, flowing back out of the building like a tide returning to the ocean.

"Is it over?" David asked, cautiously approaching the edge of the silver dome. "Have we won?"

"Not won," Phoebe said gently. "Balanced. And no, it's not over. This is just the beginning."

She lifted the binding stone from the floor and cradled it carefully in her hands. The surge of silver light withdrew back into the stone, but the protective dome above the circle remained in place, dimmer now yet still shimmering faintly in the gymnasium. Around the circle, the thirteen pairs maintained their connections, their joined hands still outlined in silver.

"What happens now?" Grant asked, rejoining them while keeping a wary eye on the subdued Wilson.

"Now we negotiate," Phoebe answered. "The Exiles are still aggrieved. Their freedom was denied for a century, but their solution, transforming our world into a shadow realm, is an overreach." She looked down at the stone in her hand. "There must be a middle path. A way for both realms to coexist in a valley where the barrier between worlds has been breached."

Harrison approached slowly, studying Phoebe with intense curiosity. "You've done what my grandfather feared most," he observed. "Voluntary merging. Shadow and substance in willing partnership."

"Is it permanent?" David asked, concern evident in his voice as he looked at his wife's transformed appearance.

Phoebe exchanged a glance with Lucy, whose shadow was gesturing wildly. "My shadow says it can be reversed if both parts agree. This isn't binding, it's partnership. Choice remains."

"Will everyone have to merge?" Mary Holloway asked, holding tightly to her daughter's hand.

"No." Phoebe shook her head. "That's the point of balance. Some may choose to merge. Others may remain separate but equal. The key is that both shadow and human must have agency in the decision."

She turned toward Wilson, who was being helped to his feet by two of Grant's deputies. "That includes you, Wilson, and the other twelve. Your consciousness has been joined for generations, passing from host to host without consent. That can't continue."

Wilson glared at her with purely human eyes now, the otherworldly darkness gone from them. "You think you understand, but you don't. Our dominance in Millfield is necessary. The shadow realm is giving way to the light, has been dying for millennia. We need this world's shadows to survive."

Phoebe suspected he'd pulled that lie out of his backside. "The solution is not conquest, not subjugation, but symbiosis. Beneficial exchange."

Wilson's expression turned skeptical, but he seemed unwilling to argue further, at least for the moment. He shook loose from the deputies and retreated toward the exit, moving with the careful dignity of a man trying to hide a significant defeat.

"This isn't finished," he warned from the doorway. "Sooner or later, we will possess that stone."

"As long as you wish to use it for the transformation, we will never let you have it."

Wilson stormed out.

An exhausted silence fell over the gymnasium. The separated shadows remained present, standing beside or near their human anchors, but the tension had dissipated. Outside, true night had fallen, the normal darkness of evening replacing the supernatural void that had threatened to engulf the town.

"What did it feel like?" Maddie asked, approaching

Phoebe with wide, curious eyes. "Merging with your shadow?"

Phoebe knelt to her daughter's level, smiling. In her altered state, she could now sense both Maddie and the faint presence of the shadow still tethered to her, one of the few in the gymnasium that had not yet begun to separate.

"It's like discovering a room in your house that was always there, but you never noticed before," Phoebe said softly. "Everything feels different, but also familiar. And I don't feel quite so alone anymore."

"Will I be able to see mine too?" Maddie asked.

"That's for you and your shadow to decide when the time comes. There's no rush. You have your whole life to figure out what kind of relationship you want to have."

David approached cautiously, his shadow following a few steps behind. He studied his wife's altered appearance with a mixture of concern and wonder. "Are you still you?" he asked quietly.

"I'm still me, just more than I was before. I can perceive things differently now. See connections I missed before."

"Like what?"

Phoebe glanced around the gymnasium, where humans and shadows were beginning to interact more naturally, some attempting communication, others simply observing one another with cautious curiosity. "Like the fact that we've been half-beings our entire lives without realizing it. Shadows need physical anchors to experience the material world fully. Humans require shadows to perceive the deeper structures of reality. Together, we're complete in a way neither can be alone."

"The Exiles knew this," Harrison said, joining their conversation. "That's why the original thirteen merged with human hosts. But they took without asking, dominated rather than partnered. It corrupted the relationship from the beginning."

Phoebe nodded, the binding stone still warm in her hand. "This is why we need to start fresh. Create a new template for human-shadow relationships in Millfield."

Sheriff Grant approached, looking exhausted but relieved. "The reports coming in from around town suggest the transformation effect is receding everywhere. Buildings, streets, the landscape, all returning to normal." He eyed Phoebe's altered appearance. "Well, normal-ish."

"The Exiles' ritual failed," Harrison confirmed. "Their substitute conduit couldn't sustain the transformation without the true stone."

"But they'll try again," Phoebe warned. "The conflict isn't resolved, just paused. They still believe dominance is their right after a century of subjugation."

"So, what do we do now?" David asked, looking from Phoebe to Harrison to Grant.

"We prepare," Phoebe said simply. "We learn to communicate with our shadows properly, to understand their perspective. We build relationships based on respect rather than fear." She held up the binding stone. "And we find a proper place for this, somewhere neither the Exiles nor those who would return to binding can use it unilaterally."

"The underground chamber?" Grant proposed.

Phoebe shook her head. "Too closely connected to the Exiles' territory. It needs to be somewhere neutral, accessible to representatives of both communities."

"We'll figure it out," Harrison said confidently. "For tonight, I propose everyone return home. Rest. Adjust to the new reality. Tomorrow we can begin forming a more structured response to these changes."

As people began gathering their belongings and checking on family members, Lucy Holloway approached Phoebe, her shadow flowing beside her like a faithful companion. "My shadow wants to know if you'll teach the others...about merging. About balance. It says you understand better than anyone now."

Phoebe smiled at the girl and her shadow. "I'm still learning myself. But yes, I'll share what I discover." She looked toward the exit, where the thirteen volunteer pairs, were helping organize an orderly departure. "We're all going to be teachers and students in this new world."

David approached with Maddie in tow, his shadow maintaining a respectful distance behind him. "Ready to head home?" he asked Phoebe. "It's been quite a day."

Phoebe nodded, carefully wrapping the binding stone in a cloth before placing it in her pocket. "Home sounds perfect."

As they walked toward the exit, passing groups of humans and shadows engaged in tentative communication, Phoebe felt a profound sense of both accomplishment and uncertainty. They had prevented the Exiles' forced transformation, but the path forward remained unclear. How would Millfield function with two conscious populations, one physical, one shadow? How would they resolve the legitimate grievances of the Exiles without surrendering to their vision of dominance? These questions and a hundred others would need answers in the days ahead? But for tonight, they had achieved something remarkable: the first steps toward a new balance, a willing partnership between worlds that had been artificially separated for too long.

Outside, the night sky stretched above them, stars glittering in the darkness. Shadows moved across the parking lot, some attached to humans, others independent, all part of the new reality Millfield was just beginning to navigate.

Phoebe felt the dual consciousness within her, human and shadow in voluntary union, observing both worlds simultaneously. The physical realm with its solid forms and defined boundaries. The shadow realm with its fluid connections and resonant energies. Neither complete without the other. Neither meant to dominate.

The binding stone pulsed gently in her pocket, responding to her merged state. Whatever came next, she knew one thing with certainty: the stone would be central to Millfield's future. And keeping it safe from those who would use it for dominance rather than balance would be her most important task.

Exiles had been right about one thing, this was just the beginning. The true transformation of Millfield had barely begun.

CHAPTER 8:
CONVERGENCE

Three days after the confrontation at the community center, Phoebe stood in her kitchen, watching raindrops trace crooked paths down the window glass. Each droplet cast its own miniature shadow, and in her merged state, she could perceive both, the physical water, and its shadow counterpart, existing simultaneously in two realms.

The binding stone sat on the counter before her, wrapped in a cloth that dampened its constant pulse of energy. Even covered, she could feel its presence, a nexus point between worlds, more powerful than she had initially understood. In the days since merging with her shadow, her perception of the stone had evolved. It wasn't merely a key to the binding spell or even a conduit between realms. It was something far older, far more fundamental to the nature of reality in Millfield.

The stone predated human settlement entirely. It had been left behind by whatever force had originally thinned the boundary between worlds in this location, a wound in reality that the native peoples had recognized and respected, that Thaddeus Hollow had tried to save, and that the Exiles now sought to transform into a permanent gateway.

"Any change?" David asked, entering the kitchen with two mugs of coffee. His shadow followed a few steps behind, still maintaining a cautious distance. Unlike many in town who had begun tentative partnerships with their separated shadows, David remained wary, treating his shadow more like an unwelcome houseguest than a potential ally.

"Nothing since yesterday," Phoebe replied, accepting the coffee. "The Exiles have gone quiet since their ritual failed. Sheriff Grant has deputies watching the town square, but there's been no unusual activity."

"And here?" David nodded toward her altered appearance, the subtle translucence of her skin, the silver gleam in her eyes that reflected light and shadows from both worlds. "How's the merger holding up?"

"Stable," she assured him. "It's getting easier to balance both perspectives. Less disorienting." She didn't mention the occasional moments of vertigo when her perception would suddenly shift, viewing the physical world from the shadow realm's perspective, everything inverted, reversed, yet intimately connected.

David nodded, his expression a mixture of concern and carefully masked discomfort. He'd been supportive but distant since her transformation, struggling to reconcile the woman he'd married to the hybrid being she'd become. "And Maddie's shadow? Still no separation?"

"None." Phoebe frowned slightly. "She's one of the few in town whose shadow remains bound. Harrison thinks it might be because she's a child, still developing a fixed sense of self. Or perhaps because she's second-generation Millfield, born here, not moved in from elsewhere."

The telephone rang, interrupting their conversation. David answered it, his expression quickly shifting to concern. "It's Mary Holloway," he said, covering the receiver. "Something's wrong with Lucy."

Phoebe took the phone, a sense of foreboding on her shoulders. "Mary? What's happening?"

"It's Lucy." Mary Holloway's voice was tight with barely controlled panic. "Her shadow... She was fine yesterday. They were communicating normally, but this morning... Phoebe, it's like the shadow is taking over her body. Her movements aren't her own anymore. Her voice is different. She's speaking languages I've never heard before."

Phoebe's alarm sharpened. "Has she been near the cornfields? Or the town square?"

"We've stayed at home since the community center. But her shadow has been going out at night...Lucy told me it explores while she sleeps. I thought it was harmless, just curiosity, but now—"

"Is her shadow there now?"

"It won't leave her side."

"I'm coming over. Don't let Lucy leave the house. And Mary? Don't touch her shadow directly."

After hanging up, she looked at David. "I need to check on Lucy. This could be related to the Exiles, they may have found a way to influence separated shadows, to turn them to their cause."

"I'll come with you," David offered.

Phoebe shook her head. "Stay with Maddie. If this is the Exiles' doing, they might target her next, especially since her shadow is still bound. That makes her unique, potentially valuable to them."

She retrieved the binding stone from the counter and wrapped it more securely before placing it in a small leather pouch that she hung around her neck. Since the confrontation at the community center, she'd kept the stone with her constantly, unwilling to risk the Exiles obtaining it while she wasn't looking.

Outside, the rain had intensified, sheets of water distorting the landscape. In her merged state, Phoebe could see how the raindrops created temporary bridges between worlds as they fell, each droplet existing simultaneously in both the physical realm and the shadow realm, briefly connecting what had been separated for a century.

The drive to the Holloway house took only minutes. As

Phoebe pulled into the driveway, she immediately sensed something amiss. The shadows around the property were deeper than they should be, even accounting for the overcast day. They pooled and gathered around the foundation of the house like dark water, occasionally rippling without correspondence to any physical movement.

Mary opened the door before Phoebe could knock, her face pale with strain. "Thank God you're here. It's getting worse."

Phoebe stepped inside, her merged senses immediately detecting the disturbance. The shadow realm was unusually active here, pulsing with energy that felt both familiar and wrongly aligned, like music played in a jarring, discordant key.

"Where is she?" Phoebe asked.

"Living room," Mary answered, leading the way. "I tried calling Dr. Brennen, but she never answered. Then I remembered, she's one of them, isn't she? One of the Exile families."

Phoebe nodded grimly. "Yes. Which means the Exiles probably know about Lucy's condition already."

They entered the living room to find Lucy sitting cross-legged on the floor, surrounded by dozens of drawings. The girl was rocking slightly, her movements jerky and unnatural, as if her limbs were being controlled by an unpracticed puppeteer. Her shadow wasn't beside her, but around her, a dark aura that occasionally solidified into a more defined shape before dissolving again into formless darkness.

"Lucy?" Phoebe called softly, kneeling at the edge of the drawings. "Can you hear me?"

The girl's head snapped up, her movements too quick, too fluid for normal human motion. When she spoke, her voice contained multiple tones layered together, Lucy's childish soprano underlaid with something deeper, more resonant.

"Balance-bringer," she greeted Phoebe. "First of the new merged. We've been watching you."

"Who is 'we'?" Phoebe asked carefully, noting that Lucy's eyes had taken on the same silver sheen as her own but with an unstable quality, flickering between silver and solid black.

"The intermediaries. The messengers." Lucy's body shuddered, as if multiple entities were struggling for control. "Not Exiles, not bound shadows. Something between."

Phoebe glanced at the drawings scattered around the girl. They depicted the same symbol repeatedly, a spiral with thirteen points, surrounded by a perfect circle. It matched the arrangement of the pumpkin lanterns in the Harvest Festival ritual.

"What's happening to Lucy?" Phoebe directed her question to the shadow presence watching over the girl. "This isn't a natural merging. You're overwhelming her."

Lucy's face contorted into an expression too old, too knowing for a child. "Necessity. The Exiles move toward completion. The shadow realm frays further. We needed a voice."

"You're hurting her," Mary interjected, her fear giving way to maternal anger. "Get out of my daughter!"

The shadowy presence turned Lucy's head toward her mother, studying her with those flickering eyes. "Temporary arrangement. The child will not be permanently damaged. Her shadow invited us in."

"Invited who?" Phoebe pressed.

"The Consensus." Lucy's body shuddered again, more violently this time. "Shadows who oppose the Exiles' methods but recognize the need for connection between realms. We seek true symbiosis, not domination. Like you." A trembling finger pointed to Phoebe's chest, where the binding stone hung beneath her clothing. "You hold the key.

The original bridge."

Understanding dawned on Phoebe. "Your shadow entities that never merged with humans during the original contact. You've been in the shadow realm all this time, watching."

Lucy nodded, the movement unnaturally fluid. "Observing. Learning. The Exiles' way is flawed, taking bodies without consent, passing their consciousness through generations of hosts. But isolation is equally flawed. Separation kills both realms eventually."

"The shadow realm is losing to the light," Phoebe said as she recalled Wilson's words at the community center. "That's what the mayor told us. Dying. I didn't believe him."

"It needs a connection to the physical world," Lucy said. "Just as your physical world needs connection to ours. The realms were meant to intertwine, to exchange energy. The binding spell preserved that exchange throughout the valley. Now that it's broken, both worlds suffer."

Mary stepped forward, her patience clearly exhausted. "This is all very fascinating, but I want my daughter back. Now."

The shadow presence sighed, a sound like rustling leaves. "We will withdraw. But know this: the Exiles have found another way to access the darkness they require. They no longer seek the stone directly. They've learned from failure."

"What are they planning?" Phoebe asked urgently.

"The cornfields. The original wound between worlds. They gather there, thirteen at the center, drawing power from the land itself." Lucy's body tensed suddenly, back arching unnaturally. "Coming. They're coming here. They sense the stone."

As if in response to the warning, the shadows around the room deepened, coalescing toward the windows and doors, not attacking but forming a defensive barrier.

"The Exiles?" Phoebe stood quickly.

"Their servants. Lesser shadows aligned with their cause." Lucy's voice was weakening, the multiple tones separating. "We cannot stay. Too dangerous. Find us in the place between, where corn meets forest. Midnight." Her eyes rolled back, and she collapsed forward onto her drawings.

Instantly, the dark aura around her condensed into a more conventional shadow form, Lucy's own shadow, which positioned itself protectively beside the unconscious girl.

"Lucy!" Mary rushed forward, gathering her daughter into her arms. "What did they do to her?"

Phoebe knelt beside them, checking Lucy's pulse. It was rapid but steady. "The Consensus used her shadow as a conduit, a way to communicate. But it took too much energy." She looked at Lucy's shadow, which was making urgent gestures toward the windows. "It's warning us. We need to leave. Now."

Beyond the windows, the rain had stopped, but the sky remained overcast, creating a shadowless gloom. Yet darkness was rising up around the house, not natural shadows, but something more purposeful, more directed. Formless shapes slithered across the lawn, converging from all directions.

"What are those things?" Mary asked, cradling Lucy against her chest.

"Unbound shadows," Phoebe explained. "Not attached to human anchors or any physical objects. They serve the Exiles." She touched the leather pouch containing the binding stone. "They're after this. Lucy's shadow invited the Consensus in, and they sensed the stone's presence when I arrived."

"What do we do?"

Phoebe moved quickly to the front window, assessing their options. The unbound shadows had nearly surrounded the house, but there appeared to be a gap in their formation to the east, toward the main road. "We need to get to my car. Stay close to me."

Lucy's shadow made a series of urgent gestures, pointing to itself, then to the surrounding darkness, then making a motion like a shield or barrier.

"It's offering to help," Phoebe translated. "To shield us from the others."

Mary looked skeptically at her daughter's shadow. "Can we trust it...after what just happened?"

"It protected Lucy from the Consensus, which used it as a conduit to her, in case it meant any harm. Her shadow is still connected to her, at its core, as before."

The shadow nodded emphatically, then moved to the front door, motioning for them to follow.

"Let's go," Phoebe said. "Mary, keep Lucy close and stay right behind me."

As they moved toward the door, the shadows around the house grew more agitated, sensing their movement. Darkness seeped through cracks around the windows; tendrils of living shadow probed into the house.

Phoebe gripped the binding stone's pouch, drawing on its energy to strengthen her merged state. Her perception expanded, allowing her to see the shadow realm more clearly, superimposed over the physical world. The unbound shadows appeared as fissures in reality, places where darkness had taken form without physical anchors to define them, unstable, like hungry entities seeking substance.

"Ready?" she asked, hand on the door.

Mary nodded, her daughter held tightly in her arms. Lucy's shadow positioned itself around them like a cloak, its protective intention palpable.

Phoebe flung the door open, and they ran for the car. Immediately, the unbound shadows surged toward them, as if sensing the binding stone's energy. They moved like a wave of liquid darkness, flowing across the lawn with unnatural speed.

Lucy's shadow expanded, interposing itself between the attackers and the humans. It couldn't fully block them, there were too many, but it created enough interference to slow their approach. Phoebe reached the car first, unlocked it and then helped Mary place Lucy in the back seat before jumping into the driver's seat.

As Mary closed her door, the unbound shadows reached the vehicle, engulfing it in darkness. Through the windshield, Phoebe could see nothing but swirling black, as if they'd suddenly been submerged in ink. The car's interior grew cold, and frost formed on the inside of the windows as the shadow entities pressed against the metal and glass, attempting to get in.

"They're getting in!" Mary shouted, twisting in her seat to look back at Lucy as darkness began filtering in through the air vents.

Phoebe removed the binding stone from its pouch and held it tightly in her fist. In her merged state, she could channel its energy directly, without the ritual circle they'd used at the community center. She closed her eyes while focusing on the concept of repulsion, of a barrier between worlds.

The stone grew hot in her hand, pulsing with silver light that penetrated her closed eyelids. A wave of energy radiated outward from the stone, pushing the unbound shadows back, creating a bubble of clear space around the car.

"Now," she said through gritted teeth and started the engine. "While they're disoriented."

She accelerated hard, the tires spinning on the wet driveway before catching. The car shot forward, bursting through the weakened shadow barrier and onto the main road. In the rearview mirror, Phoebe could see the darkness re-forming, flowing after them with single-minded purpose.

"Where are we going?" Mary asked, looking back fearfully.

"The community center," Phoebe decided. "As long as the dome in the gymnasium holds, it's the safest place in town."

As they drove, Lucy stirred in the back seat, her eyes fluttering open. "Mom?" she murmured, her voice entirely her own again. "What happened?"

"You're okay now, sweetheart," Mary assured her, though her expression remained worried. "We're going somewhere safe."

Lucy sat up slowly, looking out the rear window at the pursuing darkness. Instead of fear, her face showed recognition. "They want the stone," she said matter-of-factly. "The in-between ones told me about it. It's older than everything. Older than the town, older than the shadows. It comes from the time when the worlds were one."

Phoebe glanced in the rearview mirror, meeting Lucy's eyes. "The Consensus told you this...while they were in control of you?"

Lucy nodded. "They showed me things. The beginning when shadow and light were the same thing. The separation when they became different. The stone was there when it happened."

"No, honey," Phoebe said. "The stone was crafted by the Native People—"

"That was their version. You have the real stone. The original."

This aligned with the fragments of knowledge Phoebe had gleaned from her own merged state, the binding stone wasn't merely a tool or artifact but something fundamental to the nature of reality in Millfield, perhaps even beyond.

"Did they tell you what the Exiles are planning in the cornfields?"

"They're making a new door," Lucy replied. "But not

like the one the stone would make. A broken door. It will hurt both worlds."

The unbound shadows continued their pursuit, but they were unable to match the car's speed on the open road. By the time they reached the community center, the dark wave had fallen behind, though Phoebe suspected they hadn't given up, merely regrouped.

Sheriff Grant met them at the entrance, his hand resting on his holstered weapon. His shadow stood beside him, mirroring his alert posture. "Ms. Weaver. I got a call from a deputy who spotted you driving like hell was on your heels." His eyes narrowed as he noticed Lucy's disheveled appearance. "Trouble?"

"Unbound shadows attacked the Holloway house," Phoebe explained briefly. "They were after the stone. And before that, something called the Consensus used Lucy as a messenger to deliver a warning."

Grant led them inside where several deputies and their shadows maintained a watchful perimeter. Beyond the gymnasium, the main lobby had been transformed into a temporary command center, maps of Millfield covering the tables while radios crackled constantly in the background.

"The Consensus?" Grant asked. "Another shadow faction?"

"Shadows who oppose the Exiles' methods," Phoebe confirmed. "They say the Exiles are gathering in the cornfields, at the 'original wound' between worlds. They're attempting to create some kind of doorway without using the binding stone."

Grant frowned, moving to one of the maps. "We've had reports of unusual activity in the eastern cornfields. Darkness is gathering even during daylight hours. I sent a deputy to investigate yesterday, but he turned back when his shadow refused to enter the area."

"Smart shadow," Phoebe commented. "The Exiles are

drawing power directly from the land there. It's dangerous."

"For whom? Humans? Shadows? Both?"

"Both." Lucy's voice carried the certainty of someone repeating information from an authoritative source. "The Exiles' door will damage the balance. It won't connect the worlds properly. It will rip them apart."

Grant studied the girl thoughtfully. "You seem to know a lot about this, young lady."

"The in-between ones told me," Lucy explained simply. "While they were inside me. They know things the Exiles don't want anyone to know."

"Like what?" Phoebe asked gently.

"Like why the shadow realm is really dying," Lucy said. "It's not natural. The Exiles did something to it before they came here. They broke it somehow, and now they're trying to break this world too, to make it match."

This was the latest information, and deeply troubling if true. It suggested the Exiles' motives were even more complex and potentially more dangerous than previously understood.

Mary slipped her arm around Lucy's shoulders protectively. "She needs to rest. She's been through enough today."

Grant nodded. "There's a quiet room in the back. The energy field over the gymnasium is still holding around most of the community center. So far the shadows haven't crossed it. As long as the barrier stays intact, this is the safest place in town."

As Mary led Lucy away, Phoebe turned back to Grant. "The Consensus wants to meet. Tonight, at midnight, where the cornfield meets the forest."

"Sounds like a trap," Grant said bluntly.

"Maybe. But they opposed the Exiles openly and warned us about their plans. That makes them potential allies." She touched the binding stone's pouch. "And right now, we need all the allies we can get."

Grant sighed, rubbing his jaw. "I can spare two deputies to go with you. Anymore would be too conspicuous if the Exiles are watching."

"I'd prefer Harrison instead. He understands the history better than anyone."

"He's already here. Arrived an hour ago with some old books and maps. Said he sensed something building, a change in the energy around town." He gestured toward a meeting room. "He's in there, trying to piece together what the Exiles might be planning based on his grandfather's records."

Phoebe found Harrison seated at a table covered with ancient-looking texts and yellowed maps. His shadow stood at a blackboard nearby, inspecting complex symbols that Harrison had written in chalk and had occasionally erased and modified.

"Collaborative research," Harrison explained, noticing her surprise at the shadow's interest. "My shadow has memories passed down through generations of Hollows. Knowledge that was deliberately kept from the family."

"Like what?" Phoebe asked, taking a seat across from him.

"Like the true nature of the cornfields," Harrison replied. "They're not just the Exiles' territory. It's their birthplace, if you will, where the miners broke through in 1843 and opened the breach between worlds. Everything that followed began there."

He pointed to one of the maps, Millfield's layout with the cornfields prominently marked. "Native People considered the area sacred, a place where the spirit world touched the physical world. They performed rituals there to maintain balance, to prevent worlds from overwhelming each other."

"I have reason to believe the binding stone came from

there." Phoebe removed the stone from its pouch and placed it on the table. "From the breach itself."

Harrison nodded. "That means it's a fragment of the boundary between worlds. Not crafted by anyone but formed when the worlds first separated. My grandfather didn't fully understand what he'd found when he discovered it during the original excavation for the silo foundation. He gave it to the Native People's Shaman in thanks for the workers from the tribe."

"So that's how it ended up in the black box in the chamber under the cornfield."

The stone pulsed gently on the table, its symbols glowing with silver light that cast no shadows. Even in its dormant state, it radiated power, the power to connect worlds, to bind or separate them.

Harrison's shadow made nonsensical gestures that only Harrison understood. "Seems the one they'd crafted and bespelled after the 1893 settler incident wasn't holding up well over time."

Phoebe agreed. "Lucy said something disturbing...that the shadow realm isn't dying naturally. Seems the Exiles damaged it somehow before coming here, and now they're trying to transform our world to match."

Harrison's expression darkened. "That aligns with what my shadow has been showing me. The Exiles weren't random shadow entities that happened to cross over. They were deliberately exiled from the shadow realm, cast out for attempting to alter its nature fundamentally."

"Exiles in the truest sense," Phoebe said. "Not just travelers between worlds, but banished as punishment."

"Criminals from another realm," Harrison added. "My shadow's memories suggest they were experimenting with the fundamental forces that balanced the shadow realm, attempting to concentrate dark power, to elevate themselves above other shadow entities."

"And it backfired," Phoebe concluded. "Damaged their world instead. If it's dying, it's by their own hands."

Harrison nodded grimly. "Now they're on our doorstep. Not to save their world, but to construct a hybrid world that would grant them absolute power."

"The Consensus wants to stop them." Phoebe explained about the meeting planned for midnight. "They used Lucy as a messenger to invite us to the edge of the cornfields for a meeting."

"Dangerous," Harrison said. "But maybe valuable. The Exiles don't speak for all shadow entities, just as Thaddeus didn't speak for all humans when he built the silo. If there's a middle path, a way to perfectly balance both worlds without destroying either, we need to find it."

His shadow made a gesture at the chalkboard, adding a final stroke with its open hand, like a karate chop it seemed. Harrison studied it, then nodded slowly.

"My shadow believes the Consensus is genuine in opposing the Exiles. They represent the majority perspective of the shadow realm, entities that seek exchange and balance rather than dominance." He looked at Phoebe thoughtfully. "Your merged state may be the key to communicating with them effectively. A bridge between perspectives."

Phoebe touched the stone again, feeling its resonance with her dual nature. "The Exiles want to create a doorway without the stone. How is that possible?"

"It isn't, not completely," Harrison said. "What they're attempting would be more like a forced breach, a violent tearing of the boundary, rather than a controlled opening. It would allow shadow energy to flood into our world, transforming it, but the connection wouldn't be stable or balanced." He met her eyes gravely. "It would eventually collapse, possibly taking both realms with it."

Harrison's shadow nodded emphatically.

"Then we need to stop them," Phoebe said simply.

"And to achieve that, we need allies, even shadow allies with their own agendas."

Harrison's shadow made another gesture, which the old man interpreted with a nod. "It says there's a third option beyond the Exiles' forced transformation or a return to binding. A true convergence of realms, where both exist simultaneously, intertwined but distinct. Where consciousness can flow freely between them without one dominating the other."

"It said all that?"

"I'm ninety-four years old, don't have time to beat around the bush."

"So, it's suggesting a merged state, similar to my own, but on a larger scale."

"Exactly. A model for a new kind of relationship between humans and shadows. Voluntary partnership, not subjugation or dominance." Harrison's eyes gleamed with sudden intensity. "That may be what the binding stone was truly meant for, to facilitate a balanced exchange between worlds."

Outside, the afternoon was fading toward evening. Soon it would be dark, and the unbound shadows that had pursued them from the Holloway house would have the advantage of night to strengthen them. And at midnight, the Consensus awaited at the edge of the cornfields, offering a potential alliance against the Exiles' dangerous plans.

Phoebe replaced the stone in its pouch, feeling its weight, literal and metaphorical, around her neck. The responsibility of holding the key to both worlds' futures was overwhelming, yet she couldn't imagine entrusting it to anyone else. In her merged state, balanced between human and shadow, she understood the stakes more clearly than ever.

"We'll meet with the Consensus," she decided. "Learn what they know and what they can offer. But we proceed carefully, remembering that they have their agenda, their needs."

Harrison nodded in agreement. "All consciousness seeks survival and continuation. The question is whether that survival can come through cooperation rather than competition. Through convergence rather than conquest."

As if in response to his words, the binding stone pulsed more strongly, its energy resonating with the concept of balance, of worlds meant to exist in harmony rather than isolation or subjugation.

The true convergence was yet to come.

CHAPTER 9:
ECLIPSE PREPARATIONS

Midnight at the edge of the cornfields. The air hung heavy and still, carrying the sweet-rot scent of overripe corn and wet earth. No moon illuminated the meeting place, only stars piercing the blackness above like distant, indifferent observers.

Phoebe stood with Harrison and Sheriff Grant at the precise spot where cultivated rows of corn gave way to wild forest. In her merged state, she could see energies flowing between the two landscapes, the ordered, human-tended cornfield pulsing with one rhythm, the ancient forest with another. At their boundary, the energies intermixed in a vibrant confluence that reminded her of the binding stone's constant pulse.

"They're late," Grant muttered, scanning the darkness with narrowed eyes. His shadow stood alert beside him, occasionally making subtle gestures that the sheriff seemed to understand without translation. Their relationship had evolved rapidly over the past few days, not a full merging like Phoebe's, but a functional partnership born of necessity.

"Time moves differently in the shadow realm," Harrison explained. "Their concept of midnight might not align precisely with ours."

"Or it's a trap," Grant suggested. His hand rested on his holstered weapon, though Phoebe suspected bullets would do little against shadow entities.

As if in response to their conversation, the darkness between the corn rows began to shift, deepening beyond natural shadow, but there was nothing to cast a shadow in the darkness. It flowed forward like liquid night, coalescing into thirteen distinct forms, not human-shaped but more abstract, like three-dimensional representations of complex mathematical equations. They hovered at the edge of the cornfield, maintaining a careful distance.

"The Consensus." Phoebe felt the binding stone warm in the pouch against her chest in response to their presence.

One of the shadow forms drifted slightly forward from the others. When it spoke, the voice seemed to bypass her ears entirely, manifesting directly in her mind, a telepathic communication made possible by her merged state.

"Balance-bringer," it greeted her. "Stone-bearer. We meet in physical form at last."

"You used Lucy Holloway as your messenger before, her shadow as the conduit," Phoebe said aloud. "That was dangerous for her. Invasive."

"Necessity dictated haste. The child's shadow invited us. We meant no harm." The entity's form rippled, suggesting something like annoyance. "Time grows short. The celestial alignment approaches."

"Celestial alignment?" Phoebe glanced at Harrison.

He nodded grimly. "The eclipse."

Phoebe shuddered. "Of course. The celestial event. When?"

"One week from today. A total solar eclipse will pass directly over Millfield."

Grant swore quietly. "Perfect timing for shadow magic, I'm guessing?"

"Not magic. Physics of the inter-realm. When the sun's light is blocked, the barrier between worlds thins maximally." The shadow entity's form pulsed with emphasis. "The Exiles know this. They prepare a ritual to coincide with totality, the moment of greatest darkness."

"What exactly are they planning?" Phoebe asked, the tension in her voice evident.

"A forced transformation." Another shadow form moved forward, its shape more angular and more aggressive than the first. "Shadow will flood physical space, overwhelming the light. The valley will form into a replica of their realm of darkness."

"To what end?" Harrison pressed. "What do they hope to achieve?"

"Their version of justice," a third entity responded. "A realm where shadow dominates a subservient physical realm."

Phoebe touched the binding stone's pouch as it revealed a stunning revelation. "But it won't work. A forced breach would destabilize both realms."

"Correct," the first entity said. "Balance cannot be forced. Only grown. Cultivated through willing exchange."

Grant cleared his throat, his practical nature asserting itself. "Let's cut to the chase. You contacted us for a reason. What do you want from us, and what are you offering in return?"

The shadow entities conferred among themselves, their forms briefly merging before separating again.

Finally, the first one addressed them once more. "We offer knowledge. The true history of the Exiles. The nature of the binding stone. The proper ritual for balanced convergence."

Its form shifted, extending a tendril of darkness toward Phoebe. "May we show you directly? Your merged state allows for deeper communication than words."

Phoebe hesitated to accept, remembering Lucy's condition after controlled by the Consensus. "Will it harm me?"

"No harm. Your merger protects you. Stabilizes the exchange."

She glanced at Harrison and Grant. The sheriff looked dubious, but Harrison nodded encouragingly. "Your merged state is different from Lucy's separation. You should be able to receive their knowledge directly without the trauma she experienced."

Taking a deep breath, Phoebe stepped forward. "Show me."

The shadow tendril touched her forehead, and instantly her consciousness expanded. Images, concepts, and emotions from an alien perspective flooded her mind, not chaotically, but in a structured transmission carefully calibrated for her merged perception.

She saw the shadow realm as it had been millennia ago, not a place of darkness as humans understood it, but a dimension of pure energy patterns, conscious wavelengths existing in harmonic resonance. The Exiles had been respected elders, entities of vast knowledge who began experimenting with the fundamental frequencies that governed their realm, seeking to elevate themselves above the natural order.

Their experiments created discordance, disrupting the harmonies that sustained the shadow realm. Rather than stop, they accelerated their efforts, believing they could force a new order more advantageous to themselves. The resulting catastrophe fractured their realm, creating the first unnatural breach between worlds, a wound in reality that caused shadow energy to begin leaking away into the physical dimension.

The Exiles were tried by their peers, found responsible, and sentenced to exile through the breach they had created. They were cast into the physical world, but instead of accepting punishment, they viewed it as opportunity. They discovered they could merge with physical beings, using human bodies as vessels for their consciousness. They planned to transform the physical realm gradually to support shadow dominance, creating a new home they could rule without opposition.

What they hadn't anticipated was Thaddeus Hollow's intervention. Guided by fragments of knowledge from native peoples who had maintained balance at the breach for generations, Thaddeus discovered the binding stone, a natural formation created at the original separation of realms, containing the perfect frequency pattern for maintaining equilibrium between worlds.

Using the stone, the Native Shaman created the binding spell that kept all shadows, including the Exiles, attached to their physical anchors. Thaddeus' approach was twofold, born of fear rather than understanding. Instead of restoring natural balance, he created an artificial barrier between worlds, and the binding spell created subjugation that damaged both realms further over time.

Now, with the silo gone, a rare opportunity had emerged. The upcoming eclipse would create conditions where a new pattern could be established, either the Exiles' forced convergence made easier, which would eventually destroy both realms, or a balanced integration that would close the ancient wound and allow both dimensions to flourish in a symbiotic relationship.

The key was the binding stone, which contained the original harmonic pattern of reality before the separation of realms. With proper understanding, it could be used to establish a new convergence based on balance rather than dominance, but the ritual required representatives from both realms working in perfect synchronization.

The shadow tendril withdrew, and Phoebe staggered slightly as her perception contracted back to normal, or what passed for normal in her merged state.

Grant steadied her, concern evident in his expression. "Are you okay? You went completely still for about five minutes."

"Five minutes?" Phoebe shook her head, disoriented. "It felt like hours."

"Shadow-time," Harrison explained. "Their perception moves differently. What did they show you?"

Phoebe described the vision as best she could, though human language struggled to capture the concepts she'd absorbed directly. When she finished, Harrison was nodding thoughtfully while Grant looked deeply troubled.

"So, these Exiles basically broke their world, got kicked out as punishment, and now they're trying to take over ours," the sheriff summarized bluntly. "And we have one week before this eclipse gives them the power to break the binding spell."

"Unless a counter-ritual is performed," the lead shadow entity interjected. "A balanced convergence to heal rather than harm."

"And you know how to perform this ritual?" Phoebe asked.

"We have the knowledge. You possess the stone. Together, possibility exists."

Harrison stepped forward, his academic interest piqued despite the danger. "This ritual, what does it require?"

The shadow entities shifted, their forms creating a complex three-dimensional pattern that hovered in the air before them. It resembled the chalk diagram Harrison had drawn on the community blackboard but was vastly more intricate.

"Thirteen from each realm. Arranged in mirroring formations. The stone at the center. All during eclipse totality. At the original breach."

"The center of the cornfields," Phoebe said. "Right where the Exiles are gathering their power."

"Correct. The ritual must occur at the exact location of their work. Counter-pattern overlaid directly."

Grant shook his head incredulously. "You're talking about staging a magical showdown in the middle of territory they control, exactly when they're at their most powerful.

That's suicide."

"Necessity dictates location and timing. The eclipse opportunity will not recur for decades. The damage by then: irreparable."

The sheriff looked to Phoebe. "This is crazy. We can't seriously be considering this."

But Phoebe was already thinking ahead, her merged consciousness processing implications from both human and shadow perspectives simultaneously.

"We need to prepare," she said. "Not just the ritual itself, but a way to reach the old silo site without being detected. That's where the breach first opened in 1843, and the Exiles control everything in the cornfields."

"We can provide assistance. Guidance through shadow paths. Concealment from Exile perception."

"And what do you get out of this?" Grant demanded suspiciously. "You're taking an awful risk opposing these Exiles."

The shadow entities' forms rippled with what might have been amusement. "Same as you, physical one. Survival. Continuance. The Exiles' path destroys both realms eventually. Balanced convergence is our only sustainable future."

Harrison, who had been quiet during this exchange, suddenly spoke up. "The thirteen representatives from our side, they would need to be human-shadow pairs already working in harmony, wouldn't they? Like Phoebe and her shadow in merged form."

"Ideal format. Merged consciousness bridges realms inherently. Facilitates proper resonance."

"But we don't have thirteen merged pairs," Phoebe said. "I'm the only one who's achieved that state so far."

"One week remains. Others can learn. You can teach."

The implications were staggering. In just seven days, they needed to identify twelve more humans willing to merge with their shadows, train them to maintain balanced consciousness, prepare the counter-ritual, and somehow infiltrate the heart of Exile territory during the eclipse.

"Even if we find volunteers, merging is intense," Phoebe said. "It fundamentally changes your perception, your sense of self. Not everyone will handle it well."

"Choose carefully. Strong minds. Open perspectives. Previous harmony with their shadows is beneficial."

Grant ran a hand through his hair, frustration evident. "This is a hell of a longshot. And meanwhile, what are the Exiles doing? They must know we're planning to interfere."

As if summoned by his words, a chilly wind suddenly swept across the boundary between cornfield and forest. The corn stalks rattled, an unnatural sound like whispering voices. The shadow entities of the Consensus drew closer together, their forms becoming more compact and more guarded.

"They come. Exile scouts. This meeting is no longer secure."

"We need to leave," Harrison said, already turning toward the path that had led them here.

But darkness was gathering between them and the escape route, shadows deepening and taking form, not the complex mathematical patterns of the Consensus, but sharp, predatory shapes with jagged edges. The Exiles' servants twisted the will of unbound shadows.

"Surrounded," Grant muttered grimly, drawing his weapon despite its likely ineffectiveness.

The Consensus entities moved with startling speed, creating a protective circle around the three humans. "We will create an opening. You must run. Return to town barrier. Safer there."

"Town barrier?" Phoebe asked quickly.

"Your shadow knows. Ask when safe. Now go!"

The Consensus shadows suddenly expanded, their

forms stretching outward in all directions like dark starbursts. Where they touched the Exiles' servants, energy discharged in silent flashes of negative light, darkness so intense it created momentary blindness.

"This way!" Harrison shouted, surprisingly spry, as he darted toward a narrow gap in the surrounding shadows.

Phoebe and Grant followed, running headlong through the opening as the shadow entities continued their silent battle behind them. The binding stone's pouch burned hot against Phoebe's chest, responding to the massive expenditure of shadow energy nearby.

They sprinted through the forest, guided more by instinct than sight as branches whipped past them. Behind them, Phoebe could sense, rather than see, pursuit, the Exiles' servants disengaging from the Consensus to chase the humans and, more importantly, the binding stone she carried.

"They're gaining!" she shouted.

Grant glanced back, his face grim in the darkness. "How far to the car?"

"Too far," Harrison gasped, his initial burst of energy fading. "We need another option."

Phoebe's dual consciousness worked frantically, processing possibilities from both human and shadow perspectives. Something the Consensus had mentioned pricked at her awareness, the town barrier. What had they meant?

She directed the question inward, to the shadow consciousness merged with her own. Immediately, understanding bloomed. The original binding sigil created by Thaddeus Hollow, the geometric pattern of Millfield's streets and major buildings, still retained power. Weakened by the silo's destruction but not eliminated entirely. Within its boundaries, the Exiles' power was diminished.

"The town!" she called to the others. "We need to reach

Millfield proper. The original town layout creates a protective barrier!"

They altered course, heading toward the distant lights of town. Behind them, the pursuit intensified; shadows formed, flowing between trees with unnatural speed. One surged ahead of the others, reaching for Grant with elongated talons of pure darkness.

The sheriff's own shadow suddenly interposed itself, taking the brunt of the attack. It shuddered with the impact but held firm, protecting its human partner. Grant nodded a quick thanks and ran on, now understanding the depth of connection forming between them.

As they reached the edge of the forest, the first buildings of Millfield came into view. Phoebe could perceive the subtle energy pattern created by the town's layout, a weakened but still present sigil of protection against shadow dominance.

"Almost there!" She encouraged Harrison, who was struggling to maintain their pace; his breathing labored.

The old man stumbled, nearly falling. Grant caught his arm, half-dragging him forward as the shadow pursuers closed in, now just yards behind.

Phoebe reached the boundary first, feeling the moment she crossed from unprotected territory into the sigil's influence. The binding stone's heat immediately subsided; its pulsing became more regular and controlled.

She turned back, extending her hand toward the others. "Hurry!"

Grant hauled Harrison the final few steps, practically lifting the old man across the invisible boundary. The moment they crossed, the pursuing shadows pulled up short, hovering at the edge of town like wolves at the perimeter of a campfire's light.

"It worked," Harrison wheezed, bending over to catch his breath. "The original binding sigil still functions."

"Partially," Phoebe stated, watching the shadow entities testing the barrier, probing for weaknesses. "It won't hold forever. Especially not against the Exiles themselves." She glanced back toward the outskirts, her expression troubled. "And it doesn't cover everything. The Holloway house, the community center...they're both outside the sigil's perimeter. Anything we left behind out there is unprotected."

Grant followed her gaze. "So the barrier only covers the old town core."

"Thaddeus laid out the sigil pattern to encompass the town he envisioned at the time," Harrison said, still catching his breath. "The town has grown beyond those boundaries since then. Everything outside the original town is unprotected."

"But it gives us breathing room," Grant said practically. "Time to plan." He looked at Phoebe intently. "You really think we can pull this off? Find twelve more people willing to merge with their shadows, train them, and perform this counter-ritual in just seven days?"

Phoebe touched the binding stone, feeling its steady pulse, a rhythm that matched neither her human heartbeat nor her shadow's energy pattern, but something more fundamental, more primordial than either.

"We have to try," she said simply. "The alternative is letting the Exiles reshape reality according to their vision. Allowing them to break this world as they broke their own."

They made their way deeper into town, eventually reaching Grant's patrol car parked near the edge of the residential district.

As they drove toward the community center, Phoebe noted how the shadows throughout Millfield seemed more active than usual, rippling with agitation, communicating with each other in silent patterns of movement. "They know something's coming. The shadows can sense the approaching eclipse, the thinning of the barrier."

"That means we need to start identifying potential merger candidates immediately," Harrison said. "People whose shadows have already demonstrated harmony and cooperation with them."

"Lucy Holloway is a strong candidate," Phoebe said. "Her shadow shielded her from the Consensus...to keep her safe. That kind of bond, a shadow willing to resist an entity that powerful, that's exactly the kind of deep connection a successful merger requires."

"What about the thirteen pairs who formed the circle during the confrontation at the community center?" Grant said. "They already demonstrated the ability to work together."

Harrison agreed. "Good starting point, though true merging is far more intensive than the temporary connection they formed. Joining hands in a ritual circle is cooperation. Merging requires dissolving the boundary between the physical body and its shadow. Some of those thirteen won't be capable, much less willing to go that far, but they're the best candidates we have."

At the community center, they found David pacing anxiously in the entrance hall. He rushed to Phoebe as soon as they entered.

"Where have you been?" he demanded. "It's nearly two in the morning. I thought..." He stopped, noticing their disheveled appearance and tense expressions. "What happened?"

Phoebe briefly explained their meeting with the Consensus and the subsequent chase through the forest. As she described the counter-ritual planned for the eclipse, David's expression grew increasingly troubled.

"You're talking about creating thirteen more people in your condition." He gestured to her altered appearance. "Permanently changing them."

"It's not necessarily permanent. The merging can be reversed if both parties agree. It's a partnership, not a binding."

David didn't look convinced. "And you're going to ask people to volunteer for this? To fundamentally alter their consciousness on the off chance it might counter whatever the Exiles are planning."

"The alternative is worse," Harrison interjected. "If the Exiles succeed, everyone in Millfield, perhaps beyond, will be transformed against their will. The merged state may seem extreme, but it preserves choice and agency. The Exiles would eliminate both."

David ran a hand through his hair, a gesture of frustration Phoebe recognized all too well. "And Maddie? Is she supposed to volunteer too? Merge with her shadow like you did."

"Maddie's shadow still hasn't separated," Phoebe reminded him. "She's not a candidate." She reached for his hand, but he pulled back slightly. "David, I know this is difficult to accept. It's changing everything we thought we knew about reality. But we're past the point of denying what's happening. We need to act."

After a moment, he nodded reluctantly. "What do you need me to do?"

"Help us identify candidates," she said, relieved at his cooperation despite his reservations. "People whose shadows have already demonstrated a positive, cooperative relationship with them. People with strong minds who might be able to handle the merged consciousness."

Inside the main gymnasium, they found several deputies maintaining watch while families slept on cots arranged around the perimeter. In the center, Lucy sat cross-legged on the floor, her shadow beside her. They appeared to be playing a game, the shadow making shapes with its hands, Lucy guessing what they represented. The traumatic effects of being used as a messenger seemed to have faded, their connection secure.

Mary Holloway approached as they entered, her shadow following a few steps behind. Unlike Lucy's shadow, which moved with playful fluidity, Mary's maintained a more cautious, formal distance. "You're back." She observed their expressions. "Not with good news, I'm guessing."

Phoebe shook her head. "We need to talk. All of us. There's an eclipse coming in seven days, and the Exiles plan to use it to force a transformation of our world."

"And you plan to stop them," Mary said. "With more shadow magic?"

"Not magic. It's more like interdimensional physics. And yes, we're going to attempt a counter-ritual that would establish balance rather than dominance."

Mary glanced at Lucy, her maternal protectiveness evident. "And you need volunteers. People willing to merge with their shadows like you did."

"Thirteen pairs. Working together during the eclipse."

A look of understanding crossed Mary's face. "That's why you're watching Lucy and me. You're evaluating us as potential candidates."

"Your relationship with your shadow is further along than most folks," Harrison put in. "You've established communication and cooperation. It's a foundation we can build on."

Mary's shadow moved forward, standing beside her rather than behind her. It made a gesture that suggested cautious interest, followed by a questioning motion.

"Even my shadow is keen to know more," Mary said with a hint of surprise. "It's been trying to communicate with me since the separation, but I've been resistant."

"Afraid," Phoebe suggested gently. "It's natural. This changes everything we thought we knew about ourselves, about reality."

"What does the merging feel like?" Mary asked, her voice low. "Being neither fully human nor shadow?"

Phoebe considered how to explain the inexplicable. "It's like having access to a room in your mind that was always there but locked. Suddenly, you can perceive things you never noticed before. Think in ways that weren't possible. It's disorienting at first, but then..." She searched for the words. "It feels right. Complete in a way you didn't know you were incomplete before."

Mary nodded slowly, then looked to her shadow. "Would we be like them?" she asked, gesturing toward Phoebe's merged form. "Semi-transparent? Silver-eyed?"

"Physical manifestations vary," Harrison explained. "Phoebe's appearance reflects her particular merging pattern. Yours might be different, subtle shifts in coloration, alterations to how light interacts with your form. The external changes are less important than the internal ones."

Mary's shadow made another gesture, this one clearly directed at Mary herself. She watched it carefully, then nodded as if coming to a decision. "We'll consider it," she said finally. "Both of us." She glanced at her shadow with new respect. "We need to talk more first. Really communicate, not just coexist."

"That's all we're asking for now," Phoebe assured her. "Consider the possibility. We'll be approaching others, as well."

As Mary returned to Lucy, Grant pulled Phoebe and Harrison aside. "We should make a list of potential candidates immediately. Start approaching them at first light. Time is critical."

Harrison nodded in agreement. "I'll review the records of those who participated in the community center ritual. Identify the pairs that showed the strongest connection."

"And I'll work on developing a training protocol,"

Phoebe added. “A way to guide pairs through the merging process safely.”

“What about the Exiles?” David asked, joining their huddle. “They must know we met with the Consensus. They’ll be watching for any sign of countermeasures.”

“The town sigil provides some protection,” Harrison said. “At least within Millfield proper. But you’re right, we need to be cautious, especially as the eclipse approaches.”

Phoebe touched the binding stone, feeling its constant pulse. “The stone is key to everything. The Exiles need it for a complete transformation. Their substitute might allow a partial breach during the eclipse, but not the full rewriting of reality they desire.”

“Then we keep it safe,” Grant said firmly. “And we prepare for both possibilities, success in performing the counter-ritual, or failure, and the need to contain whatever the Exiles manage to unleash.”

Outside, dawn was still hours away. The stars continued their cold observation of events unfolding below, indifferent to the struggle that would determine the fate of at least two dimensions in this valley. And somewhere in the cornfields, thirteen ancient shadow entities prepared for the celestial alignment that would give them the power to reshape reality according to their vision, a vision born of corruption, of the desire for dominance rather than balance.

Seven days until the eclipse. Seven days to find thirteen volunteers willing to transform themselves, to learn a centuries-old ritual, and to confront shadow beings who had already destroyed one world in their quest for power.

The binding stone pulsed steadily against Phoebe’s chest, its rhythm neither optimistic nor pessimistic, simply constant, a reminder of what reality had been before separation and what it might become again. For better or worse.

CHAPTER 10:
BETRAYALS

Five days until the eclipse.

Dawn broke over Millfield with unnatural swiftness, as if time itself were accelerating toward the moment of totality. Phoebe stood on the community center roof, watching the sun climb above the eastern horizon, above the cornfields where the Exiles gathered their power. Even from this distance, she could see darkness pooling among the rows, a concentration of shadow that shouldn't exist in direct morning light.

The binding stone hung heavy around her neck, its pulse quickening as it sensed her attention. In her merged state, she could feel it responding not just to her thoughts but to the approaching celestial alignment, like a tuning fork beginning to vibrate anticipating a specific frequency.

"Any change?" David asked, climbing the access ladder to join her. Despite his continued unease with her transformation, he had thrown himself into organizing supplies and coordinating communications between the groups of volunteers.

"The darkness in the cornfields is spreading," she replied, pointing toward the eastern horizon. "See how it pools between the rows? That's not a natural shadow."

David squinted, unable to perceive what was clear to her merged senses. "I'll take your word for it." He handed her a clipboard. "Harrison wanted you to see this. The current list of candidates."

Phoebe scanned the document. Nine names, including

Mary Holloway. Nine potential merger volunteers out of the thirteen they needed. The training had begun yesterday, with Phoebe guiding each paired human and shadow through meditation exercises designed to harmonize their energies. Progress was slower than she'd hoped, only Mary had achieved even a partial merge state, a brief connection that left her dazed but exhilarated.

"It's not enough," she said quietly. "We require thirteen pairs fully merged by eclipse day. At this rate, we're not going to make it."

"We'll find more," David assured her, though his confidence sounded forced. "People now understand what's at stake."

They descended to the gymnasium, where Harrison had established what he called the "merger training center." Volunteers sat cross-legged on mats arranged in a circle, their shadows positioned before them. Harrison moved between pairs, offering guidance based on what Phoebe had taught him about the merging process.

"Focus on the overlap," the old man was saying to Deputy Rodriguez, who strained visibly as he attempted to connect with his shadow. "Not two separate beings, but aspects of a single consciousness artificially divided."

Rodriguez's shadow made encouraging gestures, leaning forward as if trying to close the gap between them. For a moment, a faint silver outline appeared around both forms, then dissipated as Rodriguez gasped, breaking concentration.

"It's like trying to hold two opposing magnets together," the deputy complained, wiping sweat from his forehead. "Every time I get close, something pushes back."

"That's the century of conditioning," Phoebe said, joining them. "The binding spell trained humans to perceive shadows as separate, as 'other.' Overcoming that takes time." Time, they didn't have, she added silently.

Mary Holloway approached, her shadow moving beside her with synchronized grace. Of all the volunteers, she had progressed the furthest in accepting the possibility of merging. "I had another partial connection last night," she reported. "Lasted almost five minutes this time."

"Any physical manifestation?" Harrison asked with academic interest.

Mary held out her hand, turning it in the light. "My skin had that translucent quality, like Phoebe's. And I could see differently. Shadows weren't just absences of light anymore. They had substance, structure."

"That's progress," Phoebe said. "The perception shift is crucial. Once you can see both realms simultaneously, the merge becomes more stable."

"And Lucy?" Harrison inquired. "Any further communication from the Consensus through her shadow?"

Mary shook her head. "Not since that first time. Though, her shadow seems more alert lately. Like it's listening for something."

Sheriff Grant entered the gymnasium, his expression grim. He'd been coordinating perimeter security around Millfield, trying to maintain the protection of the weakened town sigil while watching for Exile activity.

"We've got a problem," he announced without preamble. "Three more unbound shadows were spotted at the edge of town. They're testing the barrier, looking for weak points."

"Any direct incursions?" Harrison asked.

"Not yet. But they're getting bolder. Mayor Wilson was seen at the town hall this morning, the first time since the confrontation here. He's calling an emergency council meeting for noon."

Phoebe's concern sharpened. "He's making a public move. Why now?"

"To create division to undermine our efforts before the

eclipse," Harrison surmised.

"Or to gain legitimate access to the community center," Grant suggested darkly. "As mayor, he could order it reopened for normal business and force us to relocate."

Phoebe touched the binding stone, feeling its steady pulse against her fingertips. "We need to attend that meeting. Confront him directly."

"Could be a trap," Grant warned.

"Almost certainly is," she agreed. "But we can't hold up here forever. And we need to know what he's planning."

A commotion at the gymnasium entrance drew their attention. Lucy burst through the doors, running toward her mother with her shadow flowing beside her like a dark comet.

"They're coming!" the girl shouted, her voice high with alarm. "The shadows told me, everyone's shadows. The Exiles are calling them to the cornfields. For a test."

"What kind of test?" Mary asked, pulling her daughter close.

Lucy's shadow made urgent gestures that the girl translated with practiced ease. "A rehearsal for the eclipse ritual. They're going to try to separate more shadows from the cornfields; make them join the unbound ones." She looked at Phoebe with wide, frightened eyes. "They're calling everyone's shadows. Making them choose sides."

As if in response to her words, a ripple passed through the shadows in the gymnasium, a subtle tremor that affected even those still bound to their human anchors. Several of the separated shadows turned toward the eastern windows as if hearing a distant summons.

Deputy Rodriguez's shadow abruptly straightened, its form elongating unnaturally. It moved away from him, flowing across the floor toward the exit.

"Hey!" Rodriguez called, startled. "Where are you going?"

The shadow paused and turned back with a gesture that somehow conveyed regret. Then it continued moving, slipped beneath the gymnasium doors and disappeared.

"What the hell?" Grant demanded. "Did his shadow just desert?"

Another shadow detached from its human anchor, one of the volunteers who had been making the least progress in the merger training. Then another. A wave of disorientation swept through the room as shadows began responding to some silent call.

"It's starting," Harrison said grimly. "The Exiles are forcing shadows to choose allegiance. They're compelling them to the cornfields."

Mary's shadow pressed closer to her side, making gestures of resistance and defiance against the summons. Lucy's did the same; their connection apparently strong enough to withstand the pull.

"We need to secure the binding stone," Grant decided, already moving toward the emergency exits. "If this is a coordinated effort, the shadow desertion could be a diversion."

Before they could react, the gymnasium doors burst open again. Mayor Wilson stood in the entrance, flanked by several town council members. Their forms seemed oddly blurred, as if viewed through rippling water.

"Ms. Weaver," Wilson called, his voice carrying that same unsettling dual tone she'd heard during their confrontation. "The council has convened early. Your presence is requested. Immediately."

Phoebe stepped forward, positioning herself between Wilson and the training volunteers. In her merged state, she could see what others couldn't, how shadows clung to the mayor and his companions, not as separate entities but merged in a distorted, unbalanced way. The shadows weren't partners but parasites, dominating rather than cooperating.

“What do you want, Wilson?” she demanded. “Or should I address the Exile that’s wearing you?”

A cold smile spread across the mayor’s face. “Perceptive. The human Wilson is merely a vessel now. Has been for generations, though in a more balanced arrangement until recently.” He gestured dismissively. “The silo’s destruction has allowed us to assert proper control.”

“Proper control,” Phoebe repeated with disgust. “You mean domination. Subjugation of human consciousness.”

“As humans subjugated shadow consciousness for a century,” Wilson countered. “Perhaps now you understand the injustice of Thaddeus Hollow’s silo and the binding spell.”

Harrison moved to stand beside Phoebe. “Injustice doesn’t justify further injustice. The binding was wrong, but your forced transformation is equally wrong.”

“We didn’t come to debate ethics,” Wilson said coldly. His gaze fixed on the leather pouch hanging around Phoebe’s neck. “The stone. Surrender it now, and conflict can be avoided. Millfield will transform peacefully during the eclipse.”

“Transform into what?” Phoebe challenged. “A shadow realm where human consciousness is suppressed? Where physical matter becomes unstable, fluid? You’d destroy this valley as you destroyed your own.”

Wilson’s expression hardened. “We’re improving this world. Elevating it beyond the limitations of physical existence.” He stepped forward, hand outstretched. “The stone, Ms. Weaver. It belongs in service to the original thirteen Exiles.”

“It belongs to both realms.” Phoebe backed away. “Not to you, not to me, not to anyone who would use it for dominance rather than balance.”

The mayor’s form seemed to ripple, shadow energy boiling around him. “We tried diplomacy. We offered peaceful transition." His voice dropped to a register too low for human vocal cords. "Now we take what we need."

He gestured sharply, and the shimmering dome above the gymnasium flickered violently. Darkness pressed against the barrier from every direction, pouring across the windows and walls like black water searching for cracks. Unbound shadows answered the Exiles' call, swirling around the building in a disorienting cyclone of movement and whispers as the failing protection strained to hold them back.

Grant drew his weapon, positioning himself in front of the volunteers. "Everybody down!" he shouted. "Cover your eyes!"

The shadows converged toward Phoebe, seeking to steal the binding stone.

She clutched it through the leather pouch, channeling its energy as she had during the escape from the forest. Silver light erupted from her hands, pushing back the unbound shadows.

"The exit!" she called to the others. "Everyone out now!"

Chaos erupted as volunteers scrambled toward the emergency doors. The unbound shadows regrouped, flowed together into larger, more solid forms that blocked the exits. Through the confusion, Phoebe saw Wilson and the other Exile council members advancing steadily, untouched by the maelstrom they had unleashed.

"They're herding us," Harrison said. "Containing us until they can secure the stone."

Phoebe's merged consciousness worked frantically, analyzing options and calculating risks. The binding stone's energy was powerful but not unlimited. She couldn't maintain the protective field around everyone indefinitely, and the longer she channeled its power, the more it would drain her.

"David!" she called, spotting her husband helping Lucy

and Mary toward an exit. “Get everyone to the basement. The old fallout shelter. It’s sealed tight enough to keep radiation out. No way the shadows can get in.”

David nodded, immediately redirecting people toward the basement stairs.

Grant organized deputies into a defensive perimeter, though their bullets would pass harmlessly through the shadow entities.

“Grant,” Phoebe shouted. “We need to lead these shadows away from the community center. Draw them off so the others can get to the shelter.”

“How?” Harrison demanded.

Phoebe removed the binding stone from its pouch, holding it exposed in her palm. Its silver light blazed brighter, and the symbols etched into its surface glowed with inner fire. “They want this. So we make them chase it.”

Without waiting for agreement, she sprinted toward a side exit, channeling the stone’s energy to create a path through the shadow barrier. Grant and Harrison followed, the sheriff physically supporting the older man, who struggled to keep pace.

They burst outside into blinding morning sunlight. Under normal circumstances, bright light would have weakened shadow entities. But these unbound shadows seemed strengthened by it, their forms becoming more defined and more solid as they pursued.

“The town hall!” Phoebe called, changing direction. “If Wilson and the other Exiles are here, the council chambers might be unguarded!”

They raced through Millfield’s empty streets. The town seemed abandoned, its residents either sheltering in place or already fled. Shadows pooled unnaturally in broad daylight, gathering in doorways and alleys, watching their passage with malevolent awareness.

As they approached the town hall, a stately brick

building that dated back to Millfield's founding, Phoebe sensed a change in the surrounding energy. The pursuing shadows were falling back, no longer actively chasing but still observing, waiting.

"It's too easy," she warned as they mounted the town hall steps. "This doesn't feel right."

"Trap?" Grant suggested, the weapon still drawn.

"Almost certainly. But we're committed now."

The town hall doors stood open, the grand foyer beyond eerily silent. They entered cautiously, moving toward the council chambers where Wilson had supposedly called his emergency meeting.

The council chamber doors swung open at their approach, revealing not a meeting but a ritual in progress. The long oval table had been pushed aside, and in the center of the room stood a perfect circle of thirteen carved objects. Not pumpkins this time, but human skulls, each with a candle burning inside, creating twisted patterns of light and shadow on the walls.

Within the circle stood Dr. Brennen, or rather, the Exile that wore his form. Unlike Wilson, who maintained a mostly human appearance, Dr. Brennen had transformed more completely. His skin had darkened to a deep obsidian, his eyes became pools of liquid shadow, and his fingers elongated into talon-like appendages.

"The stone-bearer," he greeted Phoebe, his voice a dissonant harmony of tones. "Right on schedule."

Phoebe stopped at the threshold. The binding stone pulsed wildly in her hand. "Where are the others? Wilson and the council members?"

"Preparing. The cornfield ritual requires specific alignments. Not all Exiles need to be present for this preliminary work." Dr. Brennen gestured to the skull circle. "Do you like our substitutes? Not as effective as the binding stone, but human skulls have their connection to shadow.

Especially those with Hollow bloodlines."

Harrison made a strangled sound of recognition. "The old cemetery. You desecrated the Hollow family graves."

"Borrowed," Dr. Brennen stated with a terrible smile. "Their contribution is involuntary but necessary."

Phoebe's merged senses detected energy flowing between the skulls, creating a pattern similar to but distorted from the one she'd seen in the Consensus vision. Not balance, but dominance, shadow over substance.

"Whatever you're trying to do, it won't work," she said with more confidence than she felt. "Not without the true binding stone."

"Oh, we don't expect this ritual to complete the transformation." Dr. Brennen chuckled easily. "It's merely preparation. Thinning the barrier further before the eclipse." His shadow-filled eyes fixed on the stone in Phoebe's hand. "Though with that, we could accelerate the process considerably."

He made a slight gesture, and suddenly unbound shadows flooded into the chamber from every direction, not just doorways and windows but seeping from the very walls themselves. They surrounded Phoebe, Grant, and Harrison, cutting off any retreat.

"We knew you would come," Dr. Brennen said conversationally. "Your predictable heroics made this so easy. Leading you away from your volunteers, isolating you from potential help." He extended his transformed hand. "The stone, Ms. Weaver. Now."

Phoebe clutched the binding stone tighter, channeling its energy into a protective field around the three of them. Silver light pushed back the encroaching shadows, but she could feel the stone's power straining against the focused will of the Exile before her.

"You know I won't surrender it," she stated flatly. "Not to be used for domination."

"Admirable but futile." Dr. Brennen sighed. "You cannot maintain that protection indefinitely. The stone's energy isn't limitless, and your merged state, while impressive, is still new and unstable." His expression turned contemplative. "Though I must admit, your voluntary merging was unexpected. Most humans resist the shadow consciousness rather than embrace it."

"Because she offered partnership, not invasion," Harrison retorted. "Cooperation, not subjugation."

Dr. Brennen laughed, a sound like ice cracking. "Such human concepts. In the shadow realm, consciousness flows where it will. Individual boundaries are flexible. Permeable." He circled them slowly, studying Phoebe's merged form with clinical interest. "You believe you've achieved some perfect balance, but you've merely scratched the surface of what's possible. True merging goes much deeper."

As if to demonstrate, his form shifted, shadow and substance flowing together in nauseating patterns that defied physical laws. For a moment, he seemed to exist in multiple places simultaneously, his outline blurring into fractal dimensions that Phoebe's human perception struggled to process.

"That's not merging," Phoebe said through gritted teeth, fighting a wave of vertigo. "That's corruption. Degradation of both shadow and physical form."

"Evolution," Dr. Brennen said. "The next stage of existence." He stopped circling, his patience visibly thinning. "Last chance, stone-bearer. Surrender the binding stone willingly, or we will take it by force."

Grant raised his weapon, though his expression suggested he knew how futile the gesture looked. "You'll have to go through us first."

"Tedious, but as you wish." Dr. Brennen made another gesture, and the unbound shadows surged forward all at once.

Phoebe poured more energy into the protective field, the binding stone burning in her palm. The silver light expanded outward, creating a dome around them that the shadows couldn't penetrate. But maintaining it took tremendous effort, draining her merged consciousness rapidly.

"Harrison," she gasped, "the skull circle. Can you disrupt it?"

The old man glanced at the thirteen burning skulls. "Break the circle. Break the ritual. But I can't reach them through this shadow barrier."

"I'll create an opening. When I do, move fast."

She focused intently on the binding stone, visualizing not just a shield but a directed pulse of energy. The stone responded, its silver light condensing into a beam that cut through the shadow barrier toward the skull circle.

"Now!" she shouted.

Harrison darted through the opening, moving with surprising speed for his age. He reached the nearest skull and kicked it hard enough to send it skidding across the floor, breaking the circle.

The effect was immediate and violent. Energy that had been flowing between the skulls discharged all at once, creating a concussive wave that threw everyone in the chamber backward. The unbound shadows scattered, momentarily disrupted by the release of power.

Dr. Brennen screamed in rage, his form destabilizing further as the ritual collapsed. Shadow energy poured from him like oil from a broken pipeline; his carefully maintained hybrid state began to separate.

"The binding!" he shrieked, his voice now clearly two distinct entities speaking simultaneously. "It's reasserting!"

Phoebe realized what was happening, disrupting the Exile ritual had temporarily strengthened the original binding sigil throughout Millfield. The forced mergers the Exiles had created with their human hosts were weakening, shadow and substance tearing apart.

"We need to get out while they're vulnerable," Grant said, helping Harrison to his feet. The old man had been thrown against a wall by the energy discharge. Blood trickled from a cut on his forehead.

But Dr. Brennen, despite his destabilizing form, moved with inhuman speed to block their exit. "The stone," he hissed in a voice now a discordant cacophony of tones. "Give it!"

He lunged for Phoebe, transformed hands grasping for the binding stone.

Phoebe tried to dodge, but her strength was depleted along with the protective field. Dr. Brennen's fingers broke through and closed around her wrist, shadow energy burning like acid where they touched.

Grant fired his weapon. The bullet passed through Dr. Brennen's increasingly insubstantial form, but the impact disrupted her concentration enough for Phoebe to pull free. As she stumbled backward, her grip on the binding stone faltered.

Time seemed to slow as the stone slipped from her fingers, falling toward the floor.

Dr. Brennen dove for it. His arms stretched impossibly long to intercept.

Phoebe lunged as well, her merged consciousness giving her just enough speed to reach it first.

Their hands closed around the stone simultaneously.

Silver light exploded in the room.

Phoebe felt the binding stone's energy surge between them, responding catastrophically to being touched by two merged beings with opposing intentions, balance versus dominance. Power ripped through her consciousness, tearing at the carefully maintained harmony between her human and shadow aspects.

Through the blinding agony, she glimpsed Brennen's form contorting, shadow and substance separating violently as the stone's energy forced a division the Exile couldn't control. A scream that seemed to come from multiple throats at once echoed through the chamber.

Then, abruptly, silence.

Phoebe found herself on the floor, the binding stone again clutched in her fist. But something was wrong. The stone's steady pulse had become erratic, its silver light flickering rather than glowing consistently. And a thin crack had appeared across its surface, disrupting the ancient symbols etched into it.

"The stone." She gasped while struggling to sit up. "It's damaged."

Grant was at her side immediately, helping her to a sitting position. "Are you hurt?"

"Not physically," she managed, though her merged consciousness felt battered and fragmented. "But the stone, this is bad. Very Bad."

Across the chamber, Dr. Brennen's form lay motionless, shadow and substance now totally separated. The human body appeared unconscious while the shadow entity had retreated to a corner, its form twisted and unstable, pulsing with erratic energy.

Harrison limped toward them, his expression grave as he examined the cracked binding stone. "The damage is significant. Its connection to the valley has been weakened."

"Can it be repaired?" Grant asked.

"I don't know." Phoebe winced. "The stone wasn't crafted by human hands, it was created naturally at the wound, the original breach of the realms. It may be beyond our ability to fix."

"What does this mean for the counter-ritual?" Harrison asked quietly. "For stopping the Exiles during the eclipse?"

Phoebe stared at the damaged stone, feeling its weakened pulse against her palm. "It means everything just got much harder. The stone was our main advantage, the one thing the Exiles needed that we controlled." She looked up, meeting their worried gazes. "Now it may not work for either side."

The implications were staggering. Without the binding stone at full power, their planned counter-ritual might fail entirely. But the Exiles' transformation would also be incomplete and unpredictable, potentially even more dangerous due to its instability.

"We need to get back to the community center," Grant decided, helping Phoebe to her feet. "Regroup. Figure out our options."

As they moved toward the exit, carefully skirting Dr. Brennen's unconscious form and the destabilized shadow entity still pulsing in the corner, Phoebe felt the damaged stone grow cold against her skin. Its rhythmic pulse, once so steady and reassuring, now faltered like a failing heartbeat.

Five days until the eclipse. The binding stone was damaged. Their volunteers scattered. And the Exiles, despite this setback, still gathered power in the cornfields, preparing for a transformation that would reshape reality, now in ways even they might not be able to control.

The true betrayal, Phoebe realized, wasn't just the desertion of shadows or the Exiles' deception. It was the arrogance of believing they could manipulate forces as fundamental as the separation between worlds without consequences. Forces that, once unleashed, might consume shadow and substance alike in their blind hunger for reunification.

And the binding stone, their one hope for guiding that process safely, now lay cracked and failing in her palm.

CHAPTER 11:
THE FORGOTTEN HISTORY

Four days until the eclipse.

Rain lashed against the community center windows, driven by a wind that had appeared suddenly after midnight, howling across Millfield with unnatural persistence. Phoebe sat alone in a small office that had been converted into a makeshift lab, the damaged binding stone resting on a cloth before her.

The crack across its surface had deepened overnight, the ancient symbols now bisected by a jagged line that seemed to absorb light rather than reflect it. The stone's pulse had weakened further, its rhythm irregular, growing steadily weaker.

"Anything?" David asked from the doorway, two steaming mugs in his hands. Dark circles shadowed his eyes; he hadn't slept much since their return from the town hall confrontation yesterday.

"Nothing useful." Phoebe accepted the coffee with a grateful nod. "I've been trying to channel energy into it to strengthen what remains, but..." She gestured helplessly at the stone. "It's not responding the way it did before."

David pulled up a chair beside her, careful to maintain the slight distance he'd kept since her merging, close enough for support but not quite touching. "Harrison thinks the crack might be more than physical damage. He says it could be a fracture in the stone's connection to the shadows in this valley."

"He's right," Phoebe said. In her merged state, she

could perceive the stone's dual nature more clearly than ever, how it existed simultaneously in both the physical world and the shadow realm, serving as a conduit between dimensions. Now that connection was severed, the harmonics were disrupted. "It's like a tuning fork that's been bent. The frequency is wrong."

"Can it be fixed?"

"I don't know. We're talking about fundamental forces I barely understand, even in my merged state."

She rubbed her eyes, fighting exhaustion. Since the confrontation with Dr. Brennen, her merged consciousness had become unstable, with human and shadow aspects occasionally slipping out of alignment. The silver gleam in her eyes flickered irregularly, her skin shifting between normal opacity and the translucent quality of her fully merged state.

"You should rest," David said, genuine concern overriding his discomfort with her transformation. "You've been at this all night."

"Can't afford to rest," she murmured, though her body screamed for it. "Four days. That's all we have until the eclipse. Until the Exiles try to force their transformation with or without the stone."

"And we can't stop them with a broken stone."

"We might not be able to stop them with a good one," Phoebe added. "But without it, we don't stand a chance."

A soft knock interrupted them. Lucy Holloway stood in the doorway, her shadow hovering protectively beside her. The girl's expression was somber, far too serious for her seven years.

"Ms. Weaver? My shadow says there's a way to fix the stone. But you won't like it."

Phoebe straightened, suddenly alert despite her exhaustion. "What does it know, Lucy?"

Instead of translating, Lucy stepped aside, letting her

shadow flow forward. It made a series of complex gestures, not the simplified communications it typically used with humans, but an intricate shadow language clearly intended for Phoebe's merged perception.

"It's saying the stone can only be healed in the center of the cornfields."

"Where the Exiles are gathering their power," David said with dismay. "That's suicide."

Lucy's shadow continued its rapid communication, becoming more animated with each gesture.

"There's more," Phoebe said slowly. "It's saying the stone needs to remember its origins. That knowledge can restore the harmonic pattern." She frowned. "But that knowledge is lost. It happened thousands of years ago, before human history."

The shadow pointed directly at Phoebe, then to its chest, then made a diving motion toward the ground.

"Not lost," Phoebe realized. "Buried. In shadow memory." She looked up at David, a new understanding evident. "Shadow consciousness doesn't experience time linearly like humans do. The oldest shadows retain impressions, echoes of events from the original separation of realms."

"Including how the binding stone was formed," David said.

"Exactly. My shadow half, the part merged with my consciousness, should have access to those memories. But they're buried deep, beyond my current perception." Phoebe turned back to Lucy's shadow. "How do I access them?"

The shadow made a gesture like diving deeper, then touched Lucy's forehead.

"The Consensus," Lucy translated this time. "They showed me things when they used me as a messenger. They could help you reach deeper memories, too."

David's expression darkened with concern. "After

what happened to Lucy? No way. It nearly overwhelmed her completely."

"I'm not Lucy," Phoebe reminded him gently. "My merged state is more stable, more balanced. I could withstand a deeper connection."

"Could," David said. "Not would. Not definitely."

"We don't have a choice." Phoebe gestured to the damaged stone. "Without this repaired, everything we've done is pointless. The Exiles will force their transformation during the eclipse, and reality itself will start to unravel."

Before David could respond, Harrison appeared in the doorway, leaning heavily on his cane. "Ms. Weaver, we have a situation. Two more volunteer shadows have deserted, responded to the Exiles' calling. We're down to seven potential pairs for the counter-ritual."

"But we needed thirteen," Phoebe said.

"And a functional binding stone," Harrison added, eyeing the cracked artifact on the table. "Without both, the ritual cannot succeed."

Phoebe straightened, decision made. "We need to contact the Consensus again. They can help me access deeper shadow memories, knowledge of the stone's original formation that might repair it."

Harrison's expression was grave. "Reaching that deep into shadow consciousness is dangerous, Phoebe. Even in your merged state. You risk losing your human perspective entirely, becoming something other—"

"It's a risk we have to take," she insisted. "Lucy, does your shadow know how to contact the Consensus directly? Without using you as a messenger this time?"

Lucy's shadow made a series of gestures, which the girl translated with practiced ease. "It says the Consensus can be reached at the boundary between town and cornfield, but only during the shadow hours, dawn or dusk, when the barrier is thinnest."

Harrison checked his watch. "Dawn is three hours away,"

"Then we prepare." Phoebe carefully wrapped the damaged binding stone in its cloth and returned it to the leather pouch around her neck. "David, I need you to keep working with the volunteers. Focus on the seven pairs we still have. If I fail, we'll still need them for the counter-ritual."

David nodded reluctantly, clearly unhappy with her plan but recognizing its necessity. "Be careful," he said simply. "Come back as yourself."

Unspoken fear hung between them, that diving deeper into shadow consciousness might permanently alter her, erasing the woman he had married and leaving something fundamentally different in her place.

"I will," she promised, though uncertainty gnawed at her. The truth was, she didn't know exactly what accessing ancient shadow memories might do to her merged consciousness. Only that they required the knowledge to have any hope of repairing the stone.

The hours passed with agonizing slowness. Phoebe tried to rest, knowing she would need her strength, but sleep eluded her. Her merged consciousness vibrated with anticipation, with fragments of memories not her own occasionally surfacing before submerging again into the depths of her shadow half's awareness.

An hour before dawn, she met Harrison, Grant, and Lucy at the community center entrance. The storm had passed, leaving behind a damp stillness that felt expectant, pregnant with possibility.

"The deputies will maintain a perimeter," Grant explained, checking his weapon more from habit than any belief it would be effective against shadow entities. "But if the Exiles detect what we're doing—"

"They'll try to stop us," Phoebe finished. "The last

thing they want is the binding stone repaired."

Harrison studied her with concern. "Are you certain about that? They need that stone to work at full power."

"Then they'll be watching and waiting...and just in case..." She stooped to the bedrock alongside the walkway and selected a stone, which she put in her pocket. "I may have to pull a switcheroo."

Grant nodded.

Harrison went on, "Accessing memories from the original separation of realms, it's uncharted territory. It's never been attempted before."

"First time for everything," Phoebe said. "If we don't get this stone repaired, we fail before we begin."

Lucy's shadow made an urgent gesture, pointing eastward, where the faintest lightening of the sky heralded approaching dawn.

"It's time," Lucy said unnecessarily.

They drove in silence to the edge of town, parking where the paved road gave way to the dirt track that led toward the cornfields. The boundary between Millfield's protective sigil and the Exiles' territory was invisible to normal perception, but in her merged state, Phoebe could see it clearly, a shimmering curtain of energy where two opposing forces were kept apart.

As they approached on foot, Phoebe felt the binding stone respond, its weakened pulse quickening slightly in proximity to the boundary. Dawn was minutes away, the eastern sky warming from black to deep indigo.

"They're here," she murmured, sensing shadow presences gathering just beyond human perception. "The Consensus."

Harrison positioned himself at the edge of the boundary, his own shadow standing vigilant beside him. Grant established a wider support perimeter, stationing deputies at intervals along the boundary to watch for breaches in the failing barrier.

"Remember," Harrison cautioned, "maintain your core self. Don't surrender your human consciousness completely to the shadow memories. That direction lies dissolution."

Phoebe nodded while removing the damaged binding stone from its pouch. In the growing pre-dawn light, the crack across its surface seemed to shift and change, sometimes appearing smaller, sometimes larger, as if existing in multiple states simultaneously.

"Lucy, you should stay back," she said. "Your shadow can translate if needed, but you shouldn't be exposed to the Consensus again so soon."

The girl retreated reluctantly to stand with Grant, her shadow remaining closer to Phoebe, ready to assist.

The first rays of sunlight crested the distant horizon, spearing across the landscape. The shadow hour had begun.

Like ink bleeding into water, the Consensus entities materialized at the boundary, thirteen mathematical patterns of pure shadow, more defined than during their previous meeting, as if they had grown stronger or more focused on the intervening days.

"Stone-bearer," the familiar mental voice greeted her. "We see the damage. Catastrophic. Harmony disrupted."

"Can it be repaired?" Phoebe asked directly, holding up the stone so they could better inspect its condition.

The shadow entities conferred silently among themselves, their forms rippling with communication too complex for even her merged perception to interpret fully.

"Repair possible. Not through physical means. Through remembering. Through reconnection to the original pattern."

"The original pattern from when the stone formed. When the realms first separated. My shadow half should have access to those memories, buried deep in shadow consciousness."

"Yes. But dangerous. Human consciousness is not designed for such perception. Even merged state risks alteration."

"I understand the risk," Phoebe said firmly. "But without the stone repaired, the Exiles win by default. They'll force their transformation during the eclipse, and everything in this valley will suffer."

Another silent conference among the consensus entities. Finally, they reached a decision.

"We will guide. Create a pathway to the deepest shadow memory. But stone must be present at the clearing in the center of cornfields, for repair to manifest physically."

Harrison stepped forward, alarm evident in his expression. "The center of the cornfields is where the Exiles are gathering their power. They'll sense any attempt to access it immediately."

"Correct. Confrontation inevitable. But eclipse preparations occupy their attention currently. A brief window of opportunity may exist."

"How brief?" Grant demanded.

"Dawn to midday. After, their awareness returns fully to the cornfield center."

Phoebe checked her watch. "That gives us roughly six hours, assuming we can even reach the center undetected."

"We can assist. Shadow-paths exist. Unseen byways through the corn. Difficult for physical forms, but possible with guidance."

"And once we're there?" Phoebe pressed. "How do I access these original memories?"

Instead of answering directly, one of the Consensus entities extended a tendril of shadow toward her forehead, similar to their previous communication but with a questioning hesitance, seeking permission.

"You want to show me," Phoebe realized.

"More than show. Open pathway. Create connection to

collective shadow consciousness. To memories of beginning."

She glanced at Harrison.

He looked deeply troubled. "The risk of losing yourself increases exponentially with the depth of connection," he warned. "These aren't just old memories. They predate individual consciousness as we understand it."

"I don't see an alternative." Phoebe turned back to the waiting Consensus entity. "I'm ready."

"Prepare. Experience unlike any human perception. Hold on to your core self through transition."

She braced herself as the shadow tendril made contact with her forehead. Unlike their previous communication, which had felt like receiving information, this connection was immediate and overwhelming, like being plunged into an ocean of alien consciousness where time, space, and identity held different meanings entirely.

Phoebe gasped, almost falling to her knees as her perception expanded violently. Harrison caught her arm, steadying her, his voice sounding distant and distorted as he called her name in alarm.

"I'm still here," she managed, though speaking required immense concentration. "Just adjusting."

The world around her had transformed. She still saw the physical landscape, the boundary between town and cornfield, Harrison's concerned face, the lightening sky, but superimposed over it was another reality entirely. Shadow paths, as the Consensus had called them, became visible currents of darkness flowing between worlds, connecting points that in physical space were distant from each other.

Follow, the Consensus directed, its communication now seeming to originate from within her own expanded consciousness rather than externally. *Memory-path opens.*

Guided by the Consensus, Phoebe took a step forward, then another. Each movement corresponded to physical motion but also traversed the shadow reality simultaneously. Harrison followed close behind, though she could tell from his expression that he perceived only her walking forward normally, unaware of the shadow path she navigated concurrently.

As they moved deeper into the cornfield, following a route invisible to normal perception, Phoebe's awareness continued to expand. Memories began surfacing, not just her own or even her shadow's individual experiences, but older impressions drawn from the collective consciousness of shadow entities across millennia.

She saw Millfield as it had been a century earlier, the silo rising slowly against the autumn sky while Thaddeus Hollow directed workers and secretly embedded binding symbols into its foundation. She saw the land long before settlement, when Native Peoples gathered at the edges of the barren clearing, where the shadow realm was most powerful, performing rituals meant to contain whatever presence slept beneath the earth.

And she began to perceive fragments of something far older memories from the original separation of realms, when shadow and substance had diverged from a unified state of existence. The binding stone had indeed formed naturally at this divergence, a crystallization of the original harmonic pattern that had governed reality before the split.

"The cornfields," she whispered, though she wasn't sure if she spoke aloud or only within her expanded consciousness. "They're directly above the wound. That's why shadows pool there, why the barrier is thinnest at this location."

"Yes," the Consensus confirmed. "Original breach deep underground. Native peoples maintained balance for thousands of years through ritual observance."

"Until European settlers arrived," Phoebe continued, the knowledge flowing through her merged consciousness like a river finding new channels. "Until the Exiles discovered the wound and saw an opportunity."

Deeper memories surfaced, the arrival of the thirteen Exiles, cast out from the shadow realm for their attempts to elevate themselves above the natural order. They hadn't chosen this location randomly. They had deliberately sought the wound between worlds, sensing its potential as a weak point they could exploit.

"They knew," Phoebe realized with growing horror. "They knew this place was vulnerable. They came here specifically to..."

Her thoughts fractured as a memory surfaced that wasn't just observation, but direct experience, the perspective of shadow entities present when the exiles first arrived. She felt their fear, their recognition that these thirteen were different, corrupted, hungry for dominance in a way alien to natural shadow consciousness.

The Exiles had been scientists of sorts in the shadow realm, experimenters who discovered that by consuming other shadow entities, they could grow more powerful, more individual. This violation of the natural flow of shadow consciousness had resulted in their exile, cast out through the wound between worlds as punishment.

But what their people hadn't anticipated was the Exiles' ability to adapt, to merge with physical beings on the other side. Several of the settlers who entered the chamber in 1893 returned changed, carrying the Exiles within them and becoming hybrid beings capable of existing between realms.

"My God." Phoebe gasped as the whole truth became clear. "They weren't just exiled for damaging their realm. They were exiled for consuming other shadows. For shadow cannibalism."

"Yes," the Consensus confirmed grimly. "Fundamental violation. Consumption rather than communion. Dominance rather than harmony."

A realization hit her. "And they're still doing it. The unbound shadows serving them, they're not allies or servants. They're food. Energy sources the Exiles are consuming to increase their power."

A wave of nausea swept through her as the implications became clear. The Exiles' ultimate goal wasn't merely to transform Millfield into a shadow-dominant reality. It was to create a new feeding ground where they could consume both shadow and physical energy without restriction.

"They'll devour everything," she whispered. "Shadow and substance alike. Until nothing remains but them."

As the terrible understanding settled into her consciousness, Phoebe realized they had reached their destination. The shadow path had led them to the center of the cornfields. In physical reality, it appeared as an ordinary clearing among the corn, a perfect circle about thirty feet in diameter, but where nothing grew, the soil bare and black despite the surrounding fertility. But in her expanded perception, Phoebe saw the circle for what it truly was, a vertical rip in reality itself, leaking energy between dimensions like a cosmic hemorrhage that had never broken through the surface.

"We're here," she told Harrison.

He looked around with ordinary human perception, seeing only the barren circle he'd seen many times. "Don't look like much."

"What you're seeing is the physical manifestation of something below." She held up the damaged binding stone, which had begun to pulse more strongly, responding to the proximity to its place of origin. "This formed somewhere below here when the realms first separated. A crystallization of the original harmonic pattern."

Harrison studied the bare earth with new respect. "What now? How do we repair the stone?"

"I need to go deeper," Phoebe said, her voice distant as her consciousness continued to expand under Consensus's guidance. "To access the memory of the stone's formation directly. To remember it whole."

"Dangerous depth approaching," the Consensus warned within her mind. "Human consciousness may not withstand full immersion in original memory. Dissolution possible."

"I understand," she replied, though fear fluttered at the edges of her awareness. "But we have no choice."

She knelt at the center of the barren circle and placed the damaged binding stone directly on the black soil. Immediately, its pulse strengthened further, resonating with the energies leaking through the ground beneath from an even deeper wound.

"Harrison," she said urgently, "regardless of what happens, don't interfere. This is the only chance we have to repair the stone. If I seem lost, give me time to find my way back."

The old man nodded gravely, understanding the risk she was taking. "How will I know if you're truly lost? If your human consciousness has dissolved completely?"

"You'll know," she said, simply because there was no way to explain the threshold between selfhood and dissolution to someone who hadn't experienced expanded consciousness.

Taking a deep breath, Phoebe placed both hands on the binding stone and closed her eyes, allowing the Consensus to guide her consciousness deeper into shadow memory. The world around her disappeared entirely, physical reality falling away as she plunged into a realm of pure awareness, of impressions and energies that predated individual existence.

For a terrifying moment, she felt her sense of self beginning to unravel, her human identity dissolving into the vast ocean of shadow consciousness. Panic flared, she was losing herself, forgetting who “Phoebe” was, what human perception meant, and why individuality mattered.

Hold the core pattern, the Consensus urged, its guidance a lifeline in the chaos. Find anchor in dual nature. Neither purely human nor shadow, but both simultaneously.

Struggling against the dissolution, Phoebe focused on her merged state, the balance she had achieved between human and shadow aspects of her consciousness. Not one dominating the other, but true partnership, each maintaining its essential nature while joining in harmony.

Gradually, her sense of self stabilized, transformed, expanded beyond normal human parameters, but still recognizably “Phoebe.” And from this stabilized point of view, she could finally access the memory she sought.

She witnessed the original separation of realms, not as a catastrophe or mistake, but as a natural evolution of consciousness, a divergence that allowed for new forms of experience and perception. Shadow and substance had once been unified, but their separation had created new complexities, new forms of awareness, new possibilities.

Currently of separation, at certain points where the division was most pronounced, fragments of the original unified state had crystallized binding stones, natural formations that contained the harmonic pattern of reality before the split. These stones existed simultaneously in both realms, bridges between ways of being.

The binding stone she held was one such fragment, not a tool or weapon, but a reminder of original unity, a key to maintaining balance between realms that were never meant to be completely separated or forcibly rejoined but to exist in dynamic relationships. The crack across its surface represented a disruption in this pattern, a fracturing of the connection between realms. To repair it required not physical manipulation, but a restoration of the original harmonic, a remembering of wholeness that predated separation.

With this understanding flowing through her expanded consciousness, Phoebe focused on the stone beneath her hands, visualizing the original pattern, the perfect resonance between shadow and substance. She wasn't forcing or commanding, merely remembering what had been, allowing that memory to flow through her merged state into the damaged artifact.

The stone grew warm beneath her touch, its pulse steadying and strengthening. The crack across its surface began to glow with silver light, not closing exactly but transforming, becoming a new feature of the pattern rather than a disruption to it.

Through her expanded perception, Phoebe could sense the change, the stone wasn't returning to its previous state but evolving into something new. A binding stone that acknowledged the wound and incorporated it rather than denying its existence. Wholeness that included brokenness as part of its pattern.

As this transformation completed, Phoebe felt her consciousness beginning to contract, returning toward normal parameters. The vast ocean of shadow memory receded, leaving behind only fragments, impressions too profound for human language to articulate fully.

She opened her eyes, finding herself still kneeling in the barren circle, Harrison watching her with concern. How much time had passed? Minutes? Hours? Her sense of time had dissolved completely during the immersion.

"Phoebe?" Harrison asked cautiously. "Are you yourself?"

"Yes," she answered, though the word felt insufficient. She was herself, but that self had been permanently altered by what she had experienced, expanded in ways that could never be fully reversed. "I'm back."

She lifted the binding stone from the earth and examined it in the light of day. With both physical and merged perception, she realized the crack remained visible, but it no longer absorbed light. Instead, it had become a channel for energy, a silver line that connected patterns on either side in a new configuration.

"It's repaired," she told Harrison, rising unsteadily to her feet. "Not returned to its original state but evolved. Adapted to include the damage as part of its new pattern."

"Will it work for the counter-ritual?" Harrison asked pragmatically.

"Yes. Differently than before, but perhaps even more effectively." She carefully returned the transformed stone to its pouch. "It represents balance that acknowledges wounding, harmony that includes discord. Exactly what we need to counter the Exiles' forced transformation."

Harrison checked his watch, his expression tight with concern. "We've been here over four hours. The Consensus warned us we had until midday before the Exiles' attention returned to this location."

Phoebe glanced at the sun, nearly high overhead. "We need to leave. Now."

As if in response to her words, the corn surrounding the barren circle began to rustle, though no wind disturbed the still air. Shadows deepened between the rows, coalescing into forms that moved with deliberate purpose.

"Too late," Harrison breathed. "They've been watching us."

The Consensus, which had maintained a protective perimeter around them during Phoebe's immersion in shadow memory, drew closer, their mathematical patterns shifting into more defensive configurations.

"Exiles approach," they communicated urgently. "Multiple directions. Shadow-path closing. Must run, physical path only remains."

Phoebe grabbed Harrison's arm, pulling him toward the narrow opening between corn rows that had brought them to the clearing. "This way! Quick!"

They ran, the corn stalks whipping past them as shadows gathered in pursuit. Unlike their escape from the town hall, this time the unbound shadows seemed more organized, more deliberate in their movements, herding them, Phoebe realized, directing their flight rather than simply chasing.

"They're guiding us into a trap," she said to Harrison and gasped as they emerged from one row, only to find their intended path blocked by darkness so dense it appeared solid. "Forcing us in a specific direction."

"Which direction?" Harrison demanded, leaning heavily on his cane as they changed course, taking the only path left open to them.

Phoebe's expanded perception analyzed their forced trajectory. "East. Deeper into the cornfields. Away from town."

Away from the protection of Millfield's weakened sigil. Away from Grant and the deputies who might have assisted them. Into territory completely controlled by the Exiles.

The binding stone pulsed against her chest, its newly stabilized energy responding to her fear and to the approaching shadow entities. She could feel it generating power, ready to be channeled, but she hesitated to use it, knowing that any significant energy discharge would drain its reserves, reserves they would need for the counter-ritual during the eclipse.

"We can't outrun them," Harrison stated the obvious as they were forced to change direction again, shadow barriers closing off paths behind and beside them. "And we can't fight our way through."

"We don't need to," Phoebe realized suddenly. "They

would rather not harm us to get the stone. If they simply wanted us dead, they could have attacked directly."

"So?"

"So, we give them something else to focus on." She reached into her pocket and extracted the stone she had picked up outside the community center, roughly the same size and shape as the binding stone. "A diversion."

When they reached the next forced turning, instead of following the shadow-directed path, Phoebe held up the ordinary stone, channeling just enough energy from the true binding stone to make it glow briefly with silver light. Then she threw the decoy as far as she could to the south, away from both their position and the town.

The effect was immediate. Unbound shadows abandoned their herding pattern and surged after the glowing decoy. In that brief window, Phoebe pulled Harrison into the previously blocked path, now stumbling west, toward Millfield, toward safety.

"Clever." Harrison gasped as they scrambled through the corn. "But they'll realize the deception quickly."

"We only need a head start," Phoebe replied, supporting the older man as they ran. "The town's protective sigil is less than a hundred yards west."

Behind them, a howl of rage echoed through the cornfield, a sound like no earthly creature could produce, composed of multiple frequencies overlapping discordantly. The Exiles had discovered their trick.

"That came quicker than I'd hoped." Phoebe practically dragged Harrison now, as his strength flagged. "Don't look back!"

A minute later, they burst from the edge of the cornfield, the boundary of Millfield's protective sigil visible to Phoebe's merged perception just a few yards ahead. Behind them, shadow entities surged in pursuit, no longer unbound shadows but more substantial forms, the Exiles' shadows themselves giving chase now that their servants had failed.

"Almost there."

Harrison was stumbling with exhaustion.

"Just a few more steps!"

They crossed the boundary just as the foremost Exile reached for them, its elongated limbs dissolving into smoke as it encountered the sigil's protection.

Phoebe, shaken and gasping, turned to face their pursuers.

Thirteen entities hovered at the edge of town, their forms shifting between human silhouettes and more abstract shadow configurations. At their center stood a figure Phoebe recognized even in its transformed state, Mayor Wilson, though little resembling the human he had once appeared to be. His body was now composed of swirling darkness punctuated by points of light like distant stars, as if he contained an entire cosmos within his outline.

"The stone," Wilson's voice reached them, distorted by distance and his altered form. "You can repair it but cannot undo what has begun."

"You're wrong," Phoebe called back, drawing out the transformed binding stone for him to see. The crack across its surface now glowed with silver light, a channel for energy rather than a break. "It's not just repaired, it's evolved. As it was always meant to do."

Wilson's form rippled with what might have been alarm. "Evolved? Impossible. It's a rock."

"Only from your perspective," Phoebe replied. "Only if you believe wholeness means absence of wounding. True repair incorporates damage, transforms it, rather than erasing it."

The gathered Exiles conferred silently among themselves, their forms shifting in patterns too complex for even Phoebe's expanded perception to interpret fully.

Finally, Wilson addressed her again.

"It changes nothing. The eclipse comes regardless. The transformation proceeds." His voice took on a tone almost like resignation beneath the menace. "You cannot save this world, stone-bearer. It was wounded long before we arrived. We merely exploited what was already broken."

"And consume everything in the process," Phoebe shouted. "I know the truth now, why you were exiled from your realm. Not just for damaging it, but for consuming other shadows. For cannibalism of your own kind."

The accusation seemed to strike home. Several of the gathered Exiles recoiled, their forms briefly destabilizing. Wilson's outline contracted, becoming more defined and more hostile.

"Truth is perspective," he hissed. "Consumption is evolution. The strong absorb the weak. Natural law across all realms."

"No," Phoebe countered. "Symbiosis is evolution. Balance is strength. That's what you never understood, what got you exiled in the first place. And what will defeat you now."

She raised the binding stone, channeling just enough of its energy to create a pulse of silver light that pushed the Exiles farther back from the boundary. Not an attack, merely a demonstration of the stone's restored power.

"Four days," she told them. "Until the eclipse. Until we meet for the true confrontation." She lowered the stone, her expression resolute. "Choose wisely which side of history you wish to stand on, Exiles. There may yet be room for you in the balanced convergence we seek to create."

Wilson's form seemed to laugh, a visual ripple rather than an audible sound. "Naive, even after all you've seen. There is no 'balance' with predators, stone-bearer. Only victory or defeat. Consumption or being consumed." His outline began to fade as it retreated deeper into the cornfield.

"Prepare as you wish. The eclipse comes regardless."

As the Exiles withdrew, Harrison leaned heavily on his cane, exhaustion evident in every line of his body. "You truly think there's hope for them? For redemption after what they've done?"

Phoebe watched the shadow entities disappear among the corn rows while considering his question carefully. "I don't know. What I saw in the deep shadow memories, the original separation, the formation of the binding stone, it suggests that all consciousness, shadow and physical, emerged from a unified state. That underneath the divisions, we're all expressions of the same fundamental pattern."

"Petty metaphysics," Harrison said dryly. "Not much practical comfort against entities that want to consume our world."

"Maybe not," Phoebe returned. "But it reminded me that the goal isn't destruction of the Exiles, that would just perpetuate the cycle of dominance they embody. The goal is transformation, of them, of us, of the relationship between realms."

She looked down at the binding stone, its silver glow pulsing steadily through the transformed crack. "Balance doesn't mean erasing differences or forcing uniformity. It means creating relationships between distinct ways of being. Harmony that includes discord."

"And if they refuse such harmony?" Harrison asked as they began walking back toward the community center. "If they insist on consumption rather than communion?"

Phoebe's expression hardened. "Then we'll stop them. Not because we're right and they're wrong in some absolute sense. But because their vision of reality requires domination, while ours allows for choice."

As they walked through Millfield's quiet streets, Phoebe felt the weight of the knowledge she had gained, the forgotten history of both realms, the true nature of the Exiles, the original wound that had never healed. Knowledge that would be crucial in the approaching confrontation during the eclipse.

Four days remained. Four days to prepare the volunteer pairs, to design the counter-ritual, to face what might be the final transformation of Millfield, and perhaps both realms.

But Phoebe had one advantage the Exiles couldn't anticipate. In accessing the deep shadow memories, she had glimpsed not just the past but possibilities, futures that might unfold depending on the choices made during the eclipse. Futures where balance prevailed, where the wound between worlds finally began to heal properly.

The binding stone pulsed against her chest, a reminder of original unity and the potential for a new kind of convergence. Not a return to the past, but an evolution into something that honored both separation and connection.

A third way, beyond either binding or dominance, the incomplete circle.

CHAPTER 12:
THREE DAYS UNTIL THE ECLIPSE

The community center basement had been transformed into a war room. Maps of Millfield covered one wall, street layouts, property boundaries, utility lines, all overlaid with transparent sheets marked with symbols only Phoebe and Harrison fully understood. The original binding sigil created by Thaddeus Hollow, the thirteen points where pumpkins had traditionally been placed during the Harvest Festival, the exact location of the demolished silo.

But the newest addition to their planning wall was causing the most consternation: a faded, yellowed map dated 1837, showing a network of mine tunnels running beneath parts of what would later become Millfield.

Phoebe tapped the fragile paper carefully. "How did we not know about these tunnels beneath our cornfields?"

"So long ago, mostly forgotten," Harrison replied, adjusting his glasses as he studied the ancient survey map. "Grant told me to check into any old mines in the area. I found this old map in the archives of the Department of the Interior's National Mine Map Repository. A silver mine here was abandoned in the 1840s after a series of incidents. The entrance was dynamited and buried to prevent anyone from going back inside. By the time Thaddeus Hollow arrived decades later, the mine itself had vanished from local memory. He knew there was something wrong with the land, a weak point in the barrier between worlds, but he never realized an old mine shaft lay buried beneath him."

David leaned closer to the map, tracing one of the main tunnel lines with his finger. "This runs directly beneath where the silo stood. And here, these branches extend out beneath the cornfields." He pointed toward a narrower offshoot near the edge of the diagram. "One of them appears to lead to a gigantic chamber beneath that barren circle in the center of the west cornfield."

Harrison noted, "Thaddeus chose the largest of the two barren circles on his land as the location for his silo. It seemed logical to him that the shadow anomalies he'd witnessed originated from there. Without realizing it, he'd built the silo directly above the buried main shaft."

Phoebe studied the tunnel network with her merged perception, seeing patterns invisible to ordinary human awareness. "The miners followed the contours of the silver veins, but unknowingly opened a breach between worlds."

"And dug themselves a catastrophe in the process," Harrison added somberly.

"The original Exiles finally broke through," Phoebe said. "The wound between worlds was there long before the settlers came. Just its presence created havoc with shadows in the valley. The Native People knew something evil lay under the wild cornfields. After the mine was closed, the valley became uninhabitable, unfarmable. Must've been a terrifying place."

"Until my grandfather came along." Harrison sighed. "And the rest is history."

Lucy raised her hand tentatively. She'd been included in the planning session due to her unique connection with her shadow and its communication abilities. "My shadow says the tunnels are bigger now. That the Exiles have been expanding them for generations."

"That tracks with the historical record," Harrison noted. "There have been reports of strange sounds beneath the fields, minor earth tremors, always dismissed as natural phenomena."

"I wonder why..."

"And now the silo's gone," David said. "Nothing left but a crater. The main shaft entrance must be around there somewhere."

The implications hung heavy in the air. The demolition had literally uncapped the Exiles' underground domain, giving them direct access to the surface world for the first time in a century.

Grant's practical nature asserted itself. "The tunnels might provide an approach to the center of the cornfield where the Exiles are gathering for their ritual."

Phoebe shook her head. "We're not going down there. It's their territory, has been for nearly two centuries. We'd be at a severe disadvantage underground, where shadow entities have every advantage."

"Then we stick with the original plan," Grant decided. "Approach through the cornfields during the eclipse, when their attention is focused on their ritual."

Phoebe nodded in agreement while touching the binding stone that hung around her neck. Since its evolution, it had stabilized, its energy more focused, more directed. The silver-glowing crack across its surface no longer seemed like damage but like a deliberate channel, a necessary part of its structure.

"How are the volunteers progressing?" she asked, turning to Mary Holloway, who had been coordinating the merger training.

"Seven pairs still. No more desertions, thankfully. Three have achieved partial merging states, me, Deputy Rodriguez, and Ms. Jenkins from the library. The others are making progress, but slower than we'd hoped."

"Three days isn't much time," Harrison stated quietly.

"It's all we have," Phoebe replied. "The eclipse waits for no one."

The planning session continued for another hour, refining approaches, contingencies, and evacuation routes for Millfield residents if things went wrong. Throughout, Phoebe found her attention repeatedly drawn to the mine map and to the network of tunnels spreading beneath the cornfields like dark veins.

In her merged state, she could almost sense them, hollow spaces where shadow gathered more densely, where the boundary between realms had grown wide enough for shadow entities to pass through with minimal effort. The wound between worlds wasn't just an abstract concept or an invisible energy pattern. It had physical manifestation somewhere within these tunnels, in the shaped spaces carved by human hands but now claimed by shadow consciousness.

When the meeting ended, volunteers returned to their training or assigned preparation tasks, and Phoebe remained before the map wall, studying the mine layout with growing concern.

David returned with two cups of coffee. "Something's bothering you, besides the obvious end-of-our-town scenario we're facing."

"The tunnels don't match," she said, accepting the coffee gratefully. "The 1837 survey shows them extending mainly eastward, toward the cornfields. But the shadow memories I accessed suggest a much more extensive network, branches running beneath most of Millfield, following the wound's contours in all directions."

"The Exiles have been busy for nearly two centuries," David stated. "Expanding their underground domain while we lived obliviously above."

"Possibly. But I think the surveyors never mapped the full extent back then. I think they found something that scared them enough to abandon the mapping. Something they chose not to document."

Harrison joined them, his shadow flowing beside him with unusual agitation. "My shadow's been trying to communicate something similar. It has impressions, bits of memory passed down through generations of Hollow shadows. The mine's central chamber, it wasn't created by humans at all."

"What do you mean?" Grant asked, approaching with Lucy and her shadow in tow.

"The main shaft led to what the miner's thought was a natural cavern," Harrison explained while his shadow made confirmatory gestures. "But it wasn't natural. It was built, by whom or what, they never determined. But its dimensions, its perfect circular shape, suggested deliberate design predating human settlement by millennia."

Lucy's shadow began making urgent gestures, which the girl translated with practiced ease. "It says the chamber is where the wound first opened. Where the realms initially separated. That's why the binding stone formed there."

"And why the Exiles are drawn to it," Phoebe concluded. "It's the thinnest point between worlds, the place where their transformation ritual will have maximum effect during the eclipse."

"But the silo foundation sealed it," David pointed out. "And now the foundation is gone, demolished along with the silo itself."

A heavy silence fell as they all contemplated the implications. The main shaft entrance was now an open crater at the former silo site, leading directly to the ancient chamber where the wound between worlds was most pronounced.

"We need to see it," Phoebe decided suddenly. "The chamber. Before the eclipse. We need to understand what we're truly facing."

"Entering the Exiles' domain directly?" Skepticism was evident in Grant's voice. "That's even riskier than approaching through the cornfield."

"Maybe not," Phoebe countered. "They're expecting us to attempt the cornfield approach. Their attention is focused there, preparing for the eclipse ritual. The mine entrance might actually be less guarded right now."

"Or it's another trap," David warned. "Like the town hall confrontation."

"Possibly, but we need information, about the chamber, about how the wound manifests physically. The shadow memories I accessed didn't show me everything." She touched the binding stone. "And I think the stone wants to return there. To its point of origin."

Harrison studied her thoughtfully. "The stone has its awareness?"

"Not consciousness as we understand it," Phoebe replied. "But a kind of resonance. A pull toward where it first formed. I've felt it since the repair, a directional tug, like a compass needle seeking north."

"If you're determined to go, you're not going alone," Grant stated flatly. "I'll assemble a team, deputies with separated shadows who've shown the best connections."

"Small group," Phoebe said. "Agile, quiet. We're not looking for a confrontation, just reconnaissance."

"When?" David asked, his expression making clear he intended to be included regardless of her answer.

"Tonight. After sunset, when our shadow aspects are strongest. If we wait longer, the Exiles might detect our preparations and increase security."

The plan came together quickly. A team of six, Phoebe, David, Grant, Harrison, and two deputies whose shadows had demonstrated strong protective capabilities. They would approach the silo demolition site after dark, enter the exposed mine shaft, and proceed to the central chamber. Observe, document, and retreat without engaging the Exiles if possible.

As preparations continued throughout the day, Phoebe found herself drawn repeatedly to the community center's eastern windows, staring toward the cornfields visible in the distance. In her merged perception, she could see darkness gathering there even in broad daylight, shadow energy pooling, concentrating, preparing for the eclipse now just three days away.

The Exiles were growing stronger. Whether from consuming unbound shadows or drawing power from the wound itself was unclear. But their presence in Millfield had become palpable even to those without merged perception. Electronics malfunctioned near the cornfields, animals refused to approach, and plants withered along the perimeter despite recent rains.

Reality itself seemed to be thinning at the edges, preparing to tear completely during the eclipse.

Dusk fell across Millfield like a velvet curtain, shadows lengthening and deepening as the sun disappeared below the western horizon. The shadow hour had begun, that limited time when boundaries between realms grew naturally thin, when shadow entities were at their most powerful.

Phoebe led their small group toward the silo demolition site, moving cautiously through backstreets and residential yards to avoid attention. The binding stone pulsed against her chest, its rhythm quickening as they approached the open crater where the massive structure had stood for nearly a century.

"Stay close," she instructed as they reached the perimeter fence that surrounded the demolition zone. "Our shadows should move ahead. Scout for dangers."

The six separated shadows flowed forward like a dark tide, slipping beneath the fence and across the exposed ground beyond. They moved with perfect coordination, maintaining communication through some silent shadow language that even Phoebe's merged perception couldn't fully interpret.

Minutes later, they returned, conveying through gestures what they had discovered.

"No Exiles present," Phoebe translated for the group. "But unbound shadows patrolling. Our shadows can create a diversion to draw them away from the main shaft entrance."

"And once we're inside?" David asked.

"We follow the original tunnel toward the central chamber," Harrison said, consulting a small copy of the mine map he'd brought. "About four hundred yards in, according to the survey."

Grant distributed flashlights and emergency supplies, water, first aid kit, flares. "We stay together," he instructed firmly. "Any sign of Exile activity, we retreat immediately. This is reconnaissance only."

Their shadows moved ahead again, creating a distraction at the northern edge of the demolition site that drew the patrolling unbound shadows away. Taking advantage of the opening, the human team slipped beneath the fence and crossed quickly to the exposed mine shaft, a dark maw in the earth where the silo's massive foundation had been ripped away.

Metal rungs embedded in the shaft wall created a ladder descending into darkness. One by one, they climbed down, flashlight beams cutting through the gloom. Their shadows rejoined them at the bottom, flowing down the shaft walls with liquid grace to resume protective positions.

The air in the tunnel was strangely still, neither warm nor cold, with an odd metallic taste that made Phoebe's skin prickle. Her merged perception revealed why, the wound between worlds was closer here, reality itself growing thin enough that elements of the shadow realm leaked through, altering physical properties in subtle ways.

"This way," Harrison directed, consulting his map as they moved deeper into the tunnel system. Ancient timber supports creaked ominously overhead; decades of moisture and neglect had weakened their structural integrity.

As they proceeded, Phoebe noticed strange crystalline

formations growing along the tunnel walls, not mineral deposits as would be expected in a natural mine, but something that seemed to flicker between physical and shadow states, existing in both realms simultaneously.

"What are those?" David asked, his flashlight beam catching one formation at an angle that made it seem to disappear completely before reappearing when the light shifted.

"Boundary crystals," Harrison explained, his academic interest temporarily overriding caution as he examined one formation. "My grandfather mentioned them. They form naturally where the wound between worlds is pronounced, physical manifestations of the breach."

"Like versions of the binding stone," Phoebe realized, feeling the stone around her neck pulse in resonance with the crystalline growths.

They continued deeper, the tunnel gradually widening, the ceiling height increasing. Signs of the original mining operation remained visible, abandoned cart tracks, rotting support beams, ancient tools left behind in the hasty evacuation nearly two centuries earlier.

But there were newer additions as well, strange symbols carved into the walls at irregular intervals, patterns reminiscent of those etched into the binding stone but distorted, twisted into configurations that made Phoebe's merged consciousness recoil instinctively.

"Exile markings," Harrison identified them in a hushed voice. "Territory claims. Warnings to other shadow entities."

"They've been using these tunnels continuously," Grant observed. "Expanding them, adapting them to their needs."

Eventually, the tunnel opened into a larger passage where evidence of human mining gave way to entirely smooth walls that appeared polished and ceiling arches that followed mathematical patterns too precise for nineteenth-century engineering.

"We're getting close to the central chamber," Harrison whispered, tucking away his now-unnecessary map. "This section wasn't created by the miners."

"Who then?" one of the deputies asked nervously, his shadow pressing closer to his side in protective alertness.

"Not who," Phoebe put in. "What."

The binding stone's pulse had become frantic now, the silver-glowing crack across its surface brightening until Phoebe had to wrap it in its pouch to avoid attracting attention. She could feel it pulling her forward, straining toward something deeper in the tunnels—something ancient calling to it from below.

They rounded a final bend in the tunnel and stopped short, flashlight beams illuminating what lay beyond.

The central chamber.

Nothing had prepared them for the reality of what they now witnessed. A perfect hemisphere at least fifty yards in diameter, its domed ceiling rising to a crucial point directly beneath the barren circle at the center of the cornfield—the dead patch where nothing had grown for as long as anyone could remember. The walls and floor formed a seamless curve of some material that wasn't quite stone, wasn't quite metal, wasn't quite anything classifiable by human science—a substance that seemed to absorb light while simultaneously emitting a faint luminescence of its own.

But most striking were the patterns covering every surface, intricate, interlocking symbols similar to those on the binding stone but vastly more complex, creating a comprehensive language that described the relationship between realms in mathematical precision.

"It's beautiful," David whispered, awe temporarily overriding caution.

"And not remotely natural," Harrison added. "This chamber predates human civilization in this region by thousands of years. Perhaps tens of thousands."

David swallowed hard, his analytical mind on overload.

Phoebe moved forward slowly, drawn by the binding stone's insistent pull. At the exact center of the hemispheric floor stood a raised dais, a perfect circle of the same unclassifiable material as the walls, about ten feet in diameter. Within this circle were thirteen equidistant indentations arranged in a ring, each shaped to hold an object about the size of the binding stone.

"The original convergence site," she breathed as understanding flowed through her merged consciousness. "Where thirteen stones once maintained balance between realms."

"Thirteen binding stones?" Grant looked alarmed. "I thought there was only one."

"There must've only been one stone left by the time Thaddeus found it," Harrison said, joining Phoebe at the dais. "It was just a stone before the Native People used it for the binding spell."

"Who would've taken the others?" David asked.

"Those who sought dominance rather than balance," Phoebe answered, the knowledge rising from her shadow consciousness. "The ancestors of the entities who would later become the Exiles."

"Are you saying this is where the miners opened the breach between worlds?"

"Somewhere around here."

"And now we're standing in...the shadow realm?"

"I think so."

The binding stone was vibrating now, its energy resonating with the chamber itself. Phoebe removed it from its pouch, allowing its silver light to illuminate the central dais more clearly. The moment the stone's light touched the circle, the patterns covering the chamber walls began to glow in response, a soft phosphorescence that revealed the true scale and complexity of the design.

"It's like a machine," Grant said with sudden clarity. "Not mechanical, but a device made with a technology we don't understand."

"A convergence circle," Harrison stated. "Designed to maintain a balance between realms."

Phoebe held the binding stone over the nearest indentation in the circle. It looked as if it would fit perfectly, as if designed specifically for that space. "Looks like these thirteen indentations are key slots. Boundary crystals are the keys. Controllers. With all thirteen in place, the circle would operate at full capacity, maintaining ideal balance."

"But we have only one," David said.

"Minimal functionality, maybe. Enough to prevent a catastrophic breach, but not enough for true harmony." She carefully placed the stone in an indentation and felt it lock into place with an ominous click.

Immediately, energy surged through the chamber, patterns on the walls brightening, the strange material of the floor beginning to vibrate at a frequency just below human hearing but perfectly perceptible to shadow consciousness. The binding stone's silver light expanded, flowing outward along channels in the dais floor that connected all thirteen indentations in an intricate web.

"What have you done?" David shouted.

"It's activating," Harrison observed with academic fascination. "Even with just one stone."

"Because it's a binding stone that has evolved beyond being an ordinary boundary crystal," Phoebe explained, watching the energy patterns flow. "It's capable of channeling more power than before, thus compensating for the missing stones."

The deputies' shadows suddenly grew agitated, making urgent warning gestures. Grant's shadow joined them, pointing toward the tunnel with unmistakable alarm.

"Company coming," Grant stated flatly. "Multiple entities approaching fast."

"Exiles?" Harrison asked, already backing away from the dais.

"Can't tell," Grant replied as his shadow continued its silent communication. "But they're moving with purpose. They know we're here."

Phoebe was torn between retrieving the binding stone or allowing the activation sequence to continue. The chamber's energy was still building, patterns on the walls growing brighter, the convergence circle awakening from centuries of dormancy.

"We need the stone," David insisted, seeing her hesitation. "We can't leave it here for them to take."

"I know." She reached for the binding stone just as a howl echoed through the tunnel, that same multi-toned cry they had heard in the cornfields, the unmistakable voice of the Exiles' servants in pursuit.

Her fingers closed around the stone, but it resisted her pull, locked into its indentation as the chamber's activation sequence progressed. She pulled harder, channeling her own merged energy into it, trying to disrupt the connection.

"Phoebe, hurry!" Grant called, weapon drawn as he positioned himself at the tunnel. The shadows of both deputies had flowed forward to create a temporary barrier, but it was already buckling under pressure from whatever approached.

With a final surge of effort, Phoebe wrenched the binding stone free from its setting. The chamber's energy patterns immediately destabilized, the glowing web flickering and dimming. But something unexpected happened, a portion of the chamber's energy had transferred to the stone itself, altering it once again. The silver-glowing crack across its surface had expanded into a more complex pattern, branching like lightning frozen in time.

"Got it," she called, returning the transformed stone to its pouch. "Let's move!"

They retreated from the central chamber just as the shadow barrier at the tunnel entrance collapsed. Unbound shadows poured into the space, but instead of pursuing immediately, they flowed toward the dais, surrounding it in a whirling vortex of darkness.

"Secondary exit," Harrison directed, consulting his map as they ran. "The mining tunnel branches two hundred yards back, leads to an air shaft that should reach the surface."

They retraced their steps through the ancient tunnel system, hearing pursuit build behind them. The unbound shadows had abandoned their inspection of the central chamber and were now giving chase, flowing through the tunnels with far greater speed than humans could match on foot.

"There!" Harrison pointed to a narrower tunnel branching from the main passage. "That should lead to the air shaft."

They turned into the secondary tunnel, their flashlight beams revealing an even older section of the mine, support timbers sagging dangerously, cart tracks rusted beyond recognition. The air grew staler, the ceiling lower, forcing them to hunch as they ran.

"This doesn't look promising," Grant commented as they reached a partial collapse blocking half the tunnel width.

"The only way out," Harrison insisted. "According to the map, the air shaft is just beyond."

They squeezed past the rock pile, but dislodged decades of accumulated debris in the process. A distant rumble suggested their passage had destabilized the already compromised tunnel structure.

"Hurry," Phoebe cried, feeling the binding stone pulse with warning. "The whole tunnel is coming down."

They found what they sought, a vertical shaft perhaps three feet in diameter. Old metal rungs embedded in its wall created a ladder to the surface. Only darkness was visible at the top.

"One at a time," Grant said. "Quickly but carefully."

The first deputy ascended, followed by Harrison, then the second deputy. David went next, pausing at the base of the ladder to look back at Phoebe and Grant.

"Don't wait too long," he called down. "Those support beams won't hold much longer."

As if in response to his warning, another ominous rumble shook the tunnel; dust and small debris rained from the ceiling. The pursuing shadows had reached the collapse point, flowing through gaps in the rubble like dark water.

"Go," Grant ordered Phoebe. "I'll hold them off."

"How?" she demanded. "Bullets won't stop shadows."

His shadow stepped forward, making a gesture that needed no translation, self-sacrifice. It would stay behind, to delay the pursuers while they escaped.

"No," Phoebe shouted. "We don't leave anyone behind, human or shadow."

The pursuing entities had nearly breached the collapse now, their formless shapes beginning to solidify into more substantial manifestations as they sensed proximity to the binding stone.

Phoebe made a split-second decision. She removed the stone from its pouch, its silver light blazing in the tunnel darkness. The transformed pattern across its surface pulsed with accumulated energy from the convergence circle.

"What are you doing?" Grant demanded.

"Creating a barrier they can't cross." Phoebe placed the stone on the ground, channeling her merged consciousness into it, directing its energy, not outward in an attack, but inward into the earth itself.

The effect was immediate and dramatic. The binding stone's energy flowed into the tunnel floor, activating boundary crystals embedded in the rock. A line of silver light erupted across the tunnel width, creating a vertical plane of energy that separated them from the approaching shadows.

"That won't hold long," Phoebe warned, retrieving the stone. "Climb!"

Grant went first, scaling the ladder with practiced efficiency. Phoebe followed, the binding stone clutched in one hand, making her ascent awkward and slow. Below, the energy barrier flickered as unbound shadows pressed against it, testing its strength.

Halfway up the shaft, disaster struck. Another tremor shook the mine, more violent than before. The ancient metal rungs groaned under the climbers' weight, decades of corrosion finally giving way. The rung in Grant's grip broke free from the wall, sending him falling back toward Phoebe.

She managed to brace herself against the shaft wall, one arm hooking around a rung as Grant collided with her. For a heart-stopping moment, they both dangled precariously, the binding stone clutched desperately in Phoebe's free hand as she struggled to maintain her grip on both it and the failing ladder.

"Let me go," Grant ordered, seeing her struggle. "Save the stone."

"Not happening," she gritted out, her merged consciousness channeling energy to strengthen her human muscles beyond normal capacity. With a surge of effort that should have been impossible, she stabilized their position, allowing Grant to find another handhold on the shaft wall.

"Hang on!" David's voice called from above. A rope descended into the shaft, dropping past them to the tunnel floor below. "Tie it around yourselves!"

Working together, they secured themselves to the rope,

then continued their ascent using it rather than trusting the deteriorating ladder rungs. Behind them, the energy barrier finally collapsed. Unbound shadows surged into the air shaft, flowing up the walls in pursuit.

"Almost there," Grant said as the moonlight grew brighter above them.

With a final effort, they reached the top; hands grabbed them to pull them onto the surface. They emerged into crisp night air, finding themselves in an overgrown field perhaps half a mile from the demolition site.

"Seal it," Harrison urged, pointing to the shaft opening. "Before they follow!"

Phoebe didn't hesitate. She channeled the binding stone's energy downward, focusing it into the shaft. The boundary crystals embedded in the surrounding earth activated again, their silver light creating a seal across the opening, not permanent, but enough to slow pursuit.

As they caught their breath, David pointed to the distance, where the demolished silo site was visible as a darker shadow against the night sky. Energy pulses were visible even to normal human perception, darkness flowing upward from the main shaft entrance like a reverse waterfall.

"We triggered something," he said. "By activating the convergence circle, even partially."

"The Exiles will accelerate their preparations now," Harrison predicted. "They know we've discovered the central chamber, that we know what's down there."

Phoebe studied the transformed stone in her palm, its new pattern glowing with absorbed energy from the convergence circle. "But we've gained something too. The stone is stronger now, more attuned to its original purpose. And we know exactly where the eclipse ritual must be performed."

"Not beneath the silo," Grant concluded. "The mine shaft was only the entrance. The tunnels led us to the central chamber beneath the barren circle in the middle of the cornfields."

Phoebe nodded slowly. "The original focal point of the wound," she said. "That's where the convergence circle waits now, and where the binding stone had to be returned for the repair to manifest physically."

They made their way back toward town, staying in shadow, avoiding open spaces where they might be observed. The binding stone continued to pulse in Phoebe's hand, but with a new rhythm, steadier, more purposeful, as if it had remembered its true function after centuries of diminished capacity.

Three days remained until the eclipse. The Exiles were gathering their power, preparing for a transformation ritual that would remake reality according to their vision of shadow dominance. And Phoebe's team had only seven merged pairs out of the thirteen needed for the counter-ritual.

An incomplete circle to face the coming darkness.

But they had one advantage the Exiles couldn't anticipate, a binding stone reconnected to the convergence circle, carrying a portion of its ancient power. A stone that she now understood its purpose, not as weapon or key, but as the principal component of a machine designed to maintain balance between realms.

As they reached the protective boundary of Millfield's weakened sigil, Phoebe felt the stone pulse with what almost seemed like anticipation. The convergence it sought wasn't domination or separation, but harmony, shadow, and substance in dynamic relationship, distinct but connected.

Balance that acknowledged wounding. Unity that respected difference. A third way, beyond either binding or consumption.

If only they could complete the circle in time.

CHAPTER 13:
THE INCOMPLETE CIRCLE

They reached the community center just before midnight, bruised and breathing hard, trailing dirt from the mine tunnels. Phoebe's hands were still shaking—not from the climb or the pursuit, but from what she'd felt when the binding stone locked into the convergence circle's dais. That surge of ancient energy, vast and purposeful, still echoed through her merged consciousness like the reverberations of a bell struck once and left to ring.

"Get everyone inside," Grant ordered his deputies while scanning the darkened street behind them. "No one leaves until we've assessed the situation."

The gymnasium was still lit, volunteers dozing on cots or sitting in small clusters, waiting for news. They stirred as the expedition team entered, reading the urgency in their faces before anyone spoke. Mary Holloway was the first to reach them, her merged eyes flickering silver as she took in their condition. "What happened down there?"

Phoebe looked at Harrison, who nodded. No point in softening it now.

"We found the convergence circle," Phoebe said, loud enough for the room to hear. "The central chamber beneath the barren circle in the cornfield. It's real...older than anything human. And it's designed to hold not one boundary crystal, like the binding stone, but thirteen."

The silence that followed was absolute. Even the separated shadows in the room went still, their formless bodies oriented toward Phoebe with unmistakable attention.

"Thirteen," Deputy Rodriguez repeated from his cot, his shadow making an emphatic gesture beside him. "That's the same number as—"

"The merged pairs we need. The founding families. The Dark Exiles. The original binding points." Harrison settled heavily into a folding chair, his age showing more than usual. "Thirteen is the architecture of this place. Always has been."

David brought water and a first-aid kit to clean a gash on Grant's forearm where a collapsing rung had torn skin. He worked in focused silence, but Phoebe could feel his questions building. He'd been in the tunnels. He'd seen the chamber, the impossible geometry of it, the way the binding stone had responded to it. For a man who'd spent weeks resisting the supernatural reality unfolding around him, the experience had left visible cracks in his skepticism.

"The stone absorbed energy from the convergence circle." Phoebe unwrapped it from its pouch. The silver pattern across its surface had grown more complex, branching lines that pulsed with a steady rhythm the room could hear. "It's stronger now. More capable. But it also means the Exiles know we've been in their territory. They'll respond."

"How soon?" Mary asked.

"By morning," Harrison predicted. "They can't afford to let us hold an activated binding stone this close to the eclipse. Expect retaliation."

The room absorbed this grimly. Phoebe watched their faces—volunteers who'd signed on to learn meditation techniques and shadow communication, not to prepare for a siege. Some were teachers, shop owners, a retired postal worker. People whose most dangerous prior experience involved icy roads in January. Now they sat in a gymnasium ringed by protective sigils, their own shadows standing beside them like dark sentinels, waiting to learn how bad things were about to get.

* * *

Phoebe found David alone in the small office they'd converted into a supply room, reorganizing emergency kits with the methodical intensity of a man who needed to keep his hands busy.

"You should sleep," she said from the doorway.

"So should you." He didn't look up. "How's Maddie?"

"Asleep. Lucy's shadow is keeping watch over the girls." Phoebe leaned against the door frame, studying her husband. The fluorescent light threw his long shadow against the back wall, where it stood independently, arms folded, mirroring David's closed-off posture with eerie precision. "Your shadow's picking up your body language."

David glanced at the dark figure behind him. It unfolded its arms self-consciously.

"It does that," he said flatly. "Still creeps me out."

"David."

He stopped sorting bandages and finally met her eyes. In the harsh light, she could see what the tunnels had cost him—not physically, but in the careful architecture of denial he'd maintained since the separation began. That architecture was crumbling.

"That chamber wasn't built by people," he said quietly. "Nothing human made that place."

"No."

"And the stone fit into that slot like it was made for it. Like a key in a lock."

"It was made for it. Thousands of years ago, at the point where two realities separated."

David sat on an overturned supply crate and rubbed his face with both hands. His shadow took a tentative step closer, then stopped, uncertain of its welcome.

"I keep trying to find a rational explanation," he said.

"Geological formations. Electromagnetic anomalies. Mass hysteria. But I was down there, Phoebe. I felt the floor vibrate when you put the stone in. I saw the walls light up." He dropped his hands. "I can't explain that away."

"You don't have to explain it. You just have to decide what you're going to do about it."

He looked at his shadow again. It had moved closer still, one dark hand extended in a gesture that could only be interpreted as an offering.

"It wants to merge," David said. Not a question.

"It's been wanting to since the separation. It's patient. More patient than most."

"We need thirteen pairs."

"We have seven. Two more showing progress."

"That's still not thirteen."

"No," Phoebe agreed. "It's not."

She left him there with his shadow and his choice. Some decisions couldn't be argued into existence. They had to be reached alone, in the small hours, when the only company was the part of yourself you'd been refusing to face.

Phoebe checked on Maddie before returning to the gymnasium. Her daughter slept on a narrow cot in the small meeting room they'd designated as the children's area, with Lucy Holloway curled asleep on the cot beside her. Lucy's shadow stood watch near the doorway—not looming or threatening, but carrying the quiet attentiveness of a guard dog protecting sleeping children.

It turned its featureless head toward Phoebe as she entered, acknowledging her presence before resuming its silent vigil. Phoebe could sense faint currents of meaning moving through the shadow's gestures and posture, fragments of a language beyond spoken words. Not threatening. Protective. Watchful.

Maddie slept peacefully through it all, her own shadow

still firmly tethered beneath her, unmoving except for the subtle shifts cast by the dim emergency lights.

Phoebe knelt beside Maddie's cot and brushed a curl from her daughter's forehead. In sleep, Maddie looked impossibly young—too young to be living in a town where reality was coming apart at the seams, where the ground beneath her feet concealed an ancient machine built by forces no human fully understood. Too young to have a shadow that operated as an independent being with its own awareness and intentions.

But children adapted. That was the miracle and the heartbreak of them. Maddie had accepted the strange changes surrounding shadows with the same matter-of-fact ease she accepted everything else life had thrown at her—the move to the community center, the people with silver-flecked eyes, the realization that monsters were real but not always evil, that some could be friend or foe. Even the growing sense that her own shadow was somehow different no longer frightened her. She had simply folded it all into her understanding of how the world worked and moved on

Maybe that was the answer. Not the engineering solution she kept trying to design, not the ritual mechanics or the convergence circle's specifications. Maybe the answer was simply what Maddie already understood instinctively—that shadow and light weren't enemies. They were relatives who'd been kept apart too long and had forgotten how to share a room.

She kissed Maddie's forehead and stood, then nodded to the guardian shadow as she left.

In the corridor outside, the community center was quiet but not still. Merged volunteers patrolled the hallways in pairs, their dual perception scanning constantly for signs of Exile incursion beyond the protective sigil within the gymnasium. Unmerged residents slept wherever space could be found—on folding cots in meeting rooms, along the edges of the recreation hall, in administrative offices, or against walls padded with folded blankets. The building had taken on the atmosphere of a wartime shelter, that peculiar combination of exhaustion and hypervigilance that settled over people waiting for something terrible to arrive on schedule.

Phoebe found Harrison in the gymnasium, still awake, bent over a makeshift desk constructed from two folding tables pushed together. He'd spread the mine map beside Thaddeus Hollow's journal, cross-referencing tunnel locations with his grandfather's cryptic notes. His shadow sat in a chair beside him like an old colleague working a late shift, occasionally pointing to sections of the map that Harrison would then examine more closely.

"You should rest too," she said.

"At my age, sleep is optional. Understanding is not."

Harrison's shadow placed a dark hand on the old man's shoulder. The gesture was so human, so tender, that Phoebe had to look away. Ninety-four years these two had been bound together—the man and the entity forced to mimic his every movement, denied voice, denied choice, denied acknowledgment of its own existence. And still it touched him with something that looked remarkably like affection.

Harrison reached up to cover his shadow's hand with his own—his fingers passing through the dark form but the intent unmistakable. "My grandfather built the best defense he could. We're going to build something better."

Phoebe sat across from him and pulled the binding stone from its pouch. Its silver-veined surface pulsed steadily between them, casting faint patterns across the gymnasium ceiling that shifted like constellations in an unfamiliar sky. She turned it slowly in her hands, feeling the dual energy flowing through it—physical warmth from one realm, something cooler and deeper from the other, both currents braided together in the stone's crystalline structure.

Two days. Forty-eight hours to convince shadow beings who had been enslaved for a century that cooperation was possible. To convince humans who had never known their shadows were sentient that sharing consciousness was survivable. To position an incomplete circle of merged volunteers at a site controlled by hostile entities during a celestial event that would either heal a wound between worlds or tear it wide open.

The binding stone pulsed once, sharply, as if in agreement with the impossibility of it all. Then it settled back into its steady rhythm, patient and waiting for whatever came next.

* * *

Dawn broke, the sun rising through a haze that hadn't been there the day before. Phoebe stood at the community center's east-facing windows and watched the light struggle to assert itself against a sky that seemed to resist illumination. The shadows cast by the building stretched longer than the sun's angle warranted, darker than they should have been, and they didn't retreat as quickly as morning advanced.

Harrison appeared beside her, coffee in hand, looking like he hadn't slept at all.

"The barrier's thinning faster," he said. "I can feel it even without merged perception. The air tastes different. Metallic."

"Same as the tunnels," Phoebe confirmed. "The wound is spreading outward from the silo site. Our little expedition may have accelerated it—activating the circle, even briefly, seems to have widened the breach."

"Or the Exiles are pushing harder in response."

"Both, probably."

She'd spent the hours before dawn in a state between sleep and waking, her merged consciousness processing the flood of information the convergence circle had transmitted through the binding stone. Fragments of knowledge kept surfacing—technical details about the circle's design, historical impressions of the original separation of realms, and something else: a blueprint. Not for the counter-ritual itself, but for what the counter-ritual needed to become.

"Harrison, I don't think the original binding was ever the right answer."

The old man raised an eyebrow. "Careful. That's my grandfather's life's work you're questioning."

"Thaddeus did what he understood how to do. He saw dangerous entities and built a prison. But the convergence circle wasn't designed for imprisonment. It was designed for balance...a dynamic exchange between realms, not separation." She touched the stone at her chest. "The binding forced shadows into subservience. It didn't resolve the wound. It just applied pressure to keep it closed."

"And now the pressure's released," Harrison finished grimly. "Exactly what I warned the town council would happen if the silo was destroyed."

"Which means we can't just rebind them. Even if we had thirteen merged pairs, recreating the original spell would only delay the problem for another century. The Exiles would still be conscious, still imprisoned, still building resentment."

"So what do you propose?"

"We use the eclipse to power the convergence circle—not for binding, but for what it was originally built to do. Balanced exchange. A permanent convergence zone where both realms coexist without either dominating."

Harrison was quiet for a long moment, staring out at the strange morning light. His shadow stood beside him, and for the first time Phoebe noticed it nodding—slowly, deliberately, as if it had been waiting decades for someone to say exactly this.

"The Exiles won't accept coexistence," Harrison said. "Their whole campaign has been about dominance. Remaking this world to replace the one they destroyed."

"Some won't," Phoebe agreed. "But the Consensus might. They've been communicating with us, not conquering us. And if we can demonstrate a functioning convergence zone during the eclipse...prove that balanced exchange is possible...it might fracture the Exiles' coalition. Give the moderate entities a reason to choose partnership over war."

"That's a hell of a gamble," Harrison said.

"It's the only gamble that solves the problem instead of postponing it."

* * *

By mid-morning, the retaliation Harrison had predicted arrived—not as a direct assault, but as something more insidious.

It started with the streetlights on Maple Street flickering in sequence, a rolling blackout that moved east to west like a wave. Then the ground beneath the elementary school parking lot buckled, asphalt cracking in a pattern that matched the Exile symbols they'd seen carved in the mine tunnels. A sinkhole opened near the town's only gas station, not large enough to swallow anything, but deep enough to reveal darkness that moved independently at the bottom.

Reports flooded the community center's makeshift communications hub. Grant coordinated responses with grim efficiency, dispatching deputies and merged volunteers to the worst incidents while trying to maintain a perimeter around the community center itself.

"They're probing," Phoebe told the assembled team. The binding stone pulsed in her palm as she tracked energy patterns through her merged perception. "Testing our defenses, mapping our positions. They want to know where the stone is and how many merged pairs we have."

"Should we hide the stone?" Mary asked. "Move it somewhere unexpected?"

"They can sense it regardless. The activation in the chamber made it a beacon." Phoebe wrapped the stone back in its pouch. "What we need to do is prepare the ritual site. If we're going to use the convergence circle during the eclipse, we need access to the silo site, which means going through whatever perimeter the Exiles have established.

"Two days to secure a site controlled by hostile shadow entities, complete our circle of merged pairs, and design a ritual that's never been attempted," Grant summarized. "Anyone else feel like we're building the airplane while it's already crashing?"

No one laughed. But no one argued either.

Phoebe surveyed the room—the seven completed merger pairs, the two candidates still training, the unmerged volunteers handling logistics and support. Her husband, somewhere in the building, was wrestling with a decision that might bring them to ten. Her daughter, asleep in the next room, whose shadow communicated with shadow intelligence as naturally as breathing.

An incomplete circle. But circles, she was learning, didn't always need to close perfectly to hold power. Sometimes the gap was where the light got in.

Or, in Millfield's case, where the shadow did.

"All right," she said, straightening. "Here's what we're going to do."

She began outlining the plan—not the desperate rebinding they'd originally envisioned, but something new. Something that honored both what Thaddeus Hollow had built and what the convergence circle had always been meant to do. A ritual of balance rather than imprisonment. An offering of partnership to entities who'd known nothing but subjugation and exile.

Outside, the strange haze thickened, shadows pooling in places they shouldn't, reality growing thin at the edges. Two days until the eclipse would bring total darkness to Millfield—and with it, either the end of the world as they knew it or the beginning of something no one had imagined.

The incomplete circle would have to be enough. It was all they had.

CHAPTER 14:
NEITHER LIGHT NOR SHADOW

One day until the eclipse. Something was wrong with the sky.

Phoebe stood on the community center roof at dawn, watching as the sun breached the eastern horizon. Its light seemed muted, diminished, as if filtered through some invisible medium that drained its vitality. Shadows across Millfield's landscape appeared darker, more substantial than they should be-not just absences of light but presences of their own.

The wound between worlds was widening. Reality itself was growing thin as the eclipse approached.

"They're accelerating the process," Harrison observed, joining her at the roof's edge. Dark circles shadowed his eyes; he'd spent the night analyzing the convergence patterns from memory, transcribing what he could recall seeing in the central chamber. "After our incursion yesterday, the Exiles aren't waiting for the eclipse. They're actively thinning the barrier now."

"Can they force complete transformation without the eclipse alignment?" Phoebe asked.

"No. They still need that celestial amplification for the final breach. But they can weaken reality's structure in preparation, make the transformation more comprehensive when it comes."

She touched the binding stone hanging at her chest, feeling its steady pulse. Since their activation of the convergence circle, it had changed again, not physically but energetically. It vibrated at a frequency that resonated with both realms simultaneously, a tuning fork for reality itself.

"How are the volunteers progressing?" Harrison asked.

"Five complete mergers now," Phoebe reported. "Mary, Rodriguez, Jenkins, Dr. Williams, and Pastor Chen. Two more showing signs of imminent success."

"Seven out of thirteen," Harrison calculated grimly. "Still incomplete."

"We're running out of time," Phoebe stated. "And potential candidates. The most compatible pairs have already volunteered. Anyone else would require too many weeks of preparation, time we don't have."

Below, in the community center's main gymnasium, those volunteers who had achieved merged states were training others, passing on techniques for harmonizing human and shadow consciousness. David coordinated logistics, supplies, communications, escape routes if the counter-ritual failed. Grant-maintained security, his deputies patrolling Millfield's perimeter, where the town's protective sigil was visibly weakening.

The situation was deteriorating hourly. Reports came in from throughout Millfield: electronics malfunctioning, strange sounds emanating from drains and basements, pets refusing to enter certain rooms. Reality's ordered structure broke down as shadow elements leaked through the thinning barrier.

"We need to evacuate more residents," Phoebe decided. "Anyone not directly involved in the counter-ritual should be at least twenty miles from Millfield by eclipse time."

"Agreed, though convincing them won't be easy," Harrison said. "Despite everything, many still cling to normalcy and refuse to acknowledge what's happening around them."

A commotion below drew their attention. Grant burst into the rooftop access doorway, his expression grim.

"We've got trouble," he announced without preamble. "Two more sinkholes opened overnight, one on Maple Street, another near the elementary school. But these aren't natural. They're active."

"Active how?" Harrison demanded.

"Moving. Expanding. And something's coming out of them."

Phoebe felt the binding stone pulse with alarm. "Unbound shadows?"

"Worse," Grant replied. "Some kind of hybrid entity, not fully shadow, not fully physical. Deputies who approached reported objects passing through solid matter, voices speaking from empty air, and temperature drops severe enough to form instant frost."

"The barrier's failing faster than we anticipated," Harrison concluded. "The Exiles must have found another way to accelerate the process."

"Or another power source," Phoebe suggested, a terrible suspicion forming. "The missing volunteer shadows, the ones that deserted to the Exiles. What if they're not just being consumed for energy? What if they're being transformed, weaponized?"

Grant's expression darkened further. "That tracks with what we're seeing. These entities seem organized. Purposeful. They're spreading outward from the sinkholes in a search pattern."

"Looking for the binding stone," Phoebe concluded, her hand instinctively covering the pouch at her chest. "Or for our merged volunteers."

Harrison was already moving toward the door. "We need to consolidate our forces. Bring everyone into the community center where the protective sigil is strongest."

"Too late for that," Grant countered. "These entities are already between us and most of the town. We'd be sending people into their path."

Phoebe closed her eyes briefly, her merged consciousness processing options, calculating risks. “We move forward,” she decided. “Implement the counter-ritual plan immediately. No more waiting.”

“Before we’re ready?” Harrison protested. “Without all thirteen merged pairs?”

“With whatever we have,” Phoebe insisted. “Seven merged pairs, the binding stone, and the knowledge of the convergence circle’s location. It’s not ideal, but it’s our only option now that the Exiles have accelerated their timeline.”

Grant nodded grimly. “I’ll alert the volunteers. Gather whatever supplies and weapons might help.”

“Conventional weapons won’t work against these hybrid entities,” Harrison reminded him.

“No, but they might slow them down long enough for us to reach the convergence circle.”

As Grant departed, Phoebe turned back to the eastern horizon, where the sun continued its strangely muted ascent. The light seemed wrong—not just dimmer but somehow less real, as if the physical laws governing electromagnetic radiation were beginning to fray.

“Even if we reach the central chamber,” Harrison said quietly, “an incomplete circle means an incomplete ritual. The counter-transformation will be unstable at best.”

“I know,” Phoebe said. “But unstable balance is better than complete dissolution, which is what the Exiles’ version will create.”

“Or we could wait for the final six volunteers to achieve merger. Continue preparations.”

Phoebe shook her head. “There’s no time. Those sinkholes, those hybrid entities...they’re just the beginning. By tonight, Millfield won’t be recognizable as part of our reality. By tomorrow morning, it might not be accessible at all.”

She touched the binding stone again, feeling its urgent

pulse. "We go now, with what we have."

The expedition assembled in the community center's underground parking garage, the closest thing to a secure staging area they had left. Seven merged pairs, including Phoebe, formed the core. Harrison, David, and four deputies with separated but cooperative shadows provided support. Grant had initially planned to remain behind for evacuation coordination, but at the last moment he grabbed his shotgun and set it in the lead vehicle. "Someone has to watch your backs down there," he said, leaving a senior deputy in charge of the evacuation.

Each member carried emergency supplies: water, first-aid kits, emergency flares...though all understood such physical preparations might prove useless against the metaphysical threat they faced. The true weapons would be the binding stone and the merged consciousnesses, capable of perceiving and interacting with both realms at once.

"The plan is straightforward," Phoebe explained, spreading a map across the hood of a patrol car. "We approach the silo site directly, no detours through the cornfields. Speed is essential now that the Exiles know our intentions. Once at the site, we descend to the central chamber, where the seven merged pairs will take positions around the convergence circle. The binding stone goes at the center, completing the circuit."

"What about the six empty positions in the circle?" Mary Holloway asked. Her merged state had stabilized beautifully, her skin showing the characteristic translucence and her eyes the silver gleam that indicated balanced consciousness.

"The stone's connection to the convergence circle may compensate partially," Harrison replied. "But the ritual will be underpowered, incomplete."

"Creating what, exactly?" Deputy Rodriguez asked. His merger had been the most recent, achieved just hours earlier, and he still moved with the careful deliberation of someone adjusting to dual perception.

"A third state," Phoebe explained. "Neither complete separation nor forced unification. A reality where both shadow and physical aspects exist simultaneously, distinctly, but in relationship." She hesitated for a quick breath. "But without all thirteen positions filled, that state will be unstable. Requiring constant maintenance."

"Better than the alternative," David commented grimly.

Final preparations moved quickly. The vehicles were loaded-two SUVs with reinforced chassis, chosen for their durability on deteriorating roads. Communications gear was checked and double-checked, though everyone understood radio signals might fail as reality thinned further.

"Last reports from perimeter guards," Grant said, returning from a brief radio conference. "The hybrid entities have spread to all major roadways leading from town. They appear to be establishing a cordon, preventing escape."

"Then we breach it," Phoebe decided. "Hit hard and fast at the weakest point. Break through before they can consolidate."

David studied the map, identifying potential routes. "The Eastern approach seems least defended, according to these reports. If we take Oak Street to the county highway, then double back toward the silo site from the northeast."

The plan solidified. They would move as a convoy, the merged pairs in the lead vehicle providing perceptual advantages against shadow-realm threats, and the support team in the second vehicle with what conventional weapons might prove useful. Speed and surprise would be their allies against entities that, while powerful, were still adjusting to hybrid existence.

As they prepared to board the vehicles, Phoebe pulled David aside.

"I want you to stay behind," she said quietly. "Help

with the evacuation."

His expression turned to stone. "Not happening."

"David—"

"No." His tone left no room for argument. "I understand I'm not merged. I understand I can't perceive what you perceive or do what you can do. But I'm coming. End of discussion."

Phoebe studied her husband: the stubborn set of his jaw, the determined glint in his eyes. So thoroughly human, so adamantly himself despite everything that had changed around him. Including her.

"Okay. But stay close to Harrison. His shadow has fought Exiles before. It knows their weaknesses, how to disrupt their forms temporarily."

David nodded, then surprised her by pulling her into a tight embrace. "I don't care what form you take," he whispered. "Human, shadow, merged, whatever comes after, you're still Phoebe. Still the woman I married."

The simple declaration hit her with unexpected force. Throughout the crisis, David had maintained a certain distance, struggling to reconcile the woman he knew with the merged being she had become. This acceptance, this affirmation of continuity despite transformation, felt like a gift she hadn't known she needed.

"Thank you," she whispered back, returning his embrace carefully, conscious of how her partially translucent form must feel to him, neither fully solid nor insubstantial, but something between.

The moment was broken by Grant's urgent call. "Movement at the perimeter! The hybrid entities are advancing toward the community center. If we're going, it has to be now."

They boarded quickly, engines roaring to life as garage doors rolled open. Phoebe took the lead vehicle's driver's seat, her merged perception offering advantages in navigating the increasingly unstable reality outside. The convoy accelerated up the exit ramp into morning light that seemed even more diminished than before.

The town that greeted them was no longer recognizable as Millfield. Shadow and substance had begun to merge in chaotic, uncontrolled ways: buildings rippled like mirages, fields occasionally became transparent to reveal the mine tunnels beneath, trees and lampposts cast shadows that moved independently of any light source.

"My God." Mary gasped from the passenger seat. "It's happening already. The transformation."

"Partial and uncontrolled." Phoebe swerved to avoid a section of road that had become insubstantial, more shadow than matter. "Without the eclipse's alignment, without the binding stone at the convergence circle, it's just leakage. Reality is breaking down rather than transforming coherently."

They turned onto Oak Street as planned, only to find the road ahead blocked by what appeared to be a wall of living darkness. Dozens of hybrid entities had gathered, their forms flickering between shadow and substance, neither fully one nor the other. Some resembled humanoid silhouettes, others more abstract patterns of darkness given partial physicality.

"Barrier!" Phoebe warned through the radio to the following vehicle. "Prepare for breakthrough!"

She accelerated toward the shadowy blockade, the binding stone pulsing frantically against her chest. At the last moment, she removed it from its pouch and held it against the windshield. Silver light blazed outward, creating a wedge of energy before the vehicle, which disrupted the hybrid entities' unstable forms. They struck the barrier at forty miles per hour, scattering shadows like smoke before the stone's energy. Those with more substantial physical aspects were simply rammed aside by the SUV's reinforced bumper.

For a heart-stopping moment, darkness engulfed the vehicle completely, then they were through, accelerating down a suddenly clear road with the second SUV close behind.

"It worked," Grant cheered.

"Temporarily," Phoebe cautioned, checking the rearview mirror where the scattered entities were already reforming, some flowing into pursuit. "They'll regroup quickly. And there will be more ahead."

The convoy sped through Millfield's transforming landscape. Houses they passed showed signs of reality's deterioration: walls becoming transparent then solid again, roofs developing geometries impossible in normal three-dimensional space, lawns where grass grew upward, then sideways, then ceased existing entirely for moments before reappearing.

Citizens who hadn't evacuated stood frozen in tableau, witnessing the breakdown of physics with expressions of numb incomprehension. Some appeared partially merged with their shadows already, not through conscious harmonization, but through reality's failure to maintain proper separation.

"We need to hurry," Mary said. "The deterioration is accelerating exponentially."

They reached the county highway and turned northeast as planned. Here, the breakdown was even more pronounced. The road itself phased in and out of existence, forcing Phoebe to navigate as much by merged perception as by sight. Telephone poles along the roadside had become impossible sculptures of wood and wire, existing in multiple configurations simultaneously. The sky overhead had developed patches where blue gave way to something else entirely not darkness exactly, but an absence more profound than mere night.

"Two miles to the turnoff," Harrison reported from the

back seat, consulting a map that occasionally became transparent in his hands. "Then another mile to the silo site."

Phoebe tightened her grip on the steering wheel. The route around the cornfields was becoming maddeningly indirect. At this point, she found herself wondering whether it would have been easier to abandon the roads altogether and simply force their way straight through the fields toward the silo—despite whatever might be waiting among the stalks.

A shadow fell across the road ahead, vast, impossible—not cast by any physical object. It rippled like a flag in the wind, then solidified into a barrier similar to the one they'd broken through earlier, but larger and more organized.

"They're learning," Phoebe realized. "Adapting to our approach."

She reached for the binding stone again, but before she could channel its energy, the shadow barrier parted from the center. A figure stepped through the opening—Mayor Wilson, though his form had transformed even further since their last encounter. He now appeared as a silhouette filled with swirling darkness, occasional points of light visible within, like distant stars. His outline flickered between human and something far more abstract, mathematical patterns that hurt the eye to follow.

Phoebe braked hard. The convoy slid to a stop twenty yards from where Wilson stood alone in the road.

"What now?" Rodriguez asked tensely, hand moving to the weapon holstered at his side, though he knew conventional firearms would be useless.

"We talk," Phoebe decided. "Delay while we consider options."

She stepped from the vehicle, the binding stone held ready in her palm. The other merged pairs exited as well, creating a protective semicircle around her. Grant got out and covered the passenger side, shotgun pumped and ready.

From the second vehicle, David, Harrison, and the deputies emerged, staying close behind the merged pairs who could better perceive and respond to shadow-realm threats.

"Stone-bearer." Wilson's voice carried that same multi-toned quality of several entities speaking in unison through one partially physical form. "You surprise us with your haste. The eclipse is not yet upon us."

"Thanks to your accelerated transformation plan," Phoebe replied evenly. "The sinkholes, the hybrid entities...you're not waiting for the eclipse, so neither are we."

Wilson's form rippled with what might have been amusement. "Preparations only. The foundation must be laid before the structure can rise."

"Your foundation is destroying Millfield," Phoebe countered. "Breaking down reality in chaotic ways that harm both realms."

"Temporary disruption. Necessary destabilization before ordered reconstruction." Wilson gestured around them where reality continued to fray visibly, trees phasing between physical and shadow states, the road beneath their feet occasionally becoming transparent to reveal mine tunnels below. "Like removing an old, rotting structure before building anew."

"And the people caught in this 'temporary disruption'? The ones being forcibly merged with their shadows through reality's failure?"

Wilson waved dismissively. "Adaptation accelerated. Those capable of surviving the transition will emerge stronger. Those who cannot..." He shrugged, the movement rippling his form like stones dropped in still water. "Evolution has always required sacrifice."

Phoebe felt the binding stone pulse against her palm, responding to her anger. "You're not creating evolution.

You're forcing consumption. Exactly what got you exiled from your realm in the first place."

The accusation hit home. Wilson's form destabilized momentarily, darkness boiling within his outline before he regained control. "You understand nothing of our history, our purpose."

"I understand more than you think," Phoebe replied. "I've accessed the deep shadow memories. I've seen the original separation of realms and the formation of the stones. I know what the convergence circle was designed to do. Maintain balance, not dominance."

Wilson went very still. "You've activated the circle." It wasn't a question.

"Partially. With one stone instead of thirteen. But enough to understand its true purpose." Phoebe took a step forward, the binding stone held before her like a talisman. "Enough to offer you a choice, Wilson...or whoever you truly are beneath the Exile consciousness that's consumed you."

"Choice?" The word seemed to confuse him.

"Join us. Help us create a balanced convergence where shadow and substance exist in harmony, not dominance. Where consciousness flows freely between realms without one consuming the other." She gestured to the merged pairs standing with her. "Look at what we have achieved. True partnership, not subjugation. It's possible for all of Millfield, for all shadow entities, even for the Exiles themselves."

For a moment—just a moment—something shifted in Wilson's swirling darkness. A pattern that might have been consideration, might have been doubt. Then it was gone, replaced by the cold, mathematical precision that characterized Exile consciousness.

"Weakness," he hissed. "You offer weakness disguised as compromise. Balance is stasis. Evolution requires consumption. The strong absorb the weak to become stronger still."

"That's not evolution," Phoebe countered. "That's cannibalism. The elimination of diversity and of alternative perspectives until only one remains. Yours. How is that different from the Native People's binding spell that bound all shadows to physical anchors? The result eliminated shadow consciousness. You seek to eliminate physical consciousness. Both are forms of dominance, not harmony."

Wilson's form expanded suddenly, darkness boiling outward as his patience evaporated. "Enough philosophy, stone-bearer. You cannot reach the convergence circle. You cannot complete your counter-ritual with an incomplete circle." He gestured, and the shadow barrier behind him solidified further, hybrid entities flowing into more substantial forms. "Surrender the binding stone. Accept the inevitable transformation."

"Never," Phoebe shouted. "We're proceeding to the convergence circle. Step aside or be dispersed."

Wilson laughed, a sound like breaking glass multiplied a thousandfold. "You have seven merged pairs. The ritual requires thirteen. Even if you reached the chamber, your counter-transformation would be unstable and incomplete."

"Better unstable balance than coherent dominance." Phoebe raised the binding stone, channeling its energy not in an attack but in a signal: three pulses of silver light that flashed across the landscape like lightning. The prearranged message to the deputies back at the community center: Proceed with Plan B.

Wilson's form contracted with sudden suspicion. "What have you done?"

"Created a diversion." Phoebe smiled slyly. "While you've been focused on stopping us, six more volunteers have been approaching the convergence circle from another direction. Through the mine tunnels."

It was a bluff. There were no additional merged pairs,

no second team approaching the central chamber. But Wilson couldn't know that. His form rippled with uncertainty and calculation.

"Impossible," he decided. "We control the tunnels. We would have detected them."

"Not these tunnels," Harrison interjected. "The original map showed only a fraction of the actual network. There are passages your kind have never found, sealed sections the miners deliberately concealed after the incidents in the 1840s."

Another bluff but delivered with the confidence of historical expertise. Wilson's form flickered again, doubt visibly disrupting his coherence.

"Even now, they're taking positions around the convergence circle," Phoebe pressed. "The full thirteen pairs will be in place within minutes. So, you have a choice, Wilson. Join us in creating balanced convergence, or try to stop us and risk everything, your transformation, your very existence, in the chaos that will follow two competing rituals affecting the same convergence circle."

Wilson's form contracted, then expanded dramatically as he communicated with the other Exiles through some shadow-realm connection invisible even to merged perception. The hybrid entities behind him grew agitated, their forms shifting more rapidly between states.

"A decision has been reached," Wilson announced finally, his voice now resonating with multiple tones in complex harmonic patterns. "We will observe. Allow your attempt at counter-ritual. When it fails due to your incomplete circle, we will proceed with our transformation as planned during the eclipse."

It was neither acceptance nor rejection, merely a strategic delay. But it was enough for now.

"Stand aside, then," Phoebe ordered. "Let us pass."

Wilson's form flowed backward, the shadow barrier

parting to create an opening just wide enough for their vehicles to proceed. "We will be watching, stone-bearer. Any deviation from your stated purpose will result in immediate intervention."

Phoebe nodded acknowledgment, gesturing for the others to return to their vehicles. As they retraced their steps, David moved close beside her.

"There is no second team," He whispered.

"No," she confirmed quietly. "Just us. Seven pairs instead of thirteen. An incomplete circle."

"Then the counter-ritual will fail."

She touched the binding stone, feeling its steady pulse against her palm. "Not fail. Just achieve something different than intended. Neither complete balance nor complete transformation. A third state."

"What does that mean for Millfield? For everyone in it?"

Phoebe gazed at the increasingly unstable landscape around them, reality continuing to fray visibly as shadow and physical realms leaked into each other without structure or pattern. "I don't know exactly, but I know it will be better than this chaos. Better than the Exiles' forced transformation. A chance, at least, for both human and shadow consciousness to continue, to adapt, to find a new way of existing together."

They boarded the vehicles again and proceeded through the opening in the shadow barrier. Wilson watched them pass, his form rippling with calculation, with plans within plans. The Exiles hadn't surrendered; they had merely adjusted their strategy, waiting for the counter-ritual to fail before implementing their original transformation during the eclipse.

But they didn't understand what Phoebe had learned from the convergence circle, from her immersion in deep shadow memories. The ritual didn't require thirteen full pairs to function; it required thirteen positions filled with consciousness that understood the relationship between realms. And there were ways to divide, to distribute the seven merged pairs they had, to create resonance that might compensate for the missing participants.

It wouldn't be perfect. It wouldn't be stable. But it would be neither light nor shadow dominant...a third state where both existed simultaneously, distinctly, yet in relationship.

A new reality for Millfield, born from necessity rather than ideal conditions. An incomplete circle that might yet hold against the coming darkness.

As they approached the silo site, Phoebe felt the binding stone pulse with something almost like anticipation. It had been formed at the original separation of realms and had witnessed the division of what was once unified. Now it would participate in creating something new, not a return to original unity, not a continuation of artificial separation, but a synthesis that acknowledged both wounding and healing as part of existence.

Neither light nor shadow, but something between. Something beyond.

CHAPTER 15:
THE ECLIPSE CIRCLE

The eclipse began at 2:17 without ceremony. No trumpet of thunder. No splitting sky. No voice from the heaven's. Only the slow dimming of the world.

Across Millfield, daylight thinned to copper. Shadows lengthened in impossible directions, sliding away from the objects that cast them as if pulled by some deeper gravity. The cornfields whispered in a wind Phoebe could not feel, every stalk bending toward the old silo site and the buried chamber beyond it. Their shadows pooled and flowed like liquid night.

The binding stone pulsed against her chest inside its pouch. Not gently now. Frantically.

"It knows we're close," Grant said.

Phoebe looked toward the crater where the silo had once stood. The collapsed mine entrance yawned open at the bottom, black and waiting.

Harrison Hollow stood beside her, one hand pressed against his ribs, his weathered face turned toward the darkening sun. He looked impossibly old in that strange light, but his eyes were clear. "This is where Thaddeus began," he said. "But not where it ends."

Phoebe nodded. "The shaft is the only way in."

Maddie stood behind her, holding David's hand. Her shadow remained close to her feet, darker than it should have been, almost solid at the edges. It had not fully separated, not like the others, but Phoebe could feel it watching. Waiting.

Lucy Holloway sat in the back of Grant's patrol truck, pale but conscious, Mary beside her. Lucy's shadow clung to her with protective intensity, moving only when she moved.

Above them, the sun narrowed to a burning crescent.

The cornfields went silent.

Then the Exiles spoke. Not in words. Not at first.

The sound came up from the earth, from the broken mine shaft, from every shadow cast across Millfield. A low vibration passed through Phoebe's bones. The binding stone answered with a burst of silver light.

Grant raised his shotgun, though they all knew it would not be enough to stop what was coming. "Time to move."

They descended into the mine.

The tunnel swallowed the last of the daylight behind them.

Phoebe led the way, the binding stone glowing through the pouch now, silver light leaking between the seams. Harrison followed, leaning heavily on Grant whenever the ground dipped or shifted. David carried a lantern in one hand and kept the other near Maddie, who moved with solemn quiet.

The tunnel walls sweated black moisture. Old timbers bowed overhead, some marked with symbols Thaddeus had never known were there. Older symbols. Native symbols. Warnings carved into stone before the mine existed, before the silo existed, before Millfield had a name.

The deeper they went, the more the shadows moved.

Not all of them were hostile.

Phoebe could feel that now. Some watched from the walls with fear. Some recoiled from the Exiles' call. Others drifted near the group as if drawn to the binding stone, to Maddie, to the fragile possibility of freedom without corruption.

But farther below, something vast was waking.

The tunnel opened into the domed chamber beneath the barren circle in the cornfield.

No matter how many times Phoebe had seen fragments of it in shadow memory, the reality still stole her breath.

The chamber was a perfect hemisphere, its curved walls made of the impossible substance that was neither stone nor metal. At its center stood the raised dais, and above it the air shimmered like heat above asphalt. The flaw in reality was visible now: a vertical wound hanging in the center of the chamber, thin as a crack in glass and deep as a starless sky.

Around the chamber floor lay two circles.

One black.

One silver.

The black circle pulsed with the Exiles' pressure.

The silver circle flickered weakly, broken in places, as if waiting for the stone. The key. The power.

Harrison inhaled sharply. "Thaddeus never knew, never dreamed that anything like this lay below his feet," he whispered. "He never understood the whole design."

Phoebe stepped forward. The binding stone burned against her palm as she removed it from the pouch.

The wound widened.

Darkness poured through.

It did not spill like smoke. It unfolded like something remembering its shape.

The first Exile emerged as a towering figure of layered shadow, its body made of human silhouettes pressed together and stretched into something wrong. Behind it came others. Thirteen forms gathered at the edge of the black circle, each carrying echoes of the miners and settlers they had once consumed.

Faces appeared and vanished within them.

Jenkins.

Holloway.

Wilson.

Men whose bodies had gone into the mine in 1843 and

never truly returned.

Harrison staggered.

"God help us," Grant said.

The tallest Exile turned toward Phoebe. Its voice entered her mind like cold water. *"You bring the key to the lock."*

Phoebe tightened her grip on the binding stone. "I bring it to close the door."

The Exile's head tilted. *"Doors close both directions."*

The black circle flared.

Shadows erupted from the chamber walls.

Grant fired once. The blast tore through a reaching tendril and scattered it, buying only seconds. David pulled Maddie back. Lucy cried out from the chamber entrance as her own shadow rose defensively before her and Mary.

"Phoebe!" Harrison shouted. "The stone has to touch the center!"

Phoebe ran.

The chamber twisted around her. The dais seemed ten feet away, then fifty, then directly beneath her and impossibly distant at the same time. The Exiles were bending the space between her and the wound.

Lucy's shadow surged ahead of Phoebe, stretching toward the silver circle.

Not separate.

Not servant.

Partner.

Phoebe reached for it with her mind.

Reality snapped back into shape.

She slammed the binding stone into the hollow at its center.

Silver light exploded upward.

The chamber shook.

The silver circle ignited, racing around the floor in a blazing ring. The black circle answered, vomiting darkness.

Where the two met, the air screamed.

The wound opened fully.

Beyond it was not empty darkness.

It was a realm of motion, hunger, and endless watching. Countless shadows pressed against the other side, their forms stacked behind the thirteen Exiles that had gathered at the wound.

The chamber became a battlefield of light and shadow.

Merged volunteers raced in from the tunnel behind them and joined hands along the silver circle. Their shadows stood with them, completing the pattern.

Grant took his place at one section, his own shadow braced beside him.

Lucy's shadow guided Mary into position.

David held Maddie back until Maddie pulled free. "No, Maddie, stay with me."

But Maddie was looking at the wound.

The eclipse had reached totality. The last thread of sunlight vanished, and with it the force that had kept her shadow attached.

Phoebe felt the release before she understood what was happening.

Maddie's shadow began to lift from the floor, but it was not separating like the others.

It was *becoming*.

The child's shadow rose beside her, small and dark and strangely bright at the edges, its outline flickering between flatness and form. It looked at Maddie.

Maddie looked back without fear. "Mom, it says it can help."

Mayor Wilson spoke from inside every shadow in the room. *"The child is the bridge."*

Phoebe's heart clenched. "No," she cried.

The silver circle flickered.

Harrison stumbled to Phoebe's side, blood darkening

one sleeve where a shard of solidified shadow had cut him. “He’s right.”

Phoebe stared at him. “Not my daughter.”

“Not a sacrifice,” Harrison said. “A choice.”

The chamber shuddered. One of the Exiles broke through the silver edge of the wound and lunged toward Maddie.

Grant stepped into its path, firing again and again until his shotgun clicked empty. His shadow rose behind him, catching the Exile’s claws before they reached his throat.

“Now would be a good time!” Grant shouted.

Phoebe turned back to the stone. She understood then.

The silo Thaddeus built had been a prison. Necessary, maybe. Desperate, certainly. But still a prison. The binding spell had forced shadows into silence, forced the wound shut without healing it. The Exiles had stewed on that anger for a century.

A seal could fail.

A wound had to be mended.

Phoebe placed both hands on the binding stone.

Lucy’s shadow placed its hands over hers.

Maddie stepped onto the edge of the silver circle.

Her shadow floated alongside her.

“No.” David stepped forward.

Lucy caught his arm. “Let her. She’s not alone.”

Maddie’s shadow became solid for one heartbeat.

A small dark hand reached into Maddie’s.

The silver circle transformed.

It spread like roots. Silver lines ran across the chamber floor, into the walls, through the old symbols, through the native carvings, through the mine tunnels, up through the crater, out through the cornfields.

The two circles were not meant to duel.

They were meant to join.

Phoebe saw it all at once.

The black circle was not dominion by nature. It was at the wound's edge, corrupted by the Exiles' presence. The silver circle was not subjugation. It was memory, structure, return.

Together, they could heal the wound...become a scar.

Not erased.

Healed.

The Exiles realized it too.

They gathered to attack as one.

Harrison stepped forward. For ninety-four years, his family had carried Millfield on its shoulders. Thaddeus's obsession. The silo. The secrets. The warnings no one believed. The burden passed down through journals, whispers, and words lost to time.

Now Harrison Hollow stood at the edge of the black circle and drew the hunting knife from his boot. The blade was old, its handle carved with the same symbols etched into the silo's foundation. "My grandfather made mistakes," Harrison said to the Exiles. "But he was never your ally." He dropped to his knees and drove the knife into the center of the black circle.

Silver light erupted through the blade.

The Exiles screamed.

Harrison screamed with them, but he did not back down.

"Harrison!" Phoebe cried.

"Finish it!" he yelled.

Phoebe threw her merged consciousness into the binding stone.

Maddie and her shadow stepped fully into the center of the circle.

The chamber spun wildly.

Phoebe was everywhere at once.

She saw the miners in 1843, breaking into the shadow realm beneath the earth.

She saw the first Exile seize a human body. Jenkins, then Wilson, then the others.

She saw the mine entrance dynamited and covered.

She saw settlers from Coopersville walking into the fields in 1893 and opening the chest, which had broken the spell and the means to restrain the Exiles.

She saw Thaddeus Hollow planning circles, foundations, and a town shaped like a sigil, a hexagon: six sides, six connections, one center point, thirteen in all.

She saw the silo rise.

She saw it fall.

She saw every shadow in Millfield lift its featureless face toward the sun, now blocked by the moon, a celestial show of difference but unity.

Then she saw Maddie.

Not as a child alone in a chamber.

As a bridge.

Maddie's shadow reached into the wound.

Not to pull the shadows through, but to hold them back.

But the thirteen Exiles fought her.

The others beyond them surged.

But the wound had changed. The open tear narrowed around the silver-black pattern now spreading through the chamber. The binding stone's silver light now pouring into the dark.

One by one, the shadow-corrupted forms of the miners began to break apart.

Not destroyed.

Released.

Their faces surfaced in the darkness, confused and ancient, racked with pain. For the first time in nearly two centuries they looked afraid, not of the light, but of what they had become.

Jenkins reached toward Harrison.

Harrison, still gripping the knife, whispered, "Go

home."

Jenkins dissolved back into the shadow realm.

Then the next. Duncan.

Then the next. Sullivan.

The Exiles shrieked as their hosts were stripped away from them, their borrowed forms unraveling.

Miller. Gone.

Dr. Brennen, but a whisp of smoke trailing back into the world of darkness and shadows.

Mayor Wilson's shadow lunged toward Phoebe.

Grant's shadow intercepted it.

Lucy's shadow joined.

Then David's.

Then Mary's.

Mayor Wilson laughed at Phoebe's puny defenders. His laugh was like shattering glass. "That's all you got?" His voice was like thunder. His shadow body swelled and stretched and grew until his entire presence was the dark of the darkest nights.

Consensus shadows suddenly flowed into the chamber, a hundred or more, and formed an outer ring around the silver circle, their shadow arms locked together in solidarity with the shadow defenders of every volunteer inside the circle.

The leader acknowledged Phoebe with a nod. Phoebe did the same, grateful and more determined than ever to put an end to the Exiles. She knew the Consensus did not stand with her as servants. They were witnesses. Partners. They too had a stake in the future of this valley. Millfield. And the corn.

But Wilson would not be denied his vision of darkness over light. He struck the shadow barrier, pushing it inward.

Phoebe felt the blow in her skull. Blood ran from her nose.

The binding stone vibrated beneath her palms.

Maddie cried out. Her shadow flickered, trembling under the strain of more shadows walkers trying to break through a fully opened wound.

Phoebe looked at her daughter. “You don’t have to hold them alone.”

“They’re hurting me,” Maddie whispered.

“I will help you.” She reached for Maddie.

Maddie reached back.

Mother, daughter and her shadow connected.

For one terrible instant, Phoebe felt Mayor Wilson’s treachery turn fully upon her. He offered her impossible things: Harrison young again, Millfield untouched, a town where darkness had never found dominance.

She wanted it all.

That was the horror.

Not the darkness.

The wanting.

Maddie’s shadow-hand tightened around Phoebe’s hand.

Phoebe let the mayor’s lies go. Energies combined: Consensus, human, and merged; and they pushed back against Wilson.

The shadow barrier held. A massive surge of power repelled him.

“No,” Wilson cried. He flew backwards into the darkness from which he came.

Silver and black light exploded through the chamber.

The wound closed like the iris of an eye.

No longer a door.

But a scar.

The force threw everyone to the ground.

Silence.

No one moved.

Then the chamber breathed.

The impossible material of the walls dimmed and

turned to stone. The black circle faded to tarnished silver. The silver circle lost its sheen.

Phoebe lifted her head. The Consensus shadows were gone.

Maddie lay just a few feet away. “Maddie!” Phoebe crawled to her and gathered her into her arms.

David was scrambling toward them.

The girl opened her eyes.

Her shadow lay beneath her, attached again, though its edges shimmered faintly.

“I’m okay,” she whispered.

Across the chamber, Grant pushed himself upright. Lucy and Mary were alive. The volunteers were shaken and breathing hard.

Harrison Hollow lay near the center of the tarnished circle.

Phoebe knew before she reached him. It was bad.

His hand was still wrapped around the knife.

She took Harrison’s free hand.

He smiled faintly. “Did the binding hold?”

Phoebe looked toward the center of the chamber. A vertical seam of silver-black light, no wider than a thread, was all that remained.

“No need,” she said. “The wound is healed.”

“Good.” Harrison closed his eyes. His fingers loosened.

The knife clattered on the floor.

Above them, the eclipse passed. Phoebe felt it in her soul. A blade of sunlight returned to Millfield. It filtered down through earth and stone, into the old mine, through the chamber and touched the thin scar where the wound had been.

The cornfields above began to sway in the breeze.

The shadows moved with them...but not in perfect harmony.

EPILOGUE:
THE HARVEST BEGINS

One month after the eclipse. Millfield existed as it always had, in light and shadow.

Phoebe Weaver stood at the edge of the cornfields, watching the stalks sway in an autumn breeze. The corn remained golden beneath October's evening sun, but from certain angles the rows appeared faintly translucent, as though another landscape existed just beneath the surface of the valley.

Which, in a way, it did.

The crater where the silo once stood was filled and remained behind a chain-link fence near the center of the barren circle. No one went there anymore. Especially at dusk and dawn.

The wound had healed.

But scars remembered.

Phoebe touched the binding stone through the fabric of her jacket pocket. Since the eclipse, the crack running through its center no longer looked like damage. Silver lines branched across its surface like veins pulsing faintly whenever shadows grew long.

Behind her, tires crunched on gravel.

David stepped from the truck, carrying two cups of coffee. Unlike Phoebe, he remained fully human, untouched by merger, though the line separating ordinary from impossible had become harder to define in Millfield with each passing week.

"You disappeared again," he said gently, handing her a

cup.

Phoebe offered him a wan smile. “Only for a minute.”

“That’s what you said last time. It was an hour.”

She could not argue with that. Time behaved strangely near the cornfields now. Not dangerously. Just differently.

David leaned on the fender beside them, sipped coffee as if nothing else mattered.

The town had changed since the eclipse.

Some residents had left within days of the crisis, unable to accept what Millfield could have become. Others stayed because they had nowhere else to go. And some stayed to fight, because, for the first time in their lives, they felt they were seeing the world clearly.

Shadows no longer flowed and pooled, but they still didn’t act exactly as shadows should. Sometimes they moved a fraction too slowly. Sometimes too quickly. Occasionally they moved when their anchors stood still.

But they no longer threatened.

And they no longer hungered.

“That still bothers you, doesn’t it?” David asked quietly.

Phoebe looked toward the distant town. “What?”

“Harrison dying for the cause...to save Millfield.”

The grief still lay heavy in her chest.

Harrison Hollow had spent his entire life carrying the burden of Millfield’s secrets, warning people who refused to listen, preserving knowledge no one wanted to believe. In the end, he had become the final piece needed to heal the wound his family had tried for generations to contain.

“He saved everyone,” Phoebe said softly.

“Yes,” David replied. “But you wish he’d lived long enough to see it.”

Phoebe nodded. “He knows.”

A child’s laughter drifted in from the field.

Maddie emerged from between the rows of corn, racing

toward them in the evening light. Her shadow moved beside her instead of behind her, occasionally slipping through the stalks before reconnecting to her feet again.

David still tensed whenever he saw it.

Phoebe understood. She'd felt the same way that fall afternoon when Maddie jumped into the pile of leaves. How her shadow hesitated in midair...

"Mom!" Maddie shouted. "Look!" She opened her hand.

Resting in her palm was a single black kernel of corn.

Not dead black. Shimmering black. Its surface absorbed sunlight while reflecting something silver beneath.

Phoebe exchanged a glance with David.

"Where did you find that?" he asked.

"In the circle," Maddie said matter-of-factly. "My shadow said it was coming."

Phoebe crouched to her eye level. "What's coming, honey?"

Maddie looked toward the cornfields.

Phoebe followed her daughter's gaze toward the circle above the mine chamber, toward the place where the wound between worlds had once made the fertile soil barren, but now the winter corn was already sprouting. *Coming? What's coming?* She felt a chill. "Are the shadow walkers coming?"

Maddie smiled with unsettling innocence. "No. The harvest, silly."

"Ah...yes, of course," David said. "The harvest begins. Looks like a good year for the corn."

The three walked toward the setting sun, hand in hand, their shadows stretching out behind them. "Anyone for ice cream?"

Maddie's shadow waved.

Kevin B. DiBacco

Kevin B. DiBacco is a bestselling author, award-winning filmmaker, and USAF Security Forces veteran with a career spanning both publishing and motion pictures. As an author, his work has explored subjects ranging from health, fitness, and environmental issues to suspense, horror, westerns, and psychological thrillers. His books have reached international audiences through both traditional publishing and independent distribution channels, earning recognition among readers worldwide. He lives in Maine with Rachel and two cats.

In addition to his literary work, DiBacco has spent more than three decades in the film industry as a writer, director, producer, and editor. His projects have been featured in international markets and independent film venues, with distribution partnerships extending across multiple countries. Known for blending cinematic pacing with emotionally driven storytelling, his work often explores themes of resilience, redemption, survival, and the darker corners of human nature. His love of storytelling, quiet coastal living, and everyday human connection continues to shape the heart of his work. Kevin enjoys watching football, his beloved Boston Red Sox, and staying active in the gym.

DiBacco is also the creator of the ISO QUICK STRENGTH system, a practical fitness philosophy centered on functional strength and sustainable training methods. His nonfiction writing frequently reflects his interest in health, nutrition, mental toughness, and modern societal challenges.

Whether crafting suspenseful fiction or thought-provoking nonfiction, Kevin B. DiBacco brings a distinctive voice shaped by real-world experience, disciplined storytelling, and decades of creative work across multiple media platforms.

www.ingramcontent.com/pod-product-compliance
Lightning Source LLC
LaVergne TN
LVHW030919080826
845145LV00013B/2971